Books by Caroline Stafford

THE HOUSE BY EXMOOR
MOIRA
THE TEVILLE OBSESSION
THE HONOUR OF RAVENSHOLME

The Honour

SIMON AND SCHUSTER • NEW YORK

# of Ravensholme

CAROLINE STAFFORD

Copyright © 1979 by Caroline Stafford
All rights reserved
including the right of reproduction
in whole or in part in any form
Published by Simon and Schuster
A Division of Gulf & Western Corporation
Simon & Schuster Building
Rockefeller Center
1230 Avenue of the Americas
New York, New York 10020
Designed by Edith Fowler
Manufactured in the United States of America

1 2 3 4 5 6 7 8 9 10

Library of Congress Cataloging in Publication Data

Stafford, Caroline.
    The honour of Ravensholme.

    I. Title.
PZ4.S7779Hm [PS3569.T165] 813'.5'4 79-272
ISBN 0–671–24801–4

For Melinda,
who spent an unforgettable summer in northern
Germany,

and

For Martha Lynne,
who shares my abiding affection for Rutledge
Riding, where it all began . . .

The Honour of Ravensholme

1

The driver was drunk. I was certain of that now, and my heart beat wildly as the hired carriage lurched through the muddy ruts and scraped against the straggling trees choking the shoulder of the lane.

To make matters worse, I had no idea where we were or how much time had passed. We had set out from the King's Head in that strange twilight that presages a storm, and darkness had fallen quickly, speeded by the heavy black clouds building to the west. For some time I had smelled the sea, and now the salty taste of it was borne on the gusting wind that rattled the carriage windows and whistled through the cracks in the ancient doors. There was no sign at all of the vast bay, stretching somewhere to my left.

I was cold, very tired, and hungry, but at least the end of my long journey was nearly in sight. The innkeeper had impressed upon me the urgency of reaching Hest Bank before the tide had turned. The hazardous crossing over Morecambe Bay to the Kents Bank was all of nine miles, and the track over the sands disappeared with the incoming tide. There was no time to be lost if I expected to arrive at Abbot's Thorston tonight.

But my driver, Sam Hichen, cared nothing for my problems, nor, it seemed, for the dangers of Morecambe Bay. He cursed and grumbled and cajoled the two rawboned horses out of the ditches each time we came to the brink of disaster. The carriage's progress was maddeningly slow. And Hichen had paid no attention when I called out to remind him that we had a very long way to go, that the tide would surely be against us before we reached the Bank. The horses plodded along in their erratic fashion until my nerves were taut with anxiety and my head throbbing.

The carriage tilted precariously again as the nearside rear wheel ran up an embankment, and I clung wretchedly to the strap, fervently wishing that I had waited at the King's Head until the axle on the stage had been repaired. But Hichen brought the pair back into the lane after much confusion and swearing, though there was a sickening moment when the hub caught on a tree root. The rusted springs protested loudly as we settled into the ruts once more, and I could have cried with frustration.

Still, I reminded myself, the blame for my predicament was more mine than his. The man had been of two minds about taking me over the sands, much less all the way to Abbot's Thorston. And he had been sober then. The usual driver was ill, and I had insisted that a replacement be found. The reluctant landlord had finally summoned Hichen, one of his ostlers, because he had once been a freighter between Lancaster and Cartmel.

It had certainly not been my attempts to persuade him that had made Hichen agree to the hire of his services. There had been a strange expression in his eyes when we at last came to terms, but I had been too relieved to care. My meager savings were dwindling rapidly, and the route over the bay would cut at least two days from my long journey from Salisbury—not to speak of eliminating the cost of a night in the inn while the axle was replaced. And I had even been congratulating myself on my good fortune that the breakdown had occurred just outside Lancaster, I remembered wryly, because it allowed me to take this alternative! No one warned me that Hichen might spend part of his wages on drink.

Putting down the window, I gathered my courage to speak to him again, just as we finally swung west onto the strand and rolled down to the seemingly trackless bay. I could see nothing ahead, no landmarks or distant lights to guide us, not even a sliver of moonlight to point the way. But I could hear the restless tides.

As the wheels sank into wet sand and the carriage tilted and swayed, I called nervously to Hichen, "Are you certain you remember the way across?" I dared not ask outright if he was too drunk to find it. "The innkeeper said the sands were treacherous— unmarked."

"So they are," he replied, righting the vehicle as he jerked the off horse back to firmer ground.

"But do you remember the way!" I repeated in exasperation.

"Man and boy, I've crossed the bay more years than you've seen," he answered curtly. But he took another drink from the bottle he carried.

I was far from reassured, but held my tongue for fear of distracting him now. The sand sucked and pulled at the wheels as we lumbered out into the bay. Water swirled fetlock deep about the horses' legs, then moved on toward the strand we had left behind.

With the strong wind blowing, the tide seemed to be moving faster than it should, and the storm clouds that had shortened the day had also made the sea choppy. Nine miles, if we kept to the track. But what if in his drunkenness Hichen lost the way? The innkeeper had been right—I had been foolish to insist on traveling in the dark.

Behind me my trunk slithered across the boot of the

carriage. My fingers tightened on the strap and I braced my feet against the floor. The uneven shelf of sand that formed the route over the bay at low tide seemed to delight in trapping the wheels, for we jolted uncomfortably over the bars, making but a snail's pace. I suppressed my worry and tried to peer out into the empty darkness ahead. But there was nothing to see, only the sound of water moving restlessly under us.

Shaking from the cold bite of the wind, I reluctantly put up the window. Wrapping myself in my cloak, I wondered what instinct led the guides. For it could be nothing less. Even the shore we had left behind was now completely obscured. As far as I could tell, we might be headed for the open sea rather than the Cartmel peninsula and the high fells beyond! I reminded myself firmly that this route had been used for centuries, that it was far shorter and easier than the land journey around the bay.

Another fear gnawed at my peace of mind, one that had traveled with me night and day. Had my godmother really wanted me to come to her, or had she been too polite to refuse my request?

I had been driven by necessity, not choice, when I wrote to her. The headmistress had seen fit to dismiss me in mid-term—an unavoidable economy, she told me. But I had discovered quite by accident that Miss Whitmain was falsifying the account books at Trenton Academy for Young Gentlewomen, and guessed the true reason behind her hasty decision. I had no proof to support my discovery, and she was determined to send me packing before I found any.

For the hundredth time I considered the possibility that she had also given me an unsatisfactory recommendation, for I was unable to find a position as a teacher, companion, or governess. Or perhaps my age and inexperience had been against me. Indeed, the only reason Miss Whitmain had hired me three years ago was that I was a former pupil at the Academy. She had taken advantage of my circumstances and my youth—I had been scarcely eighteen—paying me a pittance for teaching deportment and drawing to the second and third forms. Even with the strictest economies, I couldn't possibly live on my slender savings while I continued my search for employment.

In desperation I had appealed to my godmother, whom I had met only once since my baptism, though she had sent a kind note at my father's death four years ago. Even so, I hadn't told her the full story of my situation, for my stubborn pride would not permit me to beg. But perhaps she saw through my thin fabrication of reasons for suddenly wishing to visit her at Ravensholme. In a letter written for her by her sister-in-law, with whom she was presently staying at Abbot's Thorston, she had merely said that she looked forward to my coming. And so I had left the Academy behind, despondent and reluctant to accept such cool charity, even though it was my only refuge.

But if Hichen succeeded in losing his way, I thought, as wind battered the old carriage, we would be caught by the rising waters and borne ruthlessly out into the Irish Sea, solving the problem of my future for me. How many graves marked the victims of the sands?

Almost as if he had read my thoughts, Hichen stopped the team with a jerk of the reins that nearly pitched me headfirst into the seat opposite.

"What's that? *Who's out there?*" he demanded roughly, his words carrying above the wind.

"Where?" I asked, opening the window to stare ahead.

"There— *there!* Don't you *see?*" There was stark terror in his voice now.

I leaned out as far as I could. "I see nothing—" Indeed, the night was empty save for us, at least to my eyes.

"We've got to turn about. I knew it wasn't safe! The dead don't *rest* in the bay!" He began to drag the team around.

"There is nothing, I tell you, only darkness!" I cried, fearful that he would overset us in his frantic haste. "It is only your drunken fancy!"

That arrested him. He hiccoughed, then peered blearily out beyond the horses' ears. "I'd have sworn . . ." he began shakily, and broke off. After a moment he looped the reins over the brake handle and rummaged under his feet.

I suspected he was searching for another bottle. "You have had enough," I insisted as firmly as I could. "Let it stay there." But I knew that I could neither order nor control him in his present state.

"I'm after a lantern, woman, not Dutch courage." And he sat up with a lamp in his hands. "I want to see where I'm going and what's out there." His fingers were trembling and clumsy, but he managed at last to light the wick and adjust the flame. Before I knew what he was about, he jumped down and sloshed through the surf to hang the lantern not by the door but on the shaft between the two horses.

"That's better," he grumbled as he climbed to the box again.

Thereafter the lamp swayed erratically as the team moved on, and I watched anxiously, shivering in the cold air as the black and turbulent water seemed to deepen before my eyes. How far had we come?

"Are you sure we haven't lost our way?" I asked at length, for the wheels were nearly axle deep at times. "Or has the tide come in faster tonight?"

"There are channels in the sands. 'Tisn't all flat."

It was then that I realized that he was indeed drunk for courage. He was as frightened as I was—but for an entirely different reason. It was in his voice now and in the way his body bent forward as if striving to penetrate the night beyond the lamp's feeble glow. He was seeking to prove something to himself, I thought suddenly, to test himself in some fashion that I couldn't begin to understand. His need, not my persuasion or my money, had driven him to take this carriage over the bay. Had his carelessness or his drunkenness caused an accident out here in the past? Or had it been a question of losing his nerve once in the face of the dangerous crossing? My fingers clenched about the strap.

The wind was still rising and whipped my hood about my face. My hands were like ice, my feet even colder. Squalls of drizzle lashed us and were as quickly gone. But I dared not close the window and sit back in my seat. Already I wondered if I would survive the crossing, much less reach my destination. Though there was nothing I could do but huddle miserably in my corner, I felt I must watch Hichen. The bobbing lantern created an island of light in empty darkness, with nothing ahead or behind to tell me where we were.

And then we churned to a halt, caught fast in shifting sand and swirling water. Hichen leaned over to look at the wheels and shook his head.

"We ought to be over the Kent channel by now. The Cartmel bar should be under us. Instead we've bogged down somehow."

My throat contracted. "What can we do?" I asked with difficulty. "Would it help if I took the reins and you led the horses?"

His red face turned toward me. "There's nought we *can* do now," Hichen said with bitter resignation. "It's too late to turn back; we've missed the track. You can see for yourself—the tides have us fast. Or else the sands have shifted since last I crossed over." He nodded suddenly, sending shadows flickering over his features in an ominous dance. "Aye, that'll be it! The sands *shift* in the winds and storms. You must walk them day in and day out, or they'll trick you. I'd forgot how they trick you!" His voice broke on the last words.

"We can't *sit* here," I said, trying to rouse him out of his wretched apathy. It was almost as if he were relieved to be brought face to face with failure, as if he had grown tired of fearing it—or waiting for it. But the tide was sucking greedily about the horses' legs, and I was frightened. Time was desperately short. My mouth was dry as I added, "There must be something. If we unhitch the team, we might be able to ride them ashore." Even faced with death, I felt the old panic rise at the thought of mounting a horse.

"We've lost the track, I tell you. They don't know no more than me how to find it again."

There was the sound of splashing somewhere near us, and harness jangled as the nearside horse shied uneasily. Sam Hichen buried his face in his hands and cringed against the box. "The dead—" he moaned in drunken horror. "They're tired of waiting. *They've come to fetch us!*"

"Hello the carriage! Are you in trouble?" a muffled voice called from the darkness beyond. "Can I help you?"

Tears of relief sprang to my eyes as a man on horseback rode into the lantern's gleam. He was wrapped in a high-collared cloak with his hat brim pulled low over his face against the rain and wind, but he was very real and clearly, blessedly stone sober.

Hichen had started violently at the first words the stranger had spoken, then straightened himself in a hurry. Whatever he was afraid of out in this wild night, it was not a flesh-and-blood man.

"We've missed the way," he began, and broke off with a hiccough.

The stranger was even with us now, staring hard at Sam Hichen on the box and then at me, framed in the open window. I felt myself flush under his regard and was glad when the wind whipped the edge of my hood across my face. For he must have seen that Hichen was disgracefully drunk and wondered why we had foolishly attempted the crossing, especially on such a night.

"I am on my way to Abbot's Thorston," I said with all the composure I could muster. "My driver appears to have gotten us caught in the sand. If you could free us and then guide us to the Kents Bank . . ."

The horse danced skittishly as his rider's cloak unfurled to catch the wind like a great black sail. The man inclined his head in an oddly graceful gesture, then rode forward to take the bridle of the nearest horse. Under his hand the team plunged and struggled against the grip of the sand. The carriage rocked precariously, nearly unseating me, and then with a jolt that brought a curse from Hichen, we rolled forward at last. Without a word the stranger began to lead the horses toward his right. I could see him in the lantern light, his cloak pulled close against the elements as he turned to fight his way to the crossing.

Sam Hichen let the reins lie slack in his fingers, his breath coming raucously in his throat. I couldn't tell whether he was angry or still recovering from his fright. In the swaying light his face was impossible to read.

The springs groaned and protested, the harness jangled and creaked, and the storm seemed to lash us with increased fury as the horses strained against the pull of the sand and tides. Then, quite suddenly, we were on higher ground, the water no longer black and deep as it raced inland. Even the splashing hoofs sounded different to my ears. With a sigh of relief I straightened my tired back and said to no one in particular, "Thank God!"

"Aye," Hichen answered, moving restlessly on the box.

In no time at all, it seemed, we were climbing the

Kents Bank to the road, the bay safely at our backs. The stranger released the bridle and let the team pass him by. As we drew opposite him, Hichen waved a hand in acknowledgment.

"You can manage from here?" the stranger asked, his voice husky, as if the dampness had affected it.

"Aye," Hichen replied grudgingly. "Thank 'e."

"I cannot tell you—" I began, trying to put all my gratitude into words, but he inclined his head in that same graceful way.

"My pleasure. A safe journey." And then he was gone, splashing out across the rising waters as he touched his heel to his horse's flanks. I felt oddly bereft, even though we were perfectly safe now. Perhaps it was only my reluctance to trust myself once more to Hichen's charge.

Hichen turned to look after the stranger. "A gurt fool, to cross now."

Unreasonably angered by his contempt, I said tartly, "After all, he was delayed because he stopped to help us. It isn't his fault. And we are very late ourselves. You must hurry, if you please!"

"Aye," he said disagreeably. "You'll not be there till long after midnight, even so." He lifted the reins. "'Twas the sands that shifted. I ought to have allowed for it. The bay is like that, claiming its own. But I'll never go back across there—not me! Not for anybody or anything!"

"So long as you take me safely to Abbot's Thorston, afterward you may go to the devil for all I care," I snapped, losing patience. As I closed the window and leaned back into my seat, he whipped up the horses.

By the time we reached Thorston Water, there were stars overhead, and I could see the lake spread before me like a black sheet. Beyond it were the great fells, brooding and silent. For a long while the land had been empty save for straggling herds of ghostly sheep. The wind was still blowing hard, but the storm had broken south of us, sparing us a thorough drenching. Even so, I wondered if it could be possible to be more miserable than I already was. Hichen had long since sobered up, but the gin or whatever it was he had been drinking had warmed him. I had no such comfort.

For an instant I pictured myself arriving late, wet, disheveled, and reeking of spirits, and I fought down the urge to laugh hysterically. Mrs. Langdale had not sounded overjoyed at the prospect of a visit from her goddaughter. She might welcome an excuse to be rid of me.

As it was, I should have reached Abbot's Thorston this afternoon, as set out in her letter. But my meager resources would not stretch to the Carlisle Mail or hired post horses. It would be difficult to explain this delay without confessing more than I wished anyone to know about my financial straits.

At long last I could see the silhouette of a house ahead, a tall pile of stone on the slope of a hill overlooking the lake. And blotting out the stars behind it was a high barren fell. There was no light burning in the windows, not even in the lodge by the gates. But Hichen turned in and I knew we had arrived. As the weary horses plodded up the drive I steeled myself to awaken the household. But my stomach twisted into a nervous knot and my mouth felt dry. I had not realized—how could I?—that the distance from Cartmel was so far or so difficult to travel, or I would have stayed the night there.

"Don't bespeak lodgings for me," Hichen said suddenly as I let down my window for a better view. "I'll see to myself."

"You must rest the horses," I said, repressing a sense of relief to be rid of his reeking, morose presence.

He shook his head. "I'll not stay here."

I made no reply, and we drew to a halt by the front

steps. Above me towered the house, its dark wet stone and severe walls staring blindly out into the silent valley.

With a tense smile fixed to my lips, I opened the door and climbed stiffly from the carriage, stumbling onto the terrace. The plain solid door appeared stark and forbidding. Taking a deep breath, I lifted the heavy brass knocker and let it fall.

The sound seemed to rend the stillness like a hundred knockers clanging against their plates. Even the horses stirred. But the house remained quiet and dark. Behind me I heard my trunk thud onto the terrace and my satchel follow.

I was debating whether to knock again or cravenly ask Hichen to take me into the nearest village when the door opened. Caught by surprise, I stood for a moment blinking into the light of a candle held high by an elderly butler wearing hastily donned clothes.

"I—— I am Miss Winton," I said with all the firmness I could manage. "I am sorry to be so late in arriving, but there was an accident to the coach."

Though true enough, the excuse sounded false even to my ears. Hichen was already turning his team, leaving me to face the butler alone.

"Come in, Miss Winton," he said, stepping aside. His eyes took in my rumpled traveling dress and my windblown hair. "The family is asleep. They expected you in time for dinner."

"I know." I followed him into the high-ceilinged hall. As coolly as possible I added, "There was no help for it."

He set the candle on a small table and went out to fetch my trunk.

As he did, another light appeared on the stairs and a woman's voice called down to him. "Who is it?" There was a moment's hesitation, and then she repeated, "Who has come, Lithwaite?"

The butler put down my luggage and closed the door. "It is Miss Winton, ma'am."

"At this hour!" She hurried down the steps in a flutter of wrapper and night dress. In the dim light of the hall I saw with disappointment that she could not possibly be my godmother. She appeared to be some nine or ten years my senior, tall and somehow rather daunting. Her hair was red-gold and her eyes were dark. "Do you realize you have awakened the entire *house?*"

"I am indeed sorry, Mrs. Ryland. The coach broke an axle and because of it we were delayed." Why, oh why, had my godmother chosen to visit her sister-in-law—for it must be she—just now? Inspiration came in the face of her cold disapproval. "Of course one can cross the sands only when the tide permits."

She stopped short at the foot of the stairs, her annoyance forgotten. "You came over the bay?" she demanded, staring hard at me.

"Why yes, it was the shortest way—" I began, but she interrupted.

"You could not have crossed alone! How did you come? Who was with you?" Behind her on the landing I saw the dark figure of a man.

"I hired a carriage at the King's Head, above Lancaster," I replied, reluctant to acknowledge any association, however brief, with the disreputable Hichen.

For an instant I thought she intended to question me further, for there was something—a guardedness, perhaps—in her expression that puzzled me. But as the man on the stairs joined us, her lips closed on whatever she was about to say. He was tall and fair, with an attractive, friendly face. Mr. Ryland, surely?

"There was a gale blowing tonight. You were fortunate that you were not caught out in it, Miss Winton." He took the candle from his wife's trembling fingers, and at his touch some of the wariness faded from her eyes.

"I nearly was," I said, too weary to sort out the undercurrents of emotion I could sense in these two people. "Fortunately, a stranger found us in time and guided us safely to the Kents Bank."

"A— A stranger?" Mrs. Ryland repeated. She glanced swiftly at her husband's profile and then added with an effort, "Indeed."

"You must be cold and very tired," Mr. Ryland said, as if he had not noticed his wife's glance. "Lithwaite will show you to your chamber and perhaps find a cup of tea for you."

The thought of a cup of tea, hot and soothing, was tempting. But I had disrupted the household enough without that. "Thank you, I mustn't disturb the servants further. It was kind of you to invite me to Abbot's Thorston. I look forward to my visit." As I picked up my satchel, I again had the feeling that Mrs. Ryland was about to speak, but she said nothing more. After a brief pause I added, "Good night," and started up the stairs.

As I reached the first landing with the butler at my heels, carrying my trunk, I looked back over my shoulder. Mr. and Mrs. Ryland were standing where I left them, staring silently after me.

At the second floor we turned into a narrow passage. Lithwaite set down the trunk and opened a door midway along the corridor. As he lighted the candles on the mantel, I looked about me. It was a plain chamber, furnished in dark woods and faded hangings. The window draperies, once a dark green, were now mellowed to fern, and those on the bed matched. There was also a worn Turkey carpet, a table and chair, a tall armoire for my clothes, and an ornate chest. The walls were a soft dusky rose. Far from elegant, but more spacious and comfortable than the bleak little room I had occupied at the Academy.

"Thank you, Lithwaite," I said, turning to the butler. "What time is breakfast in the morning?"

"Maggie will bring you a tray," he answered reprovingly, and with a chill of foreboding I wondered if I would be treated like an indigent relative rather than a guest. "If that will be all . . ."

"Good night," I replied, and turned away to remove my cloak and gloves as he closed the door.

The room had been aired, but I felt sure that no fire in the grate had warmed it since the last occupant had departed. A damp chill seeped through the walls and into the very marrow of my bones. After unpacking only what I needed, I bathed my face and hands in cold water, then undressed quickly.

As I was brushing the tangles from my hair, there was a light tap at the door and Mrs. Ryland entered.

"You have everything you need?" she asked, drawing her wrapper closer about her against the chill.

"Yes, thank you," I replied, certain that my comfort had not brought her here.

She nodded and turned to leave, saying as if as an afterthought, "This . . . this stranger. The one who guided you across the sands. Was he a dark man?" She spoke the last words with difficulty.

"I could not see his coloring," I answered. "He wore his hat low against the rain."

"No, no, I don't speak of his hair," she said irritably, as if I had deliberately misunderstood her. "Was he dark—as if he had spent some years in an Eastern country?"

"There was no way to tell," I said. "I did notice that his voice was husky, as if the raw weather bothered his throat."

She gasped, then visibly forced herself to smile. "Yes, we have been unfortunate this spring. There has been a good deal of rain." Her eyes swept unseeingly about the room. "Good night, Miss Winton." The door closed silently behind her.

When I was at last between the icy sheets, I shivered uncontrollably. But the inexpressible relief of reaching the end of my journey and being accepted—after a fashion—into the household brought exhaustion in its wake. I was soon asleep, dreaming of a dark man from the East who drove my hired carriage across shifting sands.

Maggie's knock at my door awoke me with a start. She was a fair, rawboned girl of medium height who bustled in and set my tray by the bed.

" 'Tis a fine morning, miss," she said in an accent that was nearly incomprehensible. Even Hichen, with his Lancashire dialect, had been easier to understand. As the draperies opened, a flood of sunlight warmed the room.

"We deserve a fine day after last evening's storm," I replied, sitting up against my pillows.

"Aye, you're right, miss. However, it won't last. Not up here," she said, though it sounded more like "Aa-ah, ye're reet, miss. Hooiver, it twoant la-ast. Nought oop hee-re."

She knelt to lay the fire, and soon the cheerful crackle of the blaze filled the room. As water heated by the hearth, I turned ravenously to the breakfast tray.

There was a bowl of porridge with a slab of butter and thick yellow cream, eggs, and a rasher of bacon. The tea was hot and freshly made. It was Maggie's turn to smile.

" 'Tis the air, miss. Makes you sharp set for your food, it does." She dusted her hands on her apron. "I must go to Master Philip and the little ones. You'll ring if you want anything, miss? Oh, and Mrs. Langdale will see you in the morning room at ten o'clock." And then she was gone.

I finished my breakfast, dressed by the fire, and then unpacked the rest of my luggage. Afterward I walked to the windows and looked out. My room was at the front of the house and below me lay the smooth surface of the lake, reflecting the sky. Across the water the shore was flat, with a few stands of larch here and there. Sheep dotted the empty hillsides beyond, and a bleak slate-roofed gray stone village was wedged at the upper end of the lake. There was a sensation of being completely surrounded and cut off from the outside world by the long ridges of fell. I was accustomed to the rolling Wiltshire Downs, so it was a strange, though not unpleasant, feeling. A man sat fishing from a boat near one of the islands in the lake.

All at once I felt the peculiar trill along the spine that comes from being watched without one's knowledge. Turning quickly, I found myself face to face with a slim boy who stood solemnly in my doorway.

"Hello," I said, summoning a smile to cover my start of surprise. "You must be Master Philip."

He nodded. "I'm not supposed to be here. But I wanted to see you."

Going to the fire, I gestured for him to take the small stool opposite my chair. "I'm glad you came. Sit down and tell me about yourself."

Clearly debating with himself, he stood there, a fair child with the most haunted gray eyes I had ever seen. At last with a defiant shrug of his shoulders he joined me by the hearth. "I heard you arrive in the night. The knocker woke me. It was very late."

"Yes, but there was nothing I could do to prevent it. The journey to Thorston Water is not an easy one, especially after dark."

"I wouldn't know. We go to Ravensholme—where my mother grew up—sometimes, and once my . . . my father took me to Kendal. I haven't traveled anywhere else."

"You will when you have grown to be a man," I replied, touched by the longing in his voice. "I came all the way from Wiltshire, almost the length of England. Shall I tell you about it?"

But he shook his head. "Only how you went after Lancaster." There was a strained intensity in the simple statement.

As I began to describe the last part of my journey, leaving out my difficulties with Hichen, his eyes grew large and excited.

"You crossed the bay—took the route over the sands?" he demanded, getting ahead of my story in his interest.

"Yes, it was by far the shortest way, and I was hoping to arrive—"

There was a scratch at the door and Maggie came in. "There you are, Master Philip!" she scolded. "What are you thinking of, running off like that!"

The boy was on his feet, facing her. His gray eyes were all at once expressionless and oddly vulnerable. "I wanted to say good morning to Miss Winton," he replied quietly.

"We have had a very pleasant conversation," I began, and caught the pleading glance he swiftly threw me. "There's such a lovely view from my windows. I'm eager to learn more about the Lake District," I went on, and Maggie seemed relieved.

" 'Tisn't good manners to bother guests in their bedchambers," she said. "But no harm done, I'm sure." She held the door for him and he walked out of the room, a seven-year-old boy who seemed far too quiet and self-contained. Where were the energy and enthusiasm that should be typical of someone his age?

"No harm done," I repeated, and watched them go.

Precisely at ten Maggie returned to escort me to the morning room, where Mrs. Langdale was waiting to greet me.

The house was no more than two hundred and fifty years old, if that. The staircase was handsomely carved, the dark wood polished and well cared for. The hall, so dim that I retained no impression of it from the night before, was now flooded with sunshine from the tall windows on either side of the door. It was spacious, lined with fine paneling and a handsome array of family portraits. Beyond the stairs was an open area before a wide hearth, and a rectangular table, carved and very old, held a tall silver ewer and bowl that matched the branched silver candelabra on either side. The floor was a checkerboard of black and white squares, and the high ceiling was ornately plastered, a pattern of roses entwined with ribbons.

As if she sensed my admiration, Maggie said quietly as we reached the foot of the stairs, "It's very grand, much nicer than Ravensholme. But Mrs. Ryland says all these eyes make her nervous."

I smiled, thinking of my own loneliness. "I rather like having so many associations with the past surrounding me."

"Aye," Maggie said cryptically. "When it's your own family."

She stopped at a door down the first passage off the hall, tapped lightly before entering, and announced, "Miss Winton, Mrs. Langdale." And then she was gone, leaving me with my godmother.

Mrs. Langdale sat near a window, the sunshine outlining her head and shoulders, a light shawl draped about the sleeves of her dark green gown. A much younger woman than my mother would have been had she lived, my godmother was tall and slender with brown hair and somber hazel eyes. Though I would never have described her as pretty, there was something in her face—character, perhaps even suffering—that gave it a certain quality of its own.

She smiled. "Elizabeth, my dear! Come in and sit down. Did you have too awful a journey to this far corner of creation?"

Tears sprang to my eyes at the warmth in her voice and I swallowed hastily before crossing the room to take a chintz-covered chair near hers. "From Lancaster north, I did begin to wonder if I might fall off the edges of the earth," I replied, trying to match her lightness and mask my feelings.

"Well, we are civilized here, so the poets tell us. I had hoped Freya would send a carriage to meet you at Lancaster, but she has had so much on her mind of late. One of the children has been ill. Very worrisome."

"Your children?" I asked hesitantly, for I knew very little about my godmother. Only that she and my mother had been close despite the six years' difference in their ages and that she had married late in life. She had still been Miss Deerham when she had visited us fifteen or sixteen years ago.

A flicker of sadness crossed her face. "Alas, no, I have no children. Freya has a son and two daughters, whom I spoil outrageously." Mrs. Langdale shifted in the sun. "Tell me about yourself, my dear. I gather from your letter that you have been teaching since your father's death. Do you enjoy it?"

"I find it interesting," I replied. "And I like the independence, though it isn't always pleasant to be at the beck and call of others." I had tried to weigh my words carefully, for I did not wish my godmother to think I was unhappy or asking for pity. But I must have said something wrong, for her expressive face turned suddenly away to stare at the cheerful blue and cream room behind us.

"Indeed." There was a short silence, and I didn't know how to fill it or what caused her withdrawal.

"I understand the desire for independence," she said after a moment. "And also what it is like to be subject to the whims of others." She turned back to the light, a smile replacing the strain in her eyes. "I'm very glad you have come, Elizabeth. I hope we can make your stay a happy one."

Before I could thank her, I met her glance for the first time since I had entered the room and knew why her sister-in-law had written to me for her.

Charlotte Langdale was blind.

2

As if her intuition had replaced her vision, Mrs. Langdale said wryly into the stillness, "Yes, you have guessed. I haven't learned the knack of concealing it for long. It happened several years ago—an accident." There was bitterness in her voice as she spoke the last word.

"I'm sorry," I said gently. "It must be very trying for you."

Her face brightened. "How perceptive of you! It *is* trying, yet most people don't recognize that and offer pity instead. I *detest* pity!" She stretched out her hand. "Tell me, do you look like Elaine still? Fair, with those impossible blue eyes? I was always so envious of her, you know!"

I laughed with her. "My hair is indeed very fair, and it curls, which is quite out of place for a proper schoolmistress. And my eyes are dark blue."

We spent the next quarter of an hour in very pleasant conversation until the door opened and Mrs. Ryland walked in.

"Good morning, Miss Winton. You rested well, I trust?" Her words were those of a considerate hostess inquiring after the welfare of a guest, but she seemed to cast a pall over the brightness, as if the sun had gone in. I saw my godmother lift her shawl about her shoulders, as if she felt it also.

"Very well, thank you," I replied truthfully.

"I have one of my headaches today." She sighed, took the chair beside her sewing basket, and started threading a needle. Somehow she had contrived to make my late arrival seem to blame. "I believe you are a teacher, Miss Winton?"

"Yes. I taught drawing and deportment."

"It was a charity school, I suppose? You are very young for much responsibility."

Stung by her disparagement, I said in spite of myself, "On the contrary, the Trenton Academy is well known and caters to the daughters of the best families." Almost as the words were out I bit my lip, remembering my situation. Pride and penury were poor companions, and I should have made allowances for her indisposition.

But Mrs. Ryland, fully occupied with her mending, had not noticed. She went on as if I had not spoken. "While you are with us, I hope you will make yourself useful. Mrs. Langdale—"

"I have asked Elizabeth to call me Aunt Charlotte," my godmother put in suddenly, her face turned toward the chair where her sister-in-law was sitting. Once again I was struck by her ability to appear normal.

"—Charlotte will appreciate your assistance, I'm sure."

I saw my godmother's fingers tighten in her lap. She did not want my services thrust upon her as a duty, nor her sister-in-law's patronizing reminder that she was helpless. It was, I thought, needlessly callous, if not cruel.

"Of course. I shall be happy to do whatever I can," I replied lightly.

There was a tap at the door and Maggie entered,

pulling a very reluctant Philip behind her. He was filthy, his shirt torn and hanging out of his trousers. And there was a mulish set to his jaw as he faced his mother.

Mrs. Ryland was on her feet, crying out in dismay and frustration. "You haven't been playing in those abandoned mines again!"

"No, ma'am," Maggie answered for him. "Not the mines. He was down on the mere, helping a fisherman haul in his boat. 'Twas one of the grooms that found him and brought him back."

"Fisherman? What fisherman?" Mrs. Ryland demanded, her eyes on her son's face. And I felt the same intensity in this question as I had when she had asked me about the stranger on the sands.

Philip replied sullenly, "It was only old Thomas, from the village. His leg was bothering him and he couldn't bring the boat high enough by himself. So I helped."

The tension had gone from his mother almost as quickly as it had come and was replaced by anger. "Look at you, as dirty as a chimney sweep! What am I to do with you? It is almost as if you delight in tormenting me! If you only knew how I *worry*." With an effort she brought her temper under control. Sitting down again, she took the boy's hand in hers and said earnestly, "It is dangerous to run off from Maggie and play along the mere or around those mines on the Old Man. If something happened—an accident—we wouldn't be there to help. Surely you are old enough to understand that! Why can't you be content in the gardens or running about on the grounds? Why must you frighten me so?"

"I didn't go *out* in the boat. I only helped haul her in. There's no harm in that," he answered. "And I am bored in the gardens, trailing after Dora and Nell. They are *babies*."

I saw my godmother suppress a slight smile at his last remark. It must, I thought, be a common complaint. It

34

appeared that Master Philip, quiet though he seemed, had a boy's taste for roving and exploring.

Mrs. Ryland shook her head. "You know you aren't allowed to leave the grounds. Much as I dislike punishing you, Philip, I must make you understand the seriousness of this matter. After luncheon, you will come to your father in the library."

His face was suddenly brushed clear of all expression. "Yes, Mama," he said softly. There was an uncomfortable silence as he left with Maggie.

Mrs. Ryland picked up her needle again, but she was stabbing blindly at the tiny sleeve before her, her thoughts far from the small tear in the delicate lace.

After a moment my godmother rose. "Would you lend me your arm, Elizabeth? I should like to walk in the gardens while this glorious warmth lasts."

As we stepped out the front door into the sunlight, Aunt Charlotte took a deep breath. "I can smell the earth warming. There are daffodils in sheltered corners, and violets." We crossed the lawns before the house and turned into the garden path. "What is the Old Man doing? Frowning or smiling?"

"The old man?" I asked, bewildered.

"The Old Man of Coniston. There, the high fell behind the house."

I looked up at the tall mountain rising above the lake and saw the top. "He must be smiling," I replied. "There are no clouds."

"We tell the weather by him, you know. The climate is so changeable, but the Old Man is touched first by rain or mist or snow. We always know what is in store. Great Gable, above Ravensholme, is the same."

Shading my eyes to scan the gray barren face of the mountain, I could see the scars on the slopes that must be the old mines. Fascinating for a small boy, but unsafe to explore. Turning, I looked up at the gray stone house, broad and square but rather handsomely decorated with a fine pediment above the front door and urns spaced along the gray slate roof. Matching urns, filled with soil for flowers, stood at the corners of the top step. Set among trees, mostly evergreen specimens, the house was well placed to overlook the lake.

"Good morning," a man's voice called from behind us, and Mr. Ryland came out of the shrubbery from the direction of the stables. He was dressed for riding, his high boots polished and his hair ruffled. "I've had a brisk canter along the mere," he said for Aunt Charlotte's benefit.

"It must be a perfect morning for it, Matthew," she replied as he gave her his arm. "I was taking Elizabeth on a tour of the gardens."

"Do you ride, Miss Winton?" he asked, leading the way into a rose garden.

"I'm afraid I don't," I replied, hoping he would not ask why.

"A pity. We could mount you well." He gestured toward the beds where tender leaves were just appearing on the bare stalks. "There isn't much to be seen at the moment, but in June our roses are the envy of the neighborhood." And then he added, "I hear from the grooms that Philip has trespassed again."

"I do wish there were boys his age near us," Aunt Charlotte said. "He spends so much time alone. It isn't surprising his boredom leads to mischief."

"Yes, I agree. But his mother worries. God knows, her brother—" He broke off. "I'm sorry."

"—her brother was wild enough, and she is afraid Philip will be like him," Aunt Charlotte finished for him. "You needn't spare my feelings, Matthew. Who knows more about Hal's wildness than I?"

But Matthew's face darkened. He was obviously unhappy over the slip of his tongue and wished the words unsaid.

As we turned in silence from the rose beds to a border

of Dutch bulbs, rampantly colorful beneath trimmed boxwoods, Matthew Ryland knelt to pick a small bunch of violets from a cluster at the edge of the grass. He gave them to Charlotte Langdale, closing her fingers over them as he said, "I can't imagine how violets sprang up in the path. They must have escaped the vigilance of the gardeners."

She smiled. "How wicked of them! Thank you, Matthew."

He excused himself shortly afterward, and as he disappeared in the direction of the house, I asked, "Do you visit Abbot's Thorston often?"

My godmother's arm moved beneath my fingers as I guided her along the paths. "I was plagued with a cough this winter and came here to escape the dampness of Ravensholme," she replied evasively. "Now that spring has reached us, I must begin to think of returning."

There was something in her voice that made me say diffidently, "I hope my arrival has not interfered with your plans."

"On the contrary. Your coming has brightened the darkness for me," she said gently. And I found myself wondering if she meant more by "darkness" than her blindness. "It must be nearing noon. Perhaps we should go in and change for luncheon."

As we came out onto the lawns, she halted suddenly and groped for my hand. "Don't let yourself be caught up in our problems, Elizabeth. And leave us as soon as you possibly can!"

Taken aback, I stammered a promise. But where else could I go?

Immediately after luncheon Mr. Ryland bowed politely and left the table. Nothing was said about Philip, but he must have been in everyone's thoughts. Why should a simple matter of discipline loom so large? Philip had certainly disobeyed his mother, but he had not transgressed beyond forgiveness. And Matthew Ryland had shown he understood the boy's loneliness. It occurred to me that Philip might have been rather spoiled until the births of his sisters, and was now in the painful period of adjustment after being the center of attention.

At last I pretended fatigue from my journey and went up to my room. The lovely gold and green dining room had become stifling. I was glad to leave the two women absently toying with their half-finished trifles. Aunt Charlotte was lost in her own thoughts, and Freya Ryland, a frown between her dark eyes, had evidently not recovered from her headache.

The lovely weather held, despite Maggie's dour predictions, and I slipped outside later in the afternoon to stroll in the gardens and watch the play of light and shadow across the surface of Thorston Water. My thoughts wandered to Mr. Wordsworth and Mr. Coleridge, who had first brought the beauty of this area to public notice. (Lines of their poetry, remembered from my schooldays, came back to me). As I walked on, I didn't see the child curled in the bole of a great oak until I was almost upon him.

His gray eyes, smudged with pain and tears, stared at me for an instant and then disappeared into the folds of his arms.

My breath caught in my throat. "Philip," I said, trying to keep the shock out of my voice. "Are you all right?"

"Yes," came the muffled reply. But he seemed to shrink into the crack in the wood as if he wished he could hide from me.

"There's a bird there, high above the lake. I can't quite make it out," I said, changing my tactics. "Do you suppose it is a lark?"

"I don't know."

"I'm woefully ignorant about birds and I know nothing at all about your mountains—"

"Fells. They aren't called mountains. And it isn't a *lake,* either. It is a mere or water. Or even a tarn." But he still had not lifted his head or changed his position.

"But you were born here." I moved away to seat myself on a rustic bench some ten feet from the tree. "Now if we were in Wiltshire, I could tell *you* about the lovely cathedral in Salisbury or the standing stones at—"

"We have standing stones. At Castlerigg there is a circle." He was looking at me now, easier because I had not pressed him.

"Do you believe in the legends that giants built them?"

He scowled. "Of course not. They were built by people who lived here long before the monks came to Furness—even before my mother's ancestors came from Iceland. Not even the Romans knew who they were."

Surprised, I said, "You have a fine grasp of history! You must be a credit to your tutor."

"I don't have a tutor. Herr—" He broke off and then added lamely, "A friend told me."

"Then you are very fortunate in your friendships, Philip," I said as he rolled out of the tree and came forward. There were no tears now, for he had wiped his face on his sleeve. Nor could I see signs of physical abuse. The hurt, whatever it was, came from inside. Pretending to take no notice, I made room for him on the bench.

"Is it true that you came here because you have no other place to go?" he asked with the devastating honesty of childhood.

I winced but said quietly, "There will be no place for me at a new school until the autumn term. They no longer needed me at the Academy."

He nodded. "I know what it is like not to be wanted." He looked up at me with those haunted eyes. "But I like you. You don't talk to me as if I belonged in long dresses."

For a while we sat in silence and I wondered why this

child was so different from most boys his age—why those clear gray eyes were shadowed with suffering. There was no reason for it so far as I could see. His parents seemed concerned for him, not uncaring or neglectful or cruel. Yet there were tensions in this household.

"You won't tell anyone where you found me?" he asked so unexpectedly that I was startled out of my thoughts.

"We all need our secret places. After all, you are on the grounds just as you should be."

He gave me a shy smile and then was gone, slipping away through the shrubbery. I sat where I was, trying to remind myself of my promise to my godmother. But curiosity and a natural concern for the boy distracted me.

In the days that followed I occupied myself—and avoided Mrs. Ryland's disparaging tongue—with walks on the grounds or quiet hours spent reading to Aunt Charlotte.

She had missed the companionship of books since the advent of her blindness, and it appeared that no one had the time to read aloud to her. When the weather was pleasant, we sat in the sun on a garden bench, but rain and mist were more usual.

Sometimes when we met in the gardens, Philip would talk to me, but he rarely spoke to anyone indoors. The younger children generally spent most of their day in the nursery. Two-year-old Dora, rosy and redhaired like her mother, was as friendly as a puppy. Her exuberant greetings for everyone endeared her to the household. Four-year-old Helen, who was more shy, but fair like her father, had an elfin grace. Philip, quiet and withdrawn, seemed sullen by comparison and seldom attracted attention to himself.

From his chance remarks it was obvious that he loved

Abbot's Thorston. Very little happened here that he was not aware of, and once as we watched rain clouds build over the Old Man he told me his plans for the estate. Listening to him describe a projected addition to the stables, one would have thought he expected to take charge in the near future. I smiled but said nothing to dampen his spirits.

"There's not much that will grow well up here except sheep," he went on, "but my father's estate in Gloucestershire raises cattle and horses and produce for the London markets and famous roses. I've never seen Garland, but Aunt Charlotte says it is quite beautiful. Still, Abbot's Thorston will always be my principal seat."

Then the first drops of rain drove us indoors. He slipped away, hurrying up the stairs before his mother could take note of the tear in his trousers from scrambling about in the great oak.

On Wednesday the household was disrupted by the arrival—unexpected and unwelcomed—of Mr. Ryland's younger brother Martin. A year or two my senior, brash, graceless, and obviously the black sheep of the family, he made no effort to conceal his reasons for coming.

"I haven't twopence to rub together, and my creditors think I'm in Yorkshire. By the time they've searched the dales, they won't have the energy to tackle Cumberland. You *are* spending part of the summer at Ravensholme?" he finished hopefully.

"Yes," Mrs. Ryland answered shortly. "And you will be in the way. It is gambling again, I take it?"

"Among other things," he replied cheerfully, not in the least daunted by her lack of welcome. He turned to me. "I haven't seen you before. Are you another penniless hanger-on?"

Though he couldn't possibly have meant it as an insult, I felt the hot blood in my face and was grateful when Matthew Ryland answered for me.

"Miss Winton is Charlotte's goddaughter, here for a visit and not to be taunted by your careless tongue. My dear, I have the misfortune to present my brother. If you find him troublesome, come to me."

As coolly as I could I acknowledged the introduction and soon made an excuse to leave the drawing room. Aunt Charlotte was in the hall and I warned her of the new arrival.

She grimaced. "He's young and has been allowed to grow up undisciplined. Matthew's fault, really, but he was only twenty himself when his parents died, and even as a boy Martin was high-spirited and difficult. Freya detests him. There will be no end of trouble before he leaves."

"Well," I said in resignation, "I shall avoid him whenever I can. Are you going in to greet him? Or perhaps you'd like me to read to you before tea?"

My godmother smiled conspiratorially. "I believe I shall go up to the nursery for an hour or two and pretend I don't know that Martin is here. And *he* never ventures that far from a decanter."

I laughed and watched her start up the steps, her feet and hands finding their way from long familiarity. And then a thought struck me. What of Philip? How would he respond to the presence of another rebel in the house? Martin would be a poor—but possibly exciting—example. It was really none of my affair, but I knew from my experience at the Academy how easily and disastrously a lonely, susceptible child could be swayed by hero worship.

Hurrying after Aunt Charlotte, I asked quickly, "I wonder . . . the boy is so impressionable . . ."

Aunt Charlotte's face was sober. "Martin has no influence in that direction, thank God. He really isn't interested in Philip at all."

"I'm glad," I replied, feeling a little foolish now.

As if she hadn't heard me, she went on thoughtfully. "No, it isn't Martin who holds him in thrall. It is that other man. I fear—" She stopped as one of the maids came down the stairs toward us. My godmother gave me a smile that was rather absent-minded, then went on her way again.

If Martin had no interest in the children, he more than made up for it by his interest in me. He seemed to take a perverse pleasure in teasing me, and it made my life unbearable. I had never made my debut in a London Season, never learned the clever responses one should make to gallantries, never conducted a light flirtation at a ball. Perhaps he only polished his self-esteem at my expense or wished to impress me with his rather shallow sophistication, but he merely succeeded in making me uncomfortable.

Nothing I did escaped his notice, from a bit of mud on the heel of my shoe after walking in the gardens to a curl escaping the severe knot into which I twisted my rebellious hair. Twice he called me the little Quakeress because of the plain blue and gray and brown gowns I wore. Serviceable clothes, with neatly cuffed sleeves and high collars, they were all I had except for a dark green silk for Parents' Day at the Academy. Indeed, they were ideal for teaching, but I knew very well that they appeared drab by comparison with the lovely silks and velvets that Mrs. Ryland wore at dinner. Though I avoided him whenever I could, meals always brought me within reach of his taunts.

By Friday evening, restless from being inactive and irritable from being on my guard, I forgot my resolution to ignore him, forgot even that he was a member of the family while I was a guest on sufferance.

I had been standing in the tall french windows of the crimson and white drawing room, watching the last of the sun's rays pick out the dancing crests of ripples on the mere below. Absorbed in the beauty of the scene, I didn't realize that Martin Ryland was behind me until he spoke.

"I wonder—are you really such an ice maiden?" he asked softly. "Or simply waiting for the prince to appear? He isn't Matthew, I know that. I wish he was . . . me."

Flushing hotly in spite of myself, I faced him. The twinkle in his pale blue eyes deepened and I lost my temper. "Do you consider yourself irresistible, or is rudeness the only way you can command attention?"

Martin smiled, though there were sudden spots of color high on his cheekbones as if I had touched on a sensitive subject. "I am practicing my wiles. Like Matthew, I must marry for money."

"Then you are wasting your time with me. I have none," I said bluntly. "And I wouldn't consider wedding you if I did."

"Who knows? Marriage might tame me as it did Matthew. Or like Hal Langdale, I may make a monstrous husband. Will you wager on one or the other? I warn you, it may be some time before you collect!"

"No, I won't wager," I said coldly, and crossed the room to the small gilt and damask sofa where my godmother was quietly sitting.

"Is Martin annoying you?" Matthew asked, coming to stand before the empty marble hearth.

"Miss Winton is interested in my way of life," Martin answered for me, running his fingers down the keyboard of the rosewood pianoforte.

"Must you encourage him, Miss Winton?" Mrs. Ryland snapped. "It should be apparent that we don't approve of his disgraceful behavior."

"Nor do I," I began in self-defense, but Mr. Ryland was before me.

"Try our patience too far," he told his brother curtly, "and you will find yourself back in London."

Lithwaite entered to announce dinner before anyone could speak again. We rose to follow Freya Ryland, and I caught the sullen expression on Martin's face as he allowed his elders to precede him. I was the last through the door and so heard the low words: "A brave show for a man not even in his own home!" There was a sneer in his voice that didn't quite cover the bitterness underlying his strange remark.

We retired early that evening and I found it difficult to sleep. Accustomed as I was to the frenetic pace of the Academy, the past week at Abbot's Thorston had been physically undemanding, though I worried constantly about the autumn and my dwindling finances. I lay in bed listening to the sounds of the house rather than falling into exhausted oblivion. After a time I rose and walked to the windows to look down on the moonlit lake. Though I was cold, the beauty of the night and the humped line of fells against the stars held me there.

Then, from the edge of my vision, I saw something move in the trees near the far end of the drive. It disappeared for a time, though I thought I saw it again nearer the house. Watching closely, I caught a flicker of darkness as it passed through a patch of moonlight in the circle before the door.

It was too tall and too slim for an animal. Someone, then, was creeping slowly toward the house. One of the servants, slipping home from an evening in the village? Not by the way of the front door surely!

My next thought was of Philip. Did he roam at *night* as well? The figure was too indistinct to be certain, and moonlight played odd tricks with shadows.

I stood there undecided. It wasn't my place to interfere, but in all conscience I couldn't pretend I hadn't seen him. And it wasn't safe for a small boy to wander at will until all hours.

Catching up my wrapper, I quietly made my way into the silent passage and down the dark stairs. Perhaps if I talked to him, I thought, I could convince him to stop such foolishness in return for not telling his parents.

There was a glimmer of light from the hall below, and at first I believed it was moonlight spilling through the windows near the door, though the draperies were usually drawn at dusk. But at the last landing I stopped abruptly.

Someone was there, moving quietly, a candle's glow fading into the vast darkness beyond the stairs! Surely Philip wouldn't chance being caught out of bed like this. And if it was Martin, returning from a rendezvous, I had no desire to be discovered spying on him. Lifting my skirts, I felt my way to the outer edge of the risers to prevent the telltale squeak as I leaned over the carved stair rail.

And then I could see him. A tall figure in a long cloak, silver spurs gleaming at his heels and a deep shadow obscuring his face beneath his broad-brimmed hat. A single candle burned in his gloved hand, and he was gliding about with the ease, I thought, of familiarity, not the wariness of a thief.

He paused before a portrait above the great hearth and stood for a moment staring up into the painted face. Then he turned toward the stairs. Like a moth in the darkness I fluttered up another flight to the safety of the first floor, too startled to think about anything but escape. He silently climbed a few steps, lifting the candle to look at the paintings stretching in a line up the wall. He seemed to take a strange pleasure in his surroundings, as if weighing all he saw in the light of some secret knowledge. It was with reluctance that he returned to the hall instead of continuing up the flight. Pressed against the far wall, I felt sick with relief.

I peered through the balusters as he picked up one of the heavy silver candelabra and caught my breath to cry out for help just as he set it gently back in its place on the refectory table.

Though it was my duty to summon Matthew Ryland, I had the oddest feeling that to do so would be a betrayal. So far there was no indication that the intruder had come to steal or to molest the occupants of the house. Caught up in the spell of that winking candle's gleam, torn by doubts and curiosity, I did nothing but merely watch carefully from a safe distance. My heart, thudding in my breast, seemed overly loud in the stillness.

Once, as if he sensed eyes upon him, he paused to look up into the blackness of the stairwell, calmly searching the darkness. I shivered as his glance swept past me. After a time he seemed satisfied that he was indeed alone and walked into the drawing room. My throat was dry.

Suddenly it came to me who he was: the man that night on the sands, the stranger who had found us floundering in the stormy darkness and set Hichen's team safely upon the right track once more! There was something about him, some strange and unsettling force that reached out to me then as now, an odd attraction that was as elusive as it was unreasonable. I had never even seen his face!

Why should he coolly enter the house while the owners slept? Who was he? And what must I do?

He was gone as quickly as he had come, for I *sensed* the emptiness before I could be certain of it. The front door had not been opened, yet the hall and drawing room no longer held his presence. Frightened by the unexplained ease of access, the almost ghostly appearance and disappearance of the intruder, I found myself shaking in the darkness and clinging to the newel post for support. The spell was broken.

The recollection of Mrs. Ryland's tense questions about the dark man from an Eastern country sent me flying to the master bedroom. It was wrong to conceal what had happened. Only the Rylands could know if this man threatened anyone at Abbot's Thorston.

Knocking on their door, I tightened the sash of my wrapper and tried to think what to say. But when Matthew Ryland, his fair hair tousled with sleep, stood before me I could only stammer, "There—there was someone in the hall. I—I saw him."

He put his hand on my shoulder. "Have you had a nightmare, Miss Winton? What's wrong?" Behind him I heard his wife fumbling for a candle.

"I thought I saw something on the lawns—a man. When I came down the stairs to investigate, I found him already in the hall, walking about. I—I think he has gone. I hope he has," I ended, shivering again.

"Wait here," he said quickly, closing the door. When he returned a few moments later, he was dressed in shirt and trousers. Mrs. Ryland followed, her face white in the candle's light.

"Did you see him?" she asked, grasping my arm with trembling fingers as Matthew Ryland hurried on ahead of us.

I shook my head. "He wore a cloak and a hat with a wide brim. He—he was tall. And he wore spurs, silver ones—"

"Dear God in heaven!" For an instant I thought she would fall at my feet in a faint, but she pushed me aside and raced after her husband.

We must have searched the ground floor for nearly half an hour, but there was no sign of forced entry, indeed, no sign of entry at all. The man had gone, leaving no trace behind.

"Are you certain it wasn't a nightmare?" Matthew Ryland asked, coming back from the front lawns and closing the heavy door behind him.

"No! He was *here,* walking about, looking at the portraits, touching those silver candlesticks—"

But this time Mrs. Ryland sank to the floor in a

huddle of silk. With a sharp exclamation her husband knelt beside her just as Martin, fully dressed, called down from above, "What the hell is going on? Do you know what *time* it is?"

His brother ignored him, lifting Freya in his arms after passing the candlestick to me. We went upstairs to lay her on her bed, and I loosened the ties of her wrapper while her husband poured a little brandy into a glass and held it to her lips.

"Will someone tell me what has happened?" Martin was demanding from the foot of the bed.

Freya moaned, her hand fluttering across her eyes as she struggled to sit up. "Oh, God," she said weakly. Then she seemed to gather her wits with an effort and added, "I—I can't bear the thought of a *thief*—"

"A thief?" Aunt Charlotte repeated, standing in the doorway.

"Miss Winton thought she saw someone in the house," Matthew Ryland said, turning toward the blind woman in an attempt to sound soothing. And so he missed the fleeting look of relief in his wife's eyes, as if she welcomed the brief distraction.

"I'll call out the grooms. We'll search the grounds!" Martin exclaimed in excitement.

"You'll do nothing of the kind," his brother ordered. "If there *was* someone in the house, he has long since left Abbot's Thorston. You may be sure of that. I won't drag the servants from their beds for your amusement. In fact, there is every likelihood that Miss Winton imagined the incident." As he wheeled toward me, the protest died on my lips. Matthew Ryland believed me, it was there in his face, but he didn't want Aunt Charlotte or his wife to be frightened.

"In—Indeed, it seemed very real, but dreams sometimes are," I said, trying to infuse sincerity into my voice for my godmother's sake.

"Then we shall all return to our beds," Matthew said, taking his brother's arm and leading him firmly to the chamber door.

As I followed, I felt Freya Ryland's eyes burning into my back. She too knew that I had spoken the truth about the strange visitor, though I couldn't be certain how—or why.

It was cool and cloudy the next morning. Very little was said at breakfast about the night's events, though they were far from forgotten. And it was clear that the servants knew nothing about the incident.

But Mrs. Ryland, her dark eyes looking determined in her pale face, announced that we were leaving at once for Ravensholme.

There was consternation at the table. Only Martin seemed pleased. Aunt Charlotte, her face drawn, picked at her food and said nothing after her first shocked protest. Matthew argued with his wife, but she was not to be dissuaded.

"It *isn't* a sudden notion," she said angrily. "I have had it in mind for some time. I need the change. My headaches—" Her hand touched her temple automatically, as if this was an old complaint—or weapon.

"We usually go to Ravensholme in July. Hal doesn't expect us now, and Charlotte will certainly need time to prepare for guests."

"I sent a groom with a message this morning. Hal knows we are coming. As for the house, Torver runs it, not Charlotte. It won't make a particle of difference to *him!*"

"It doesn't make sense!" Matthew replied curtly, a flush rising in his face at her high-handedness. "And we couldn't possibly be ready to leave for several days."

"We can—and will—leave this morning. I've told the servants to pack what we need for a day or two. The rest can follow. I will not spend another night here. I want to go *home!*" And to my shocked surprise she burst into tears and fled the room.

We finished our breakfast in an uncomfortable silence, and immediately afterward Matthew had a violent quarrel with his brother behind the closed doors of the library. Freya, head high, went about the preparations for departure as if it had been arranged for weeks. My godmother had gone to her room, and so I hastily set about packing my trunk.

Only an hour behind schedule, we climbed into the carriages waiting beside the front door and discovered for the first time that Philip was missing.

Maggie, flushed and breathless, had searched everywhere before she came to the boy's mother. "Indeed, he's not in the house, nor in t' gardens."

"You saw him this morning? He *was* in his bed?" Freya Ryland asked sharply.

"Oh, aye, he was in his bed right enough. And after breakfast one of the gardeners saw him tossing his ball outside the library windows."

Matthew Ryland swore. "I'll have the grooms look along the mere. Do you suppose he went up the Old Man?"

"Not as clarty as it be today," Maggie replied doubtfully, glancing toward the cloud-rimmed fell.

"I'll look in the gardens," I told my godmother quietly, suddenly remembering the crack in the oak tree. She nodded as I hurried away.

But Philip was not there. I had walked as far as a stand of larches before I heard the sound of a shoe scuffling. Whirling about, I saw no one, then looked up in time to catch a glimpse of the boy cowering in the upper branches of the oak, his brown suit nearly the color of the great limbs.

I called up impatiently, "Philip Ryland, you should be ashamed—"

He came slipping and sliding down the tree with a

speed that left me speechless. As I ran to catch him if he fell, he tumbled down the trunk and threw himself at me, his fists pummeling me and his face twisted with grief and pain.

"Don't call me that!" he cried. "Don't ever do it again!"

Catching the flailing wrists, I held him at arm's length. "Stop that!" I ordered sharply. "Behave yourself at once!"

"I am *not* his son! My name is Philip *Carrock!*" He was weeping so hard that I could scarcely make sense of the jumbled words.

Kneeling beside him on the path, I tried to make him hear me. "What are you saying? I am willing to listen, Philip, if you will explain."

He choked in his effort to stifle the harsh, wracking sobs, and then leaned his forehead against my shoulder, exhausted. "I am not his son! I never was. My mother was married to Charles Carrock first, so my name is Philip Carrock."

I drew the thin shivering body into my arms. "I didn't know. No one had ever told me, you see. I didn't mean to hurt you, Philip."

He gulped something and then took the handkerchief I held out. "It's all right," he said with the quick forgiveness of a child. "I shouldn't have hit you. It was wrong. But I heard them talking in the library about the man last night." He had refolded the handkerchief and returned it as we started slowly back toward the house. "My . . . my stepfather thought it was his brother pretending to be a thief so he could steal something. He needs money badly. But it wasn't him. I know it wasn't."

"Who was it?" I asked gently, driven by the intensity in him. "Why did he come here? What does he want?"

"They want me to believe my father is dead. I even put flowers on his grave each year. But he isn't. I know he isn't. And last night he came for me. Only he had to leave before he reached the nursery." His voice broke.

Stunned, I could think of nothing to say to the child, no word of comfort or even of explanation to dispel his wild fancy.

When we reached the carriages, I said only that Philip had taken a tumble. Because of his tear-streaked face and rumpled clothes no one doubted me. His mother took him in charge, scolding furiously, while Martin hurried off to call in the searching grooms. Fifteen minutes later we closed the door of Abbot's Thorston and drove off on the journey to Ravensholme.

3

We turned into the long narrow valley of Wastwater as the last rays of the sun touched the peaks about us with golden fire. The empty land appeared desolate and rocky above the black finger of the mere, and yet invested with a majesty that was a little frightening. Flocks of sheep dotted the slopes of the fells, with a shepherd's hut sometimes visible in the high reaches. But there were no people—no friendly villages clustering by the twisting, dusty road. At the far end lay the frowning mass of Great Gable, isolated, like some ancient Icelandic god left to guard the dale. Thorston Water had been impressive, beautiful, and yet approachable. Wasdale was awesome.

Freya Ryland sighed with relief. "We will arrive before dark. I was afraid—" She broke off and after a moment added, "It *is* good to be home!"

"Yes," Aunt Charlotte agreed quietly. But her hands were locked together in her lap.

All day the crosscurrents of emotion in the carriage had left me on edge, uncertain how to deal with them. Freya had been by turns silent and irritable. I wondered if she was thinking about the man I had seen last night, and how much he had to do with our precipitant departure for Ravensholme. Whoever he was, she knew him and feared him.

Philip too believed that he knew the man. I couldn't forget his heartbroken confession, the suffering in his gray eyes as he told me about his father. It was only a child's illusion, born of loneliness and dreams of what might have been. All the same, to Philip it was real.

I looked at Freya, sitting across from me, her pale face turned toward the window. In her green velvet traveling dress she was slim and elegant, a very attractive woman. Whatever she was frightened of, it was not her dead husband. Then who in her past wore spurs and was in some way connected with a pair of silver candlesticks? And Matthew Ryland, grim and taciturn as he rode beside our carriage, was still furious with Martin and blamed *him* for that nocturnal visit. Martin had long since given up trying to talk to him and had spurred on ahead. Only Aunt Charlotte seemed unconcerned about the stranger. Whatever worried her lay at Ravensholme, and I was beginning to suspect it was her homecoming.

Almost as if she sensed my endless speculations and wished to put a stop to them, Freya leaned forward to point ahead. "That's Scafell Pike—the ridge beyond the shoulder of Great Gable," she said with more warmth in her voice than I had yet heard. "And you can see the Screes over there, like a cascade of rock reaching from Scafell's flanks almost to the mere's southern edge. Wastwater must be the deepest lake in England. I find it cold even in summer. You are fortunate—there is no mist this evening to mar the view. Even Scafell itself, the second highest peak of the ridge, is clear."

"I've never known anyplace quite like it," I replied.

"You won't. Not until you visit Iceland. That's why my ancestors, marauders from the sea who pillaged and fought their way inland, decided to settle here. It was like their homeland, only not as harsh. Tradition says they brought the first Herdwick sheep with them. Of course, many of the dalesmen claim descent from Norse rovers," she added fairly.

I stared out the carriage windows at the bleak scenery, relieved when at long last I saw a village spreading over the flat wedge of land between Great Gable and the head of Wastwater. Stone walls marked fields, houses stood gray and sturdy in tiny patches of flower beds, and silent, dignified people watched us pass, nodding to Mrs. Ryland and my godmother with a grace that was never servile.

The dale ended in a cul-de-sac, as if Gable had been set down to block the way out. Like some slumbering giant, he brooded over the mere, dominating the valley with a presence that was almost tangible. Or perhaps it was only a trick of the fading light.

Beyond the village, on the first slopes rising from Wasdale, stood a long, rambling gray stone house, slate-roofed and ageless as if it had grown out of the rock and soil around it. Even the spacious gardens failed to soften the strength and severity of it.

"Ravensholme. The very first house is still here, a stone room in the cellars below where we store wines today. Charlotte and I welcome you to our home."

"Yes," my godmother echoed, breaking her long silence. "I hope your stay will be a happy one." But I thought she shivered as she spoke.

Harald Langdale was out when we arrived.

A thin gray-faced man stepped out of the shadows of the paneled hall and greeted Aunt Charlotte with stiff formality. "The master is away but will return for dinner," he said briefly, then added, "If the ladies care to go to their chambers, the luggage will follow."

"Thank you, Torver," Aunt Charlotte replied and turned to show me the way.

The children had already preceded us up the twisting

staircase and were strangely subdued now, though they had been lively enough in the nursery carriage. The house was typical of many old homes—rooms and passages, some narrow and dim, others cavernous and gloomy, were jumbled together with no logical sequence. The furnishings were all of dark woods and somber velvets, surrounded by heavy paneling, but they were far from shabby.

My room was just down the passage from Aunt Charlotte's suite. Though the windows were small and set high in the thick stone walls, yellows, ranging from the primrose of the draperies to buttercup in the bed hangings and marigold in the Belgian carpet, brightened the dark woods of the tables and chests and chairs. The hearth, with its ornate mantel of Irish marble, held a small but welcome fire. There was a chill in the air after the sun's warmth had vanished.

I bathed and changed into a gown of dark blue wool and afterward, uncertain of the time, found my way downstairs again.

The front door opened just as I reached the hall and a man strode in, slamming it behind him. He stopped short and stared at me for an instant. "Who are you?" he demanded.

He was a tall, heavy man of perhaps thirty-five or forty, with Freya's red-gold hair. His light brown eyes, high-bridged nose, and thin lips gave his face a cruel cast in the flickering light of the sconces. Hal Langdale, surely.

"I am Elizabeth Winton," I said, involuntarily stepping back. "I—I have come to visit Aunt Charlotte." When he said nothing, I added, "She is my godmother."

His glance swept me from head to foot. "Indeed." There was silence between us, for I could think of nothing to say, and then he repeated, "Indeed," before brushing past me to mount the stairs two at a time.

Uncertain how to take his cold reaction, I hesitated. A

thin voice almost at my elbow said, "The drawing room is down the passage to your left."

Startled, I turned to see Torver standing in a doorway. I thanked him with a brief nod and followed his directions, finding the chamber easily enough. It was long and dimly lit. The oak paneling, ornately carved, met ice blue damask walls halfway to the arched and beamed ceiling. Midnight blue draperies had been pulled over the windows. The several branches of candles seemed lost in the overwhelming gloom. Only the fire burned cheerfully and I crossed to it to warm my hands.

I hadn't seen Martin standing at the far end of the room. He turned at my step and said, "Oh, it's you." With his hands shoved into his pockets and his mouth sullen, he looked more like a disgruntled boy than a London sophisticate.

When I said nothing, he came down the room to the fire, adding, "I wish you would tell my brother that it wasn't *me* you saw last night!"

"I never said that it was."

"Well, he thinks I'm to blame. Oh, I know, in the past I've helped myself when Freya shortened the purse strings. What choice did I have? And it isn't her money anyway! But I haven't stooped to robbery in the disguise of a thief!"

"Nothing was taken," I said. "He knows that."

"Only because—according to Matthew—I didn't have time." He swung around to pace restlessly. "And if it *was* a thief, and he comes back, *I'll* be made to answer for it." He stopped before me. "Or are you filling *your* pockets? No one else saw this intruder. We have to take your word."

Any sympathy I might have felt for him vanished. "That's vicious!" I cried furiously.

"Well, that's the answer I intend to give if anything is missing!" he snapped. "I've lived on the ragged edge of debt ever since I was sixteen. All of them profited from Charles Carrock's death except me—and I'll have my share somehow, wait and see! But I'm not stupid enough to risk prison by pinching those damned candlesticks of Freya's. I'll find another way. And I warn you, don't try to spoil it for me!"

He was gone before I could say anything. Aunt Charlotte came in almost at once, staring over her shoulder at the sound of the door slamming in the hall.

"I came down a little early," I said, mastering my anger and discreetly trying to let her know I was in the room. "Torver directed me in here."

"Was that Martin?" she asked, still frowning.

"Yes. He is still in a bad temper after his dressing down this morning. Or so I gathered."

She sat beside me on a gilt sofa. "Matthew deplores his brother's way of life. But the answer isn't in scolding him. Martin needs some occupation for his energy and time. A position or career, perhaps. His father intended him to read for law, but nothing has ever been done about it." She smiled at me. "Do you like the Yellow Room?"

"Yes, I'm very comfortable."

"I'm glad. Elizabeth, if there had been time, I'd have told you something of my circumstances here before we arrived—"

She broke off as the door opened and Hal Langdale entered, followed by the Rylands.

Mr. Langdale greeted his wife with little show of warmth. "You seem to have recovered from your cough, I see."

"Yes, thank you, it is much improved. Hal, I should like to present my goddaughter—"

"We've met," he said shortly, and Aunt Charlotte turned to me with a look of surprise.

"Mr. Langdale returned home just as I came downstairs," I said.

"Hal, where is the goblet?" Freya interrupted, her hand on the mantel. "Surely you haven't taken it to your room!"

Her brother wheeled slowly to stare at the empty spot just above the flames. "I've been cleaning it," he said. "It will be there tomorrow."

"I've never seen it missing," she went on, her fingers nervously running over the carved wood. "The 'Honour' has always been here as long as I can remember."

"Don't be a fool," he said shortly. "It needed to be cleaned."

At my look of puzzlement, Matthew, standing near my sofa, said in explanation, "It's an ancient goblet, handed down through the family. No one knows where it came from, but it is generally called the 'Honour of Ravensholme.' Superstition, of course, but legend has it that the Langdales will always prosper as long as they keep it."

Torver came in to announce dinner, and Martin, calmer after his walk, joined us in the hall. The dining room was decorated in a rich brown brocade that matched the exquisite Turkey carpet on the floor. A chandelier of Venetian glass, old and very ornate, filled the long Chippendale table with light. The food was plain but rather good, a roast of ham with side dishes of creamed chicken and freshly caught fish.

Conversation was desultory. Mr. Langdale made no effort to fulfill the duties of host, and his detached silence made any other attempt fail after a few brief sentences.

Freya, looking up from a chocolate mousse flavored with rum, said to her brother, "Have you gotten rid of that horrid schoolmaster?"

"The German? No, why should I? He's cheap enough, God knows, and the villagers have come to tolerate him in spite of his accent."

"You know I don't care for his influence on Philip!"

"Then keep the boy away from him. I don't inconvenience myself for your whims, my dear. Find me another schoolmaster at his price and then I shall send this one packing."

Her dark eyes swung down the table toward me. "Miss Winton is a teacher. And searching for a place. Let her take his."

"Impossible!" Aunt Charlotte and Matthew cried at once. "Do you realize what you are saying?" Matthew went on. "She couldn't possibly cope with the problems of discipline. She's too young, and inexperienced—"

"The villagers wouldn't accept a woman, anyway," Hal Langdale said, sardonic amusement flaring in his light eyes. "I had trouble enough making them swallow a foreigner. And he minds his own business, I give him that. I doubt if I've clapped eyes on him twice in the eighteen months he's been here. That's the way I prefer it."

Shaken by Freya's suggestion, I tried to speak in my own behalf, but Freya cut me short. "Then, Miss Winton, I charge you to see that Philip stays where he belongs. And I shall hold you responsible if he disobeys."

"That's unfair," Aunt Charlotte said, her voice firm and decisive. "She is a guest, and I remind you that I am mistress here."

There was a cold silence. Freya obviously expected her brother to take her part, but he said nothing, still smiling with amusement at some private jest.

To ease matters, I said earnestly, "Indeed, Mrs. Ryland, I have no authority over the boy, nor any influence either. But I shall do what I can, naturally, to help you amuse him."

"I hope it is enough," she said ungraciously, flinging an angry glance in her brother's direction. "It isn't as if the man cared for Philip. He is merely trying to ingratiate himself in the hope of being appointed the child's tutor!"

"Has he told you this?" Aunt Charlotte asked. "The schoolmaster?"

"I've never spoken to him," she answered contemptuously. "It is what they all want, to escape the drudgery of village schools."

Bored with the subject, Langdale signaled Torver to clear the table. When Freya and my godmother rose to leave the men to their port, I pleaded fatigue and went up to my room. Both of them seemed glad to see me go.

I rose early the next morning and, after a hasty breakfast of tea and toast, decided to venture outside. A chill wind was blowing as I wrapped my dark blue cloak about me and slipped out the front door.

The morning mists were dispersing rapidly before the wind, though they lingered still in pockets. The mere was invisible, while Gable surveyed the dale with the same lordly disdain I had felt last evening, and the village chimneys seemed to float in a white sea. I had taken the first path beyond the gardens, and this soon became a rough track circling a slight rise. I didn't see the stone house until I was almost upon it, it blended so well with its surroundings. A low stone wall and a stand of yew loomed out of the gray light, and only then did I become aware of it.

Not wishing to trespass, I turned aside, climbing a branch of the track that followed the wall in the direction of Gable. And so it was that I looked back the way I had come in time to see someone standing in the open gate before the house and Philip racing down the path I had left to fling his arms about the man, babbling incoherently.

He was about thirty-five, tall and gaunt, dressed in a shabby black coat. Below the dark glasses he wore to protect his eyes, his beard was neatly trimmed. I needed no one to tell me that this was the schoolmaster, for he fit the description of hundreds like him. He stood there, his dark head bent to hear the boy's words, his fingers still resting lightly on the latch of the gate. Hardly the Pied Piper sort, I thought, and yet as Philip stepped back to take the man's hand I saw him look up with a wide and trusting smile that changed the thin little face almost beyond recognition.

I wished suddenly that I had come another way. Because of my foolish promise to Freya Ryland, I couldn't walk on and ignore this forbidden meeting. And yet it was almost more than I could bear to interrupt the child's happy reunion with the "friend" he had once mentioned to me.

But the choice was not mine, after all. The man saw me first, and Philip, sensing his distraction, turned after a moment. As the mists shifted in a vagrant breeze, I saw the smile fade and despair take its place. I moved reluctantly toward them.

"Miss Winton," Philip began, and then simply stood there waiting wretchedly for me to reach the gate.

"Have you had your breakfast, Philip?" I asked, ignoring the man.

"No." It was barely a whisper. And then his eyes lifted to mine, fear and hope vying in the gray depths. "Are you going to tell Mama?"

"You know you shouldn't be here," I said gently. Promises or no promises, I refused to be harsh with him.

He nodded, the toe of his shoe scuffing at the stone wall. "Please, if I come back with you, will you not say where you found me?"

I hesitated, uncertain what the best course was, trying to find a compromise of sorts.

The man spoke for the first time, his voice low and heavily accented. "You are his governess, Fräulein?"

I looked up at him. He was not at all as unprepossessing as he had seemed at first glance. Though his ill-fitting clothes emphasized his height and slenderness, he was actually broad-shouldered and muscular. He was also younger than I had realized. Behind the scholar's smoked lenses, the color of his eyes was nearly extinguished. I could not tell if they were blue or dark in the gray light, but I knew they were holding mine.

"No. I am a visitor at the house. But last evening Mrs. Ryland asked me to keep an eye on Philip. He is not permitted to wander on his own."

"Not permitted to wander—or to come here?" he asked.

"Both," I replied, aware of Philip beside me, silently listening.

"And so you have followed him—"

"No!" I said, stung by the accusation. "No, I have done nothing of the sort. It was only by chance that I walked this way. And I didn't know Philip had left the house."

"So." He turned to the boy. "You must return with Fräulein Winton."

Philip's eyes darkened. "Yes, Herr Raeder."

He stumbled toward me, his head bent down to hide the tears of disappointment, and we started back to Ravensholme. But before we had taken a dozen steps he tugged at my hand and pleaded desperately, "Could we not stay for a *very* few minutes?"

Deeply moved, I answered more harshly than I intended. "No."

He followed the rest of the way in silence. I was furiously angry now, for somehow I had been made to feel cruel and heartless. I resented the schoolmaster's influence on Philip and his mother's thoughtlessness in thrusting me into such a situation in the first place. And now Philip himself held me to blame. As soon as we reached the drive before the house, he released my hand and raced on ahead. I saw nothing of him for the remainder of the day.

I told no one about my encounter with Philip. It was one thing to keep a promise, another to bear tales.

Instead I spent the morning in Aunt Charlotte's cheerless sitting room, reading to her while her restless fingers busied themselves with knitting. A watery sun gave no warmth to the cream walls, and several times I found myself shifting closer to the fire.

There was the sound of argument in the passage, Freya's voice and then Martin's raised in anger. As I read aloud, my thoughts wandered from the story to the people in the house. Whatever else they might have, they had not found happiness or peace.

My godmother's hand covered the page before me. "It's no use," she said ruefully. "I haven't heard one word in ten."

I glanced doubtfully toward the windows. "Would you prefer to walk in the gardens?"

She shook her head. "No. When do you expect to hear from your applications for the fall term?"

"Not until May or even June," I replied.

"So long? Oh, my dear, I do wish I could help in some way!"

"There is nothing for it but to wait," I said, wishing I had not heard the disappointment in her voice.

Her fingers picked at the yarn in her lap. "It isn't easy for me to say this, Elizabeth, but I worry about you here. Hal is so unpredictable."

I thought of the cold man who was her husband and wondered how such a marriage had come about. My godmother had been an heiress and could surely have made her choice from scores of suitors. Why had she accepted Harald Langdale?

Aunt Charlotte said, "He can be very persuasive—and charming—if he wishes." She smiled sadly. "He went through my fortune very quickly. It was the only reason he married me—my money. He is single-minded in his devotion to himself and to Ravensholme."

Unable to answer such devastating honesty, I stared at the dancing flames. After a moment she continued. "As long as you have nothing to offer Ravensholme—or represent no threat to it—you will be safe enough from him."

My eyes flew to her face. "Surely—" I began, but her hand groped for mine and she cut my protest short.

"I am blind," she said gravely, "because one night, angry that my fortune was gone and that I was barren into the bargain, Hal threw me down the stairs. He expected me to die. But I didn't. Instead, my head struck that carved newel post. The blow itself cost me my sight."

I stared at her in horror. "And yet you have stayed here, *lived* here all this time as if nothing had happened?"

She shrugged. "Like you, my dear, I have no other place to go."

When we gathered for luncheon, Freya was relieved to find the missing goblet back in its accustomed place on the drawing-room mantel.

It was an odd piece in heavy gold, an ornately chased bowl on a stem, jewels crusted about the rim and the base. Freya's hands ran over it with loving reverence while her brother, his arms folded as he leaned against the door, watched cynically.

"It is beautiful, isn't it?" she asked, turning eagerly to me. "The first of the Langdales to settle here, Harald Bluespear and his son, carried it with them—plunder from some Irish abbey, no doubt. But it had already brought them luck, saving their long ship in a fierce storm and then leading them to this dale. They treasured it, passed it down from generation to generation, along with the story of its origin and the exhortation to preserve it. It wasn't called the 'Honour' until about a century ago, when such things became fashionable. Actually it has always been, quite simply, the Ravensholme Goblet. There are two other such talismans in Cumberland—one at Penrith and the other at Muncaster. But the goblet is older by over six hundred years."

"It's extraordinary," I replied, watching the firelight wink in the polished jewels as she held it up for me to see more clearly. But when I reached out to touch it she stepped back possessively and set it once more in its proper place.

It began to rain in the afternoon, a steady downpour that continued for the next three days. Little Helen developed a fever, and when Freya complained, Matthew told her bluntly that it was her fault for bringing the children to Ravensholme so early in the spring.

Freya and Martin quarreled again over money when she refused to pay his most pressing debts or make him a loan.

"You'll only gamble it away," she told him contemptuously. "You ought to know by now that you are unlucky at cards!"

"*I* wasn't the one who lost the Ryland estates!" he flung back at her. "I've lived damned well by my wits. God knows, I've had to learn how."

They were in the hall, where all the house could hear them clearly, and they did not think to lower their voices.

"You've wasted your life and used Matthew as the excuse for it long enough. He owes you nothing. And neither do I!"

Martin laughed harshly. "Nothing? We'll see about

that. Somehow I'll find a way to make you pay. Or rather Charles Carrock's money will pay, won't it? Just as it always has."

The quarrel ended only when Martin shouted for his horse and disappeared for two days. He was still in his brother's black books too, for there was a continued coldness between them, even before he left.

I tried to think of a way to broach the subject of the intruder with Matthew, to tell him that Martin couldn't have been the man I saw. But it proved to be impossible. A fleeting reference to that night brought only a curt reminder that the matter was closed.

To my relief, Hal Langdale seemed to be as anxious to avoid me as I was to stay away from him. It was difficult at meals to keep my knowledge of his cruelty out of my eyes and voice. I could so easily picture him, flushed with anger, deliberately shoving my godmother down the twisting stairs, coldly watching her fall in the hope that she would die. The wonder was that Matthew and Freya allowed her to live here, helpless as she was. Or perhaps she had hidden the truth from them. Such a secretive family, I often thought during the next few days. It might even be unsafe for anyone who knew too much about one of them.

Philip and I had little to say to each other. We met one morning in the passage near my room, and he sidled past as quickly as he could. But not before I had seen the dark circles under his eyes and realized with a shock that the child was grieving for his lost "friend."

"Philip—" I began, but he said hastily over his shoulder, "Mama wants me. I can't stay."

In the evenings I sometimes played chess with Matthew while Freya sewed or accompanied herself on the pianoforte. Her voice was well trained, though low. Aunt Charlotte, her hands folded quietly in her lap, sat by the fire, staring into darkness. Once I saw her husband's eyes on her in speculation, and shivered as I returned to my endangered queen.

When on the fourth day I awoke to find the mists opal with hidden sunlight, I was eager to pull on my boots and hurry outside. There was a freshness and a warmth in the air that took my breath away. Avoiding the path that led to the schoolmaster's cottage, I climbed a rough track behind the stables that led to a vantage point from which I could look down on the village and Wastwater. Birds were singing and daffodils nodded in the borders, with raindrops like diamonds sparkling in their cups. Sighing with pleasure, I stood for a long time watching the mists recede and the dark waters of the mere reflect the golden light of the sun. No wonder poets were inspired here, I thought fleetingly as the grays, greens, and purples of the fells came to life.

There was a crunching step on the loose chippings behind me and the schoolmaster spoke. "It is lovely, ja?"

I whirled, startled, and he nodded in greeting. "How long have you been here?" I demanded, disliking being watched.

"I have only just come this way. In the mornings before my classes begin I often walk to clear the mind of . . . other things," he replied mildly. As I turned to walk away, he said, "Tell me. Was the boy punished? I have not seen him since you took him away."

"Not that I know of," I said, facing him. "I didn't betray him, if that's what you wish to imply."

He frowned. "You do not approve of me, Fräulein. Why?"

I shrugged. "I know nothing about you. Only that Philip's parents don't wish him to spend his time with you."

"And have they bought a pony for him, then? Or found a tutor to develop his mind? Does his father take an interest in him now? Or found a school for him where he will be happy with other boys his age? Tell me, Fräulein, what have they done to fill his days? Or have they merely ordered him to stay in the garden and left him there to brood?"

I met his rising anger with anger of my own. "And what have you done? Besides take advantage of his loneliness in order to find yourself a place as his tutor?"

Behind the smoked glasses his dark eyebrows flew up, and then to my shocked surprise he laughed deep in his throat. "Is that what they tell you? That I wish to become Philip's tutor? Nothing on earth could take me into that house of darkness. I try instead to bring the boy into the light. What have I done? I have opened his mind where they have left it closed. I have given him a retreat that is far safer than these fells when he must escape Ravensholme for a time. And I try to understand his needs as well as I can. It is not easy with a child like Philip. But if someone doesn't try, he will destroy himself with his terrible fears and sorrows."

"And you have taken his love," I added, holding my ground.

There was a long silence. "Yes. It is so," he said at length. "Only because he has given it freely, of his own accord. I did not ask for it. I had not wanted it." There was something in his voice that made me, against my will, believe him.

"Now he grieves because he can't come to your cottage. Do you think *that* is good for him?" I went on, pursuing my advantage.

But an eyebrow quirked and behind the dark lenses I had the feeling he was again mocking me. "Perhaps he is afraid of you. Perhaps he believes that you'll not tell so long as he does not repeat his error. And you hold this weapon over his head like a sword."

"It's not true!" I cried. "I *never* threatened him!"

"It only matters if he *believes* that you have," he replied coolly. "Good morning, Fräulein." And he left me standing there, my pleasure in the gossamer light lost in my sudden realization that what he said was very likely true.

Martin Ryland returned from Cartmel, where he had gone to sulk after his quarrel with Freya Ryland, in better spirits and bearing an invitation to a betrothal dinner.

The bridegroom-to-be, a cousin of the Langdales, had written expressly to Freya and she felt compelled to attend. Hal Langdale was curiously eager to go, and it was clear that his decision was based on the premise that my godmother would remain at Ravensholme.

Freya, worried and tense, wanted no part of leaving the security of Wasdale, and to my surprise, part of her concern was directed toward Philip.

"You *will* promise not to let him out of your sight?" she repeated, having summoned me to the bleak green morning room and asked me to take charge of him in her absence. "Maggie has the girls to care for and Nell is still sleeping badly. As for Charlotte, you know it is impossible for her to take such responsibility."

"What can I do—" I began.

"I don't want him to leave the house alone. Not even to go into the gardens. Under no circumstances! Nor must he leave the grounds. I cannot stress the importance of this enough!" Her hands twisted together in her agitation.

"I shall do my best," I assured her, moved by her evident distress.

"And do not allow *any* strangers near him, whatever excuses they may give you," she went on, rising to walk to the windows, her back to me.

"Of course not," I replied, then added diffidently, "If I knew what you were afraid of—"

She turned on me then. "It is none of your affair. I am afraid of nothing, of no one! Just see that you keep the boy under your eye at all times!" Her dark eyes held pride and anger, and bitterness as well.

"Yes. I shall." When she said no more, I walked to the door, and as my hand touched the handle, she called my name, her emotions brought under control once more.

"Miss Winton. I remind you that Philip is the heir to wealth and large estates. And if my brother has no children, Ravensholme comes to him as well. Such a child is vulnerable. Unscrupulous people would not hesitate to use—or abuse—him for the sake of gain. Do you understand?"

"Yes, I understand." Though it was strange to hear her voice such concerns in so isolated a part of the country. But there was the man from the East, the man Philip desperately wanted to believe was his father. And he had entered Abbot's Thorston in the dead of night. I couldn't reconcile my impression of him with Freya's fears. Yet I knew so little about any of these people, how could I *truly* judge? "I will take very good care of him, I promise you," I added firmly.

"You won't regret it," she said, and let me go.

The four of them left for Cartmel early on the following Monday. Matthew appeared to look forward to the change. Ravensholme seemed to depress him. Hal Langdale was impatient to be off. Freya, her face ashen as if she had not slept well, stared out of the carriage window at the rambling gray house as if she were leaving behind her anchor in a desolate world. Martin, his horse prancing nervously, had been on his best behavior for three days, as though he feared he might at the last moment be left behind. He had confided to me that luck had been with him on the last visit to Cartmel—he had won a hundred pounds at cards. Obviously he expected to repeat the performance.

Aunt Charlotte sighed as they disappeared from view down the drive. I turned to her in surprise, for I thought she might welcome even this brief respite from her husband's presence.

She smiled as she took my arm. "I still enjoy parties. It isn't easy to be left out. And yet I'd be miserable most of the time. Here I can *pretend* a little, I know my surroundings so well. Blindness is very real when you stumble over unfamiliar obstacles and blunder into people you don't know." She paused as Torver closed the door behind us. "Freya gives a ball at Abbot's Thorston each spring. And that is enough of a trial, even though Matthew sees to it that I never lack partners for the dancing. He's very kind."

As we entered the morning room, she crossed to the fire and held her hands out to the warmth. It was a tragedy, I thought for the hundredth time, for such a woman to be tied to Harald Langdale. She needed the warmth and compassion of a man like Matthew.

Changing the subject, I said, "Tell me what you know about the schoolmaster. Is he truly bad for Philip?"

"I don't know." She frowned thoughtfully. "For one thing, I feel it is wrong for him to take the affection that Philip *ought* to give to Matthew. No child could ask for a better stepfather. It is so unfair! For another, I don't trust the man. Perhaps it is only because he is a foreigner and different from us—cold and reserved and impossible to understand with that accent of his. Somehow he frightens me in a way that Hal never has, for all his cruelty. There's a . . . ruthlessness about him."

Good reasons, but not sound enough to deter me from a project that had been revolving in my mind for days.

That afternoon Aunt Charlotte went to lie down after luncheon. Maggie was occupied with Nell, who was restless and irritable in her mother's absence. Torver, that peculiar little man whose silent movements about the house made me uneasy, was down in the wine cellars doing an inventory. My chance had come.

I found Philip in his small room reading a book and told him to put on his coat for a walk. His thin pallid face nearly broke my heart, but I said nothing as I waited for him. There was no enthusiasm in his step as we left the house and turned into the garden path.

I stopped by a bed of pink hyacinths, their scent heady in the light breeze, and took his hand.

"Philip, I can't really give you a reason for what I'm doing. Perhaps it is because I like to find my own answers when I'm caught in the middle of a problem. But I want you to understand that I have not and will not shut my eyes to disobedience."

He nodded, his gray eyes enormous beneath the fine golden hair that blew across his forehead.

"Your mother forbids you to run off to the schoolmaster's cottage. She has said nothing about my taking you there." A flush had risen to the high cheekbones now, and his fingers trembled in my grasp. "Shall we pay a brief call on Herr Raeder?"

Philip's eyes came to life and it was all I could do to hold back the tears at the change in him. With a brief prayer that I was doing the right thing, we walked down the track toward the schoolmaster's cottage.

4

It was with some misgivings that I opened the gate and let Philip race ahead to disappear inside the cottage. But the decision was already out of my hands. It was too late to turn back.

The stone-seated porch was deeply recessed, and as I slowly came up the walk I realized that the schoolmaster was waiting just inside the iron-bound oak door, watching me narrowly.

He said nothing until I had stepped into the porch and then only a reserved "Welcome to my house, Fräulein" as he swung wide the door.

I entered the square stone-flagged kitchen and looked about me in surprise. The thick walls were spotlessly whitewashed, with dark green curtains at the small windows. A fire burned cheerfully on the great open hearth, cheeses rested on the broad beam just above it, and hams were suspended from others, beside loops of dried sausages and bunches of herbs. A gallery ran around two sides, with stone stairs leading up to it and a door to the sleeping loft at the top. Beneath the stairs was a passage widening into a tiny dairy. The simple but comfortable furnishings—a table, dresser, several chairs and benches—were well polished, and a rag rug was spread before the hearth. A kettle was already simmering on the black hob, and the smell of fresh bread filled the room from the ovens at one side. In spite of my resolve not to be drawn into taking sides, my first reaction was "No wonder Philip likes coming here!"

Something of my thoughts must have been reflected in my face, for Herr Raeder's wariness changed to amusement.

"A man alone," he said whimsically, "soon learns to manage. Or else he resigns himself to squalor." He offered me a chair by the fire and turned to show an impatient Philip a shelf of birds' nests that he had collected for him since last summer.

They were soon lost in a discussion of building techniques and materials, giving me an opportunity to observe them together. Philip was fascinated, absorbing details in a way that spoke well of the schoolmaster's ability to teach. I had never held a class of giggling girls enthralled with such seeming ease.

The kettle's whistle finally interrupted them and Herr Raeder moved to the dresser to set cups and plates upon the table. "You will have tea with me, ja? And"—he lifted a napkin from a dish—"currant pasties."

Philip cried out in delight and hurried to help arrange the table. His eyes were bright, his cheeks glowing. Would the excitement be too much for him? I had not considered the possibility of it making him ill. And then he laughed, a strange sound from that solemn child, but completely natural and relaxed. The schoolmaster's eyes met mine over the fair head and I looked quickly away.

As we took our places at the table, he gestured to the pasties. "My culinary skills do not extend to these. One of the village families sent them. Although Herr Langdale pays my wages, the parents of my pupils settle their accounts in their own fashion. In my turn I am grateful."

"What brought you to England?" I asked as I filled their cups.

He shrugged. "For over a hundred years Hanover has provided your kings and fought your wars. It changes now only because England allows women to rule and Hanover does not. But the Queen speaks German and has married a German prince—the ties are still there. When a man must leave his home, he searches for another like it, or as near as possible." Behind the smoked lenses his glance was unreadable. I resented the fact that he could so easily hide his thoughts while mine were vulnerable. "There was a vacancy here. The position was not attractive, the salary small. I was the only person who applied, and only because my accent was not acceptable elsewhere."

Philip, his mouth stuffed with currant pasties, clamored for attention and Herr Raeder turned back to him.

"A gentlemen does not overfill his mouth. It is seen only in the nursery," he said calmly.

Philip blushed and replied sheepishly, as soon as he decently could, "I beg pardon. But I *like* them very much!"

The schoolmaster chuckled. "So it appears. The dish is bare." As the child became engrossed in his treasures once more, Herr Raeder asked quietly, "Why are you here, Fräulein? Have you changed your mind about my influence on the boy?"

I looked down at my empty cup. "I am trying to keep an *open* mind, that's all. Coming here meant so much to him. I wished to see for myself whether it was wrong."

"And your promise to Frau Ryland?" he persisted.

"I don't know," I said truthfully. "She is very worried for him. At the same time I can see . . . other concerns, equally important."

I couldn't tell him of that harrowing morning when Philip believed his dead father had come to find him. It hadn't been mentioned since, but the child had not forgotten, I was certain of it. An unhealthy obsession for a boy starved for love and left alone to brood. After my encounter with the schoolmaster on the hillside above Ravensholme I had tried to find an answer to Philip's dilemma, weighing two evils as it were.

"Why does his mother fear for him?"

"I don't know," I said again. "She does not confide in me. I don't think she particularly likes me."

"Yet you are her guest."

"No," I said, rising. "I am visiting Mrs. Langdale. She is my godmother."

"Ah. So." He would have said more, but Philip had noticed my preparations for departure.

"Must we go now? I . . . I have only just begun to study these."

"I am afraid we must. Your aunt will not know where we are."

Disappointment filled his eyes, but he found his coat without protest. As I moved to the door, he turned and caught the schoolmaster's hand. Speaking rapidly, as if this might be his only chance to tell his news, he said, "My father has come for me. He's here."

The schoolmaster looked sharply at him, then glanced toward me for verification. "What is he saying?" he asked abruptly when I remained silent.

"He— There is some confusion about what really occurred," I replied slowly. "A man came to the house—"

"And his mother? What does she say?" he demanded, interrupting me. "She confirms this?" There was a forcefulness in him now that filled the quiet room.

"How can she?" I answered, angered by his interrogation. Philip, wide-eyed, was listening to our exchange, believing it confirmed his own conclusions. And that could do irreparable damage. "Charles Carrock is *dead*."

He made an impatient gesture with his hand. "This will not matter to her. Or to Askham."

I shook my head. "I don't know what you are talking about."

"Where is Askham now?"

"I don't know anyone named Askham! I thought I saw someone in the house—Abbot's Thorston—one night, very late. It was . . . only a dream. But Philip misunderstood a conversation between his stepfather and Martin Ryland concerning the incident and convinced himself that Carrock was somehow still alive and searching for him."

Herr Raeder stared blankly at me. *"Carrock?"* he repeated in bewilderment. "I do not understand this."

Before I could reply, Philip said, "Everyone was asleep but Miss Winton, and she said she saw a man enter the house. She called my . . . my stepfather, and so the man left before he found me. My stepfather thought it was only Uncle Martin pretending to be a thief, and Miss Winton said it was a nightmare. But Mama was frightened and left for Ravensholme anyway. *I* know it was my father," he ended earnestly. "And he *isn't* dead!"

The tension in the cottage had vanished as quickly as it had come. The schoolmaster dropped to one knee and said, "Why do you believe this? You have not told me of it before." His voice was very gentle.

"It's a feeling I have. People don't like to talk about him. Or if they do, they sound as though they are hiding something. Then, this winter Mama began to worry about strangers and wouldn't explain to my stepfather. Why should she do that if my real father was truly dead?" he asked with all the logic of childhood.

"Why, indeed?" Herr Raeder repeated dryly. "But I think you are mistaken, Philip. As for your mother, it is possible that she is afraid for other reasons entirely."

"Ye-es," Philip said doubtfully, obviously clinging to the comfort of his longing.

"We will talk of this another time," the schoolmaster

said, rising. "But hear me, Philip. Charles Carrock would not steal into the nursery like a felon if he came to seek his son. He would pound on the door and ask openly. When—if—that day comes, you may believe that he is indeed alive."

I opened my mouth to protest, preferring bluntness to these evasive half-truths. Only then would Philip realize he was clinging to a dream. But when I saw his face, the pride vying with disappointment, I knew that the schoolmaster had been wiser than I. He had closed the door on hope more gently than I might have, and yet had managed to make it a shield as well.

As we left the cottage and started down the path, the schoolmaster lightly touched my arm and his voice was pitched for my ears alone. "Safeguard him, Fräulein. He is more vulnerable than you know."

All the way home a question repeated itself over and over in my mind, frightening me with its implications: Who is the man from the East and why should he threaten this child?

My godmother had not missed us. She was still lying down when I tapped at her door on my return. The draperies had been drawn and her face was a white blur in the semidarkness.

"Come in, Elizabeth," she called as I hesitated, unwilling to disturb her. "You would not believe how my heart has fluttered since luncheon. But I'm easier now. Sit and talk with me for a while."

"I didn't know you were ill!" I said quickly, remorseful that I had been too full of my own projects to take notice of her needs.

"It is nothing, I assure you." She smiled wryly. "Whenever I am not well and Hal is away I work myself into a state wondering if he has tried to poison me."

I cried out in disbelief, but she shrugged. "He's a strange man. As cold and ruthless as his Viking ancestors. And as acquisitive. He has no heir, and at his age mortality looms large. I don't think he would hesitate to rid himself of me if he thought another wife would be the answer. And he can't bear to see a Carrock ruling Ravensholme."

Too shocked to think what I was saying, I blurted, "He doesn't have much choice in the matter."

"Hal *makes* his fate, Elizabeth. He doesn't wait until it comes to him. That's why he is dangerous." Her fingers picked at the satin coverlet and I cast about for a change of subject, unhappy to see her distressed.

"Aunt Charlotte, why is Mrs. Ryland afraid of strangers? She bade me watch Philip closely while she was away."

Her face turned toward me in that uncanny way she had of looking directly at the person speaking to her. "I'm not sure I know. She won't discuss it with me and denies it if Hal or Matthew broaches the subject. But according to the London papers, George Askham is back in England after an eight-year tour of duty in India. He arrived in October, as I recall."

George Askham. The man from the East. So he had a name and a face, a personality—a reality.

"Who is he?"

"George is a captain in a cavalry regiment but was posted to India. Freya was very much in love with him at the time. She was certain that he would marry her and take her with him. She should have known that any friend of Hal's was not to be trusted. There was a scandal over money—I never knew the details. George simply walked out on her. I thought she would never recover from that blow, but a few weeks later she had married Charles Carrock. I was never so surprised."

A man who had lived in an Eastern climate. A man who wore silver spurs. "And what had he to do with the ornate silver candlesticks in the hall at Abbot's Thorston?" I asked.

Her brows rose in astonishment. "However did you know of those? Charles won them from Askham in a card game. The only time Hal ever succeeded in cajoling Charles into playing. It was a wild night. I wasn't here, thank God. I'd gone into Kendal to stay with friends. There was drinking, gambling, all manner of vice. Freya told me about it later—I hadn't been able to persuade her to leave with me. Matthew lost the Ryland estates that same night and Hal was so drunk he used the Ravensholme Goblet as a stake. It must have brought him luck."

So Freya was waiting for George Askham to return, but in terror, not in joy. It made no sense.

"Has he tried to reach her—a letter perhaps?"

Aunt Charlotte was feeling for her wrapper and I handed it to her. "No. I don't believe he has. I don't see why he should, come to that. You know, I seem stronger. This spell was my imagination, I expect. Shall we have our dinner here by the fire? So much nicer than that empty dining room. And we can dispense with Torver too."

I smiled. "A very good idea."

But Aunt Charlotte continued to feel ill. There was little I could do for her and she refused to summon a doctor. Her symptoms were slight nausea and a fluttering pulse, neither of them severe enough for me to act on my own and seek professional advice. It crossed my mind that Torver might be tampering with her food, but we ate from the same dishes at every meal. One murder was unlikely enough. Two would be impossible to deal with, even if my suspicions were true.

Philip asked hopefully if we would return to the schoolmaster's cottage, but I was unwilling to leave my godmother. "Another time," I said, hardening my heart against the look in his eyes. "We will go back, I promise," I added, relenting. "Meanwhile, we must make Aunt Charlotte well again."

He nodded and was on his best behavior in the expectation of hastening our expedition. Even Maggie commented on it, torn between disbelief and pleased surprise. "To be sure, the lad must be sickening for something! I'll keep my eye on him."

The Rylands and Hal Langdale returned just before sunset on the third day. Martin had lingered in Cartmel. Aunt Charlotte, improving at last, was in the hall to greet them. Freya was glad to be home, but her brother was taciturn, going directly to his room as soon as Torver had taken his cloak and gloves. Matthew drew my godmother into the drawing room, telling her about the betrothal party, the dinner and the dancing afterward. Freya, frowning slightly, watched them go and then turned to me.

"Philip is well? Safe?"

"Yes. He has been very good while you were away."

"No strangers?"

"I haven't seen anyone," I assured her.

She nodded. "Perhaps I was mistaken—" Breaking off, she excused herself to change for dinner.

As I turned to join my godmother and Matthew Ryland in the drawing room, Hal Langdale passed me without a word. Then, pausing at the door to the kitchen, he looked at me for a moment.

"Freya tells me you have no close relatives living?" It was a question rather than a statement.

I hesitated, somehow unwilling to admit that I was completely alone in the world, especially to this strange man.

"It is true then." With a smile that sent a chill through me, he disappeared through the door.

For dinner there was ham baked with sweet pickled damsons, potted char, and preserve tarts. Aunt Charlotte, who had minced at her food for three days, had more appetite and I ate my meal with greater pleasure. Conversation centered upon the betrothal celebration, though Freya spoke disparagingly of the "dab of a girl" her cousin was to marry. It occurred to me then that she was accustomed to praise for her own beauty and disliked any other woman who might represent a challenge to her.

Tall, graceful, rather Junoesque, she wore her clothes with style and excellent taste. The thick coils of red-gold hair, the dark eyes, the haughtiness in her manner, would appeal strongly to many men, and like her brother, she could undoubtedly be very charming if she so chose. Worry had left her pale and irritable. I hadn't really seen the woman behind the tension that now held her in its grip. It was a revelation.

The door swung open and Martin strode in, his mouth set in sullen lines that indicated he hadn't been very successful in whatever games of chance he had played at Cartmel. Flinging himself into his empty chair, he irritably told Torver he would skip the soup and begin with the ham.

"You needn't take your ill humor out on the servants," Freya said coldly. "I warned you that your luck was out. You should have left then."

"So I should have," he answered sourly. "Well, I was not the only one out of luck," he went on as Torver served his plate. "Remember the drunken fool who nearly fell under the Fredericks' carriage? Seems he turned up at his sister's door several weeks ago after disappearing years back. She'd given him up for dead. And now he is. He tried to cross the bay, probably too intoxicated to know what he was doing, and the tides by some fluke washed him up rather than taking him out to sea. What was his name? Higgins . . . Higham . . ."

"Hichen," I said, not even aware I had spoken aloud. I hadn't thought of the man since the night of my arrival, but I knew with a shiver of foreboding that it could be no one else. The sands had claimed their own, as he had dreaded they would. "Sam Hichen," I went on into the stunned silence. "But he swore he would never cross again."

They were all on their feet, five pairs of eyes—one pair blank and unseeing—staring down the length of the table at me as I sat there dazed. Freya's chair had gone over, the sound loud in the stillness, but almost unnoticed.

"Who are you?" she demanded, bending toward me like a snake about to strike. *"Who sent you here?"*

"Why have you come?" Matthew asked harshly. "How did you know this man?"

"I— He drove the hired carriage from the King's Head . . . the night we lost our way," I stammered, suddenly afraid. "I had never seen him before, but he was drunk even then. He— He told me that nothing in this world would make him cross the bay another time. And for some reason, I believed him."

But Freya wasn't listening. She had turned on my godmother. "How can you be sure this is truly Elizabeth Winton? You are the only one who would know, and you are blind!"

"Don't be foolish!" Aunt Charlotte answered, frowning deeply, as if she were trying desperately to penetrate the curtain of darkness that lay between us. "Who else could she be!"

"But she is the only one who has 'seen' that man—first on the sands and then in the house! What if she is lying?"

"Sit down!" Hal Langdale ordered. "You can prove nothing. If she *is* lying, it will soon come to light. If not, you are behaving irresponsibly." But there was an ugly expression in his light eyes as he watched me. I began to tremble uncontrollably.

Martin, waiting out the tumult, turned triumphantly toward me. "That isn't all of the story. It appears that Sam Hichen—who ought, by now, to have been lost in the Irish Sea—was stabbed twice before he was left to drown. Now why would anyone have wanted to do that?"

They had forgotten me. As Martin finished, Freya covered her mouth with her hands, sinking down into her chair as if her bones had become water. Matthew, his face parchment white, stared at her as if he were seeing a ghost. There was a dull flush in Hal Langdale's cheeks and flecks of anger in his light eyes. Aunt Charlotte searched the table with her sightless glance, making a supreme effort to sense each reaction. No one spoke.

Martin took his seat again and jabbed viciously at a gooseberry tart. "I lost three hundred pounds at faro," he said softly, "but now I expect it was to my advantage to have stayed on. I enjoy being the bringer of tidings." His eyes lifted to the circle of faces. "There's always a reward."

"In the old days," my godmother said uneasily, as if she were finishing something that was there in every mind, "those who brought *bad* news perished for it."

Martin's face stared blankly at her for a moment. And then he choked on the tart. Before Torver could step forward to slap him soundly on the back, he had recovered, tossed his serviette into his plate, and fled the room. I fought down the panic that urged me to leave also.

In an uncomfortable silence we pretended to finish the meal, but no one cared what he or she ate. It was a face-saving gesture only.

As we left the dining room I touched my godmother's arm and said softly, "Please, I must talk to you."

She hesitated. "Is it wise, especially now?"

" 'Now' is the very reason I must. Please?"

We went to the morning room, unpleasantly cold without a fire in the grate. Aunt Charlotte drew her shawl about her shoulders and waited.

"I didn't know what to say or do in there! Or why they

were so upset. I'm frightened!" Pacing the floor before her, I tried to shut out the scene I had witnessed and think clearly. "It is something to do with Hichen, I am aware of that. But I scarcely spoke a dozen sentences to the man, and then only to urge him to be more careful." But he had been reluctant to take me to Abbot's Thorston. And he was deathly afraid of something out there on the bay.

"It has nothing to do with you, Elizabeth. Not really."

"Doesn't it? I thought Freya would strike me. Even Matthew looked at me as if I were someone *monstrous*."

"Oh, Elizabeth, I didn't want you to become involved!" Aunt Charlotte all at once had tears in her eyes. "If we had only stayed at Abbot's Thorston until July, possibly none of this would ever have happened!"

"We are here and I'm involved very deeply. For my own safety I must know what is happening. I should never have mentioned Hichen."

"How could you know?" she said sadly. "It is an old story. Charles Carrock married Freya and everyone thought they were happy, especially when Philip was born in that first year. But after that they drew apart—quarreled. They had come to Ravensholme to celebrate Freya's birthday. Matthew was here. He often visited us. I think he was a little in love with her even then. Perhaps he always had been." She paused, sighing.

"After the dinner party Freya and Charles began to bicker. Hal didn't help matters. He seemed to take a vicious pleasure in baiting Charles. They argued and Hal left the house. He often walks the fells at night. I've never seen a man so at home on them. Freya and Charles went upstairs but apparently in the course of preparing for bed Freya said more than she meant. I've always suspected she threw Askham in his face."

"He knew about their relationship?"

"Everyone did. But perhaps not how . . . close they

were. He struck her, there was a struggle, and she tried desperately to defend herself. According to Matthew, who came to her rescue, Charles was in a black fury and would have killed her. There was a silver paper knife in his hand, blood everywhere. Matthew succeeded in disarming him after a struggle on the stairs. Charles broke away and fled. Matthew went after him. I had run to Freya's aid. She was hysterical and kept repeating something about Philip—he was at Abbot's Thorston—and trying to dress. She's quite strong, you know, and I couldn't prevent her from leaving alone for Thorston Water. I sent Torver for Hal, but he wasn't to be found."

She stopped, her thoughts back in that dreadful night. After a moment she looked at me and said, "You can't imagine what I suffered, helpless to do anything, endlessly waiting. Matthew, looking like death itself, came back at dawn. He said he hadn't found Charles, though he had searched as far as Cartmel. As it turned out, Hal had gone after Freya and lost her in the dark. He finally came up with her as she was riding back here with Philip, still in his nightshirt, before her on the saddle. Charles had simply vanished. The first notion we had of his fate came from Sam Hichen. He'd been taking a load of household goods across the bay and late that same night saw a man struggling in the water. The moon was full and Hichen *swore* there were *two* people. He was drunk, frightened. You really can't blame him for what he did. Instead of investigating, he turned back to Cartmel for the constable. But there was no sign of anyone by the time they had reached the spot. Two weeks later Charles' battered body washed up outside Liverpool. Freya fainted when Hal took her there and he himself made the identification, such as it was. Fortunately he recognized some of the clothing too. The sea isn't kind to its victims. To save Freya a great deal of suffering we had already let it be known that Charles had gone to Lancaster. So it appeared that he lost his way on the sands. Philip worships his father's memory. He has never guessed the truth, and I pray he never will. Charles is the shining knight, the golden idol, not a would-be murderer."

I sank down in one of the fine green velvet chairs, remembering the drunken fancies Hichen had suffered. No wonder he was afraid to cross the bay! Whether there was one man or two, their ghosts had haunted him and in the end brought him to his death. But who had stabbed him? And why?

"They were certain . . . it *was* Charles Carrock's body?" I asked.

"Oh, yes. There's no question about it. Charles is dead. The question has always been Did he drown trying to escape across the bay? Or was someone else there when he died?"

I shivered. "They suspect I might have an answer, don't they?"

Her hand groped for mine, and the fingers were icy. "Elizabeth, if you could leave tomorrow morning—" she began earnestly.

"How can I?" I asked bitterly. "I haven't enough money to last a month. And no prospect of a position. I don't know which is more frightening— destitution or their hatred."

"I have nothing of my own. Even my jewelry has been sold. Or I would gladly give you all I have."

"What has Mr. Langdale done with it all?" I asked. "Gambled it away?"

"I don't know what he does with his money—or mine. Once I thought he was being blackmailed. More likely he has his Viking ancestors' desire to hoard. He should have lived a thousand years ago and gone *i viking* with the rest. Shiploads of plunder, bloodlust, roving—these would have appealed strongly to him. By some ironic twist of time he's caught in the nineteenth century instead."

"I need to think," I said, rising and going to the door. "And I'll feel safer in my room. Do you mind?"

"Go along. And don't worry. After the first shock has worn away, they will all see that this has nothing to do with you," she promised reassuringly.

"I hope so," I replied and shut the door behind me, hearing an echo of her voice not five minutes ago urging me to leave at once if I could.

I slept poorly that night, starting at every sound. But no one came to my door and at breakfast the next morning there was no mention of what had occurred. It was almost as if I had imagined it all.

Relieved, I told myself that I had been too ready to see threats in what was only surprise and uncertainty. It was natural for Freya to be upset by the unpleasant reminder of the past and for Matthew and Hal Langdale to wonder how I could possibly have come by such unexpected knowledge. Martin hadn't helped matters with his sly innuendos.

All the same, I breathed more comfortably when out of the house altogether. Philip and I took to roaming the tracks above the gardens. If Freya knew, she said nothing. After all, she had left Philip in my care during her absence. Whatever she might think of me, she surely realized that I would never harm him.

There were many routes up the fells, most of them probably sheep tracks that had been followed for centuries. I had grown accustomed to the stark severity of the scenery but I felt it unwise to venture too high without a map or a guide. Still, it was pleasant to look down the length of Wastwater or to watch the tiny figures in the village going about their everyday affairs. Philip was content to follow my lead and we cajoled the dour cook into preparing sandwiches and tarts for our first outing. After that I hadn't the courage to ask.

On the second afternoon we met the schoolmaster on a flank of Great Gable. According to Philip, the route to the top via Sty Head Pass would take no more than an hour, but my skirts and light boots made a quarter of the distance heavy going. Mist had settled over the top of Scafell and was drifting lazily toward Gable as we laughed over my efforts. The schoolmaster hailed us then and we waited while he scrambled down to us.

"You are not thinking of an ascent?" he inquired, concern in his voice.

"Not really. We were out for a walk."

"So. One must have stout shoes, a working compass, and a packet of food. Also warm clothing. It is cold when the mists descend, and if one must stay the night unexpectedly, these preparations can make the difference between living and dying."

"Yes," I replied soberly. "I would not care to be lost on these fells." Sheep, like a herd of dirty ghosts, trooped past us. A splash of blue on one shoulder proclaimed their owner, but there was neither shepherd nor dog with them.

As if he had understood my unspoken thought, the schoolmaster smiled. "Where could they go? And who would molest them?"

"Who indeed."

Philip, listening silently, could contain himself no longer. "Please, may we go see the birds' nests again?"

"Not today. It is well past teatime. Your mother will wonder what has become of us."

"She doesn't care. I heard her tell Uncle Harald that she wished she had seen the last of you. But I like you, and so does Aunt Charlotte, so you mustn't feel badly about it," he ended kindly.

Herr Raeder glanced at me. "So. You are in disgrace?"

"In a way," I replied evasively. "Come along, Philip."

The schoolmaster's long slender fingers ruffled the boy's hair. "You will do as Miss Winton asks you. Tomorrow there will be rain. On such a day it will be better to look at birds' nests than to climb the fells, ja? If you are good today."

Philip grinned crookedly. "I'll try to be good."

We walked together down the track, Philip racing ahead and then stopping to wait for us to catch up. Herr Raeder watched him for a time and then reached into his pocket.

"I can do nothing about your boots or those abominable skirts. But I would feel better if you had at least this."

He held out a worn gold case inscribed with the initials KHR. As his finger touched the hidden spring, the top flew up to reveal a very ornate old compass. The points were written in a very fine copperplate hand, scrolled and delicate. The blue needle quivered in the pale afternoon light, steady on north.

"You know how to use this?" As I nodded he continued "It has seen much use, but I assure you it is very trustworthy."

"I cannot accept this," I protested.

"Why not, Fräulein? I have another one, newer and better suited to my needs. It is imperative that you take it, since no one at Ravensholme has thought to offer you one. The mists come swiftly. One can be lost in the blink of an eye. If you wish, you may return it as soon as you have a compass of your own."

I hesitated. What he said was very true. And I had the odd feeling that someday I might need it. Enclosed in Wasdale with only one road leading out to the rest of the world, surrounded by the bleak and pitiless fells, I had no escape. Sam Hichen had been stabbed and left to drown. But by whom? The same person who had killed Charles Carrock?

"You are frightened, Fräulein?" the schoolmaster asked softly.

"No. Certainly not. Why should you think that?" But my smile was false. "Thank you. I shall consider the compass a loan. For the present." I took the gold case from his palm and slipped it into my cloak pocket.

We had reached the fork in the path. He bowed formally and turned away. I watched him walk on, tall and shabby, but not a man to cross lightly. There was a strength of purpose in him that would brook no interference.

We hurried on our way as the first fingers of mist drifted toward Ravensholme. Philip gave me a smile and darted through the garden door just as Martin came around the corner of the house, his boots muddy and scuffed.

I had nothing to say to him and was not disposed to linger, but he called to me before I could escape.

"I want to speak to you," he snapped breathlessly, catching up with me. As he closed the door on the gray afternoon his voice echoed in the flagged passageway. "About Hichen."

"What about him?" I asked coldly.

"Why don't we share what we know? Who can tell, it might be more profitable for both of us."

"I know nothing. Hichen drove me from the King's Head to Abbot's Thorston. He was so drunk he could have killed both of us crossing the bay. I had as little to do with him as I possibly could."

He looked me over. "You play a deep game, don't you? I couldn't understand before why you were always so cold—an ice maiden in Quaker's dress. You have no intention of sharing because you are greedy, selfish—"

"You are describing yourself. Please stand aside. Aunt Charlotte will be wondering what has become of me." I spoke with a coolness I was far from feeling. I disliked being cornered in this dimly lit passage and I resented his callous assurance that I was hiding something. He was, above all, putting me into danger with his ridiculous suspicions, and that frightened me.

"What I want to know most of all is how you found Hichen in the first place," he went on, ignoring my protests.

"I didn't *find* him!" I said sharply. "When I hired a carriage after the stage broke an axle, he was assigned to drive!"

"Of all the incredible luck!" he marveled. "And drunk as he was, he told you the story?"

"How often must I repeat it before you believe me? I don't know anything! No one confided in me, least of all that dreadful old man! I am not hiding something and I want nothing! I am here only because I can't find a position until the autumn and I would leave tomorrow if there was only some place I could go!" Shoving him aside, I ran down the passage, thinking only of reaching my room before he could stop me again.

There was a slight movement in one of the side corridors, a twisting arch of darkness that led down toward the cellars. I barely noticed, intent on Martin, who was shouting something after me.

It was not until I had closed my door and leaned against it gasping for breath that it occurred to me that someone had been standing there in the archway, out of sight but not out of earshot. Whoever it was had been listening to the exchange between Martin and me, then taken care not to be seen as I rushed by. Had he been motivated by courtesy, curiosity, or some darker purpose?

I had never felt so alone and vulnerable in all my life, not even after my father's death. And my only allies were a blind woman and a haunted child.

5

It was unnerving to live in a house with people who carefully avoided speaking of the suspicion that filled their thoughts and yet who watched me like cats at a mousehole. Even Aunt Charlotte, who had shown me warmth and affection since I had arrived, sometimes seemed to be staring at me across a room, as if a seed of doubt had been planted in her mind and refused to be uprooted.

It was only natural; I was as much a stranger to her as I was to any of the others. She knew my mother, of course, and had visited me when I was no older than Philip was now. But people change. Even if I could prove that I was indeed Elizabeth Winton, it would mean nothing. I might still be an agent for another party or determined to use my supposed knowledge for my own purposes. A penniless teacher might not boggle at blackmail, if it came to that. How could they read what was in my heart?

I lay awake that night counting over my meager savings, trying desperately to think of ways to augment my income until—if—a position could be found by the autumn term. But it was hopeless, and I found that a bitter truth to face. Hundreds of women with better connections, more experience, and longer years were available for the hiring. And I still had doubts about the recommendation that Miss Whitmain had given me. It would have suited her well to see me refused by other schools. She would not have wished even the faintest hint of her bookkeeping schemes to reach other ears. Indeed, I might have talked out of simple spite. How could she be sure that I wouldn't? She would have had no hesitation blackening *my* character if positions had been reversed! It was the sort of woman she was.

All of which left me exhausted and back where I had started from. For a moment I toyed with the idea of asking Freya or Matthew for the loan of enough money to tide me over the summer. But I had the feeling they would very much prefer keeping me under surveillance until they were satisfied that I was harmless. Indeed, such a request might appear in their eyes as the first step in a long series of demands for money, once I was safely away.

But what were they so afraid of? I wished I knew, so that I might be on my guard; then instantly I was grateful for my ignorance.

Someone had killed Sam Hichen. And that same someone might have been struggling with Carrock in the waters of the bay when the drunken freighter had passed those many years ago. It didn't matter whether the person with Charles Carrock was trying to murder him or drag him back to the safety of the shore. Carrock was dead, and *that* would only make matters worse, since no one had come forward—for whatever reasons—at the time. The weight of evidence might easily go against the other person, especially if he or she had benefited by the outcome of that struggle.

All the same, I knew there was more to the story. I could feel the tension in this household just as readily as I could feel the presence of Great Gable out there in the mist and rain.

The next morning I found Matthew alone at the

breakfast table. We spoke of commonplace matters, while Torver moved about the room with his silent, lurking tread.

It occurred to me that the manservant might well have been in the passageway near the cellar arch when Martin confronted me the day before. Then Matthew was saying that a warm fire burned in the library.

"It's not a day for an outing," he added, gesturing toward the windows, where rain made rivulets down the glass panes. "I had thought of taking the children down to the mere for an hour or two." As he held my chair and followed me from the dining room he smiled. "Dora will be disappointed. The rowboat is quite a favorite of hers, because she has a small one just like it for her bath."

I smiled in return. Aunt Charlotte had described more than once Dora's enthusiasm for water in large quantities and for the small gray boat that sailed in puddles on the floor as often as it did in the tub.

There was no reason not to accompany him into the library. The firelight sent dancing shadows along the dark shelves of books and rusted weapons that gleamed dully above the mantel and between the windows. Spears and ancient battle-axes, mostly, though there were two or three swords as well, heavy ugly blades scored with channels that protected their hilts from becoming slippery with blood.

He noticed my gaze and grimaced. "Hal's father developed an interest in his Icelandic heritage. He brought those back from a visit there. Hal went with him and for a time it seemed that he shared the interest. Then, about ten years ago, he dropped it entirely. But the weapons stayed on the wall in spite of Charlotte's protests." He took a winged chair by the fire and said easily, "You are from Wiltshire, I think?"

"Yes. My father owned a small estate not far from Salisbury. My mother was from Gloucestershire—"

Too late I remembered Philip saying once that the Carrocks had land there, and a house called Garland. Trying to retrieve my error, I went on into the stillness: "—but she had married against her family's wishes, and so I never knew them."

The fire crackled cheerfully and Matthew stared thoughtfully into the red-gold heart of it. "What was your mother's maiden name?" he asked when the silence had stretched uncomfortably long.

"Horton." Taking a deep breath, I added as casually as I could, "I understand that Philip has estates in Gloucestershire. Are they in the south, near Horton Court?" He could find the location of my grandparents' home easily enough for himself if he looked in Debrett's.

To my relief, he glanced at me and said, "No, Garland is near the Herefordshire border. Philip has a second cousin who lives in Gloucester. In fact, he is heir to Garland and Abbot's Thorston after the boy. A rather pompous, puritanical old man who has never approved of Freya's second marriage."

And did they suspect that I had come here to spy for the cousin? "I don't see that it could be any of his affair," I replied firmly. "She certainly hasn't neglected Philip. And you have been a kind stepfather."

He frowned. "Philip isn't easy to deal with. He's imaginative, sensitive, and resentful. If he is sent to me for punishment, it is a crushing blow to him, for it represents an authority and a relationship that he refuses to recognize as often as he can."

Which explained the day I had found him in the oak tree, so distressed that at first I believed he had been severely beaten.

"Children sometimes feel left out when a parent remarries."

Matthew shook his head. "It is more than that. He is morbidly attached to his father, though he can remember nothing about him. He was younger than Dora when Carrock died, after all." As he paused, I thought about Philip's eager questions on the bay crossing I had made and his silent pleading for me not to betray him to Maggie. Morbid was the correct word. "Sometimes I wonder if Langdale—" he broke off and got to his feet. "Why can't people leave well enough alone? Let the past stay buried! It is the only way any of us can find peace!" And he turned on his heel, leaving me there in the gloomy library, his curiosity unsatisfied and his questions unanswered.

I stared at the door, wondering if this attractive, shallow man had taken advantage of his opportunity and killed Charles Carrock on the sands of Morecambe Bay. He was not a murderer by nature, but my godmother believed that he was in love with Freya long before that night of violence, and he was in need of money, surely, if Martin's present circumstances were any indication. The Ryland estates had been gambled away in this very house. Would he have killed Sam Hichen also to protect his marriage?

Freya came into the room, her dark amber skirts swinging about her amber slippers. "What have you said to Matthew?" she demanded.

"Nothing." I rose to face her, startled and uncertain.

Her fingers bit into my shoulders and for a dazed instant I thought she would shake me. Her dark eyes blazed with anger as they held mine. "You are a troublemaker! I guessed it from the beginning. Well, it is a dangerous game, my girl, and you may come by your just deserts. I'd give a great deal to know how Askham got around you. But he was a charming devil even when I knew him—and dangerous. Remember that! Because when he discovers he is wasting his time here, he'll be finished with you too!"

And she was gone, leaving bruises aching on my shoulders as I caught the mantel to steady myself. I was no match for her strength, not when anger moved in her like a dark tide. But I knew that she was terribly frightened, which might easily place me in greater jeopardy than if she had killed Carrock herself.

Luncheon was an uncomfortable affair that left my nerves taut and my stomach in knots. Hal Langdale was in a foul mood, and Martin didn't help matters by badgering him to play cards in the evening.

"It's pouring rain and there's nothing to do in this godforsaken dale anyway. Why not a friendly game to pass the time?"

"This 'godforsaken dale' serves you well enough when your creditors are after you," Freya put in. "If I recall correctly, you came here of your own choice."

"Because I *had* no choice," he snapped pettishly. "And Hal gambles the night away when he takes the notion."

"I never gamble. I play only to win," Hal replied, his light eyes lifting to stare pointedly at Martin. "What can I win from *you?*"

"Yes, well, I know I'm under the hatches now," Martin answered. "But you could make me a loan."

"Why should I waste the time of playing for my own money?"

It was obviously an old struggle between these two men, for Martin flung himself back in his chair and said testily, "What do you do with the thousands of pounds you win? Sit in your mountain stronghold and gloat over your gold?"

There was a sudden stillness in Langdale. "What do you mean?"

"I mean you are a miser, counting over your guineas like some City merchant, filling bags and strongboxes when you could be enjoying Paris, Vienna . . ."

Langdale relaxed. "I have seen Paris and Vienna. Ravensholme is more to my taste." His eyes once more flickered contemptuously over the younger man. "We'll play for high stakes when you have a fortune of your own to lose."

Martin subsided, signaling Torver to refill his glass once more. He had already partaken freely of the excellent Rhine wine that had been served with the roast chickens, and I was glad when Freya gave the signal for the ladies to withdraw.

Longing to escape this bleak, forbidding house with its secretive passageways and silent servants, I gave in to Philip's persuasions and agreed to visit Herr Raeder in the afternoon.

I had not been willing to return too soon—if at all—for I still had not made up my mind about the schoolmaster. It was true that he was kind to Philip and showed more interest in him as a person than either of his parents did. And yet I could not disregard Freya's prohibition on the basis of a first impression. The fact was that the man irritated me and at the same time troubled me. He was not at all like meek little Herr Friedrich, the German master at the Academy—quiet, unassuming, his eyes uncertain behind their thick lenses. Indeed, Herr Raeder reminded me forcibly of the handsome German diplomat, a former Junker officer, whose daughter attended our school for some six months. Arrogant, mocking, and formidable even at sixty, he had quelled me with a glance and demolished Miss Whitmain's pretensions in three terse sentences. And Gretchen had been enrolled in spite of her predilection for every activity except her studies. Herr Raeder might be half the diplomat's age, but he was just as accustomed to having his own way.

Rain was falling in gray sheets, sweeping down from Scafell as if it would never stop. My half-boots squelched along the path as Philip and I hurried toward the cottage, and the rising wind tore at my cape and hood. We were laughing and nearly soaked through by the time we reached the sheltered door.

"So. It is you. From the clatter I thought several of my students had decided to call."

Philip tumbled across the threshold and pulled off his dripping coat and cap. "The villagers never come *here!*"

"There is a first time for everything, my friend," the schoolmaster replied calmly, lifting the cloak from my shoulders and spreading it over a chair to dry. "Why do you wear your hair in that appalling knot, Fräulein? It is more becoming like this—curling about your face."

My hands went quickly to the unruly strands, smoothing them back into place. "I don't care to have it untidy," I replied coldly.

He stared at me for a moment. "I am not speaking in compliment. Merely stating an obvious fact. You need not be offended."

I was grateful when Philip, who had been exploring with his usual impetuosity, chose that moment to squeal with delight. "Oh, look! Look, a *cat!*"

And there on a rug in the chimney corner was a large yellow and white cat, pretending to sleep.

"He followed me home two days ago and asked shelter from the storm. I could not refuse him," the schoolmaster explained. "Perhaps he has decided to stay."

Philip, squatting by the rug, gently smoothed the twitching ears and ran a finger down the soft back. The cat, an opportunist, opened his yellow eyes and stretched, then rose to wrap himself around the child's shins. Philip sank down and grinned in pleasure as the cat climbed into his lap.

Herr Raeder turned to me. "I call him Bismarck, for he can be very charming when he pleases and very single-minded when he wishes to have his own way."

I smiled. "Exactly like most *people*."

"It is whispered in the village that all is not well at Ravensholme. Is this true?" He had lowered his voice.

Dismayed at his presumption, I said stiffly, "I don't

discuss the affairs of a house in which I am a guest."

"That is as it should be," he answered, unabashed. "I have not asked you to gossip. Merely to confirm or deny this rumor."

"It is none of your affair," I told him coldly, wishing we hadn't come here.

"Which tells me precisely what I wish to know." I stood up angrily and reached for my cloak, but he stopped me with a firm hand on my arm. "You are being very foolish, Fräulein. I hear the children talking in school, and see the women with their heads together in quiet corners, the men standing together in the fields. There are dark circles under your eyes as if you do not sleep soundly. And Philip is thinner than he was last summer. Should I turn my back, ignoring what is plainly there?"

"You have no right—"

"Only that of a friend. Philip comes and goes from this house as freely as the cat. While he is here I do what I can for him. How does that interfere?"

Suddenly it occurred to me that Bismarck might have had a bit of encouragement to follow the schoolmaster home. To help Philip forget the tensions and suspicions of Ravensholme? Or to forge the bonds more tightly between the man and the child? I watched the schoolmaster's long slender fingers toy with the gold fob of his watch chain.

"I don't understand anything any more," I said at last, tired of struggling to find answers. "But I've grown quite fond of Philip. And I want whatever is best for him. If only he were an ordinary little boy in a cheerful village in Wiltshire or Devon, not the heir to several estates and caught up in the middle of whatever is happening! Most of all I wish neither of us had ever heard of Ravensholme or even Abbot's Thorston!"

Here Raeder, his mouth grim, led me back to my chair.

"Sit down, Fräulein," he commanded and went over to the tall oak cupboard. He returned with a glass of dark red liquid. "Drink this." At my obvious hesitation, he said curtly, "It is a mild wine made by one of the goodwives of the village. Scarcely vintage, but palatable and an excellent restorative. It cannot harm you."

I did as I was told only because it seemed simpler than refusing. The wine was indeed mild and sweet, but its warm glow spread through me and stopped the tremors in my hands.

He left me sitting there and went to show Philip how to cast a bit of string for the cat to play with. The cat, wise in the way of its gypsy kind, performed brilliantly, abandoning its mature dignity and scrambling about the kitchen with the verve and agility of a kitten. Soon we were all breathless from laughter and Philip subsided in a giggling heap at Bismarck's graceful but impressive disappearance through the dairy archway.

The schoolmaster's eyes met mine as he collapsed gasping into the other chair. Behind the dark glasses they seemed to ask, Where is the harm, Fräulein? Tell me that.

We left as soon as Philip had collected himself. The wind had dropped, leaving a misting rain behind. Herr Raeder offered us a lantern, but I refused, wishing to slip unnoticed into Ravensholme. He stood in the bright rectangle of the cottage doorway watching us disappear.

We followed the track to the garden path and found the mist heavier here, blended with the smoke from the chimneys. Putting his hand in mine, Philip guided me between the flower beds, past the hyacinths and to the flagstone circle before the garden door. The thick branches of ivy that climbed to the roof at the corner of the wing rustled as if birds fluttered in the leaves, settling for an early night.

Philip pushed open the door and we stepped inside the dark passage just as a deafening clatter behind me brought us both up short. I whirled to see a heavy slate from the roof lying shattered on the flagstones. Philip, his face white, stared down at it in disbelief.

Finding my voice with difficulty, I said, "The rain must have loosened it—rusted the nails perhaps. How fortunate that it missed us!"

"It might have hurt you," he said, squatting down and reaching out to finger the sharp edges of the pieces. "We didn't even hear it *slide*."

"Well, no harm done," I said as lightly as I could. "But you will take a chill if you stand about in those wet shoes. Upstairs with you, and don't forget to set your coat by the fire to dry."

He stood up and looked at me. "I'm very glad it missed you," he said shyly, and then was gone.

I followed more slowly, thinking about the rustle in the ivy and the fact that the slate had made no sound as it slithered down the steeply pitched roof. Had it really been an accident? And if it hadn't, who was the intended victim? Philip—or me?

The next morning when the rain slackened briefly, I walked out the front door and strolled casually through the muddy gardens until I had a clear view of the door leading to the narrow passage.

The roof sloped sharply on this side of Ravensholme, though there was a single dormer high up among the slates and just above the doorway. The vine, its branches as thick as a man's wrist, climbed the corner of the house and then separated to ramble along the gutters. A gulley, cupped to channel the rain water, ran from each side of the dormer to the corners of the roof.

Someone might well have been waiting in the dormer for our return. We would have been clearly visible until we came within the last few feet of the door, and anyone in the open window would have had to guess at the best moment to drop the slate upon our heads. That would also explain why we had heard nothing until it crashed upon the flagstones.

And he would have known at once that he had missed. We had not cried out. Perhaps he had even intended to miss, hoping only to frighten us. Well, he had succeeded in that!

The ivy was strong enough to have supported someone's weight, and the gulley running to the side of the dormer would have made walking on the roof a simple matter, unlike negotiating the slippery slates. Just because the window was there, it didn't necessarily mean that someone had used it. I didn't even know what room lay behind it.

Afraid to be seen staring up at the roof, I quickly moved on.

Why, I wondered miserably, couldn't I persuade myself that it was indeed an accident? A loose slate, precariously balanced and jarred free as Philip swung open the door? We had had so much rain of late. Try as I would, I remained unconvinced—and very frightened.

It began to rain again as I turned back toward the house, and I quickened my pace, my head down. And so I didn't see the horsemen until I had left the garden path and stepped out onto the flagstones leading to the front door. Hal Langdale and his sister had been out riding and were returning by way of the drive. They made a handsome pair, both in elegant black that set off their red-gold hair. I hurried on my way, hoping to reach the safety of the hall before the horses caught up with me. But they too were hurrying, for the drizzle was fast becoming a hard shower.

Swept by panic as the horses came snorting and prancing toward me, I hesitated, realized it was too late to return the way I had come, and darted frantically toward the front door. Langdale's mount shied, and he shouted at me for startling the creature. Pressing myself against the wet stone wall as I fumbled for the latch, I watched as Freya drew up by the steps and slipped from her saddle quite as capably as a man, tossing her reins to her brother.

"There's no need to ruin my habit," she said, and then added to me, "What have you been up to? You are as white as a feather."

"I . . . nothing . . . the horses . . ." I stammered, fighting to control my breathing as the door opened at last beneath my shaking fingers.

She wheeled, her eyes scanning the hill above the gardens. "Did you meet someone? Is someone up there?"

Langdale had turned to look also before touching his mount with an impatient heel and moving off toward the stables.

"I had walked in the gardens for a few minutes," I said, backing into the hall. "The . . . the horses frightened me, that's all."

"Nonsense!" she said sharply. "I can see it in your face. You needn't try to lie. You didn't expect to be caught, did you?"

"I merely walked in the gardens when the rain stopped! If I had planned to slip away to meet someone, do you suppose I would choose to leave and return by the front door, for all to see me?" Pressing my advantage, for she had glanced at the door as if considering the point, I continued earnestly: "If only I could make you understand. I know nothing about Hichen or this man Askham! I'm not a part of *anyone's* plot."

Freya looked me up and down, contempt in her dark eyes. "I'm not a fool, Miss Winton. Nor am I a green girl of twenty, so wildly in love that she would do anything to keep a man to his promise! That was eight years ago, and eight years can be a lifetime. George Askham may take whatever revenge he pleases against Hal. I am well aware now that it was my brother who persuaded him to pay his gaming debts with those regimental funds. For all I know it was Hal who turned him in to his colonel afterward, to get rid of him so that I would have no choice but to marry Charles Carrock. But there is nothing left between George and me. *Nothing!* The sooner he realizes that, the better for all of us. If— When you see him, give him my message. Tell him too that a frightened woman can be driven to desperate measures. He—and you—would do well to remember!"

And she left me standing there in the hall staring after her as she swept up the stairs. Then, as reaction set in, I leaned weakly against the door.

"Is that you, Elizabeth?" my godmother called as the silence lengthened in the dimly lit hall. She was standing in the passage from the drawing room.

"Yes." With an effort I brought myself under control and went on brightly, "I took advantage of a break in the storm to enjoy a breath of air. But it has begun to rain once more, I'm afraid."

As I came near her, she smiled and nodded. "I can smell the damp wool of your cloak. Was that Freya on the stairs?"

"She had just come in from a ride with Mr. Langdale."

She sighed and turned back the way she had come. "I do miss that. But I feel it is . . . unwise . . . to ride these days. Matthew took me out once, and Hal often asks. The temptation . . ."

As I followed her into the drawing room, she picked up a slim volume of Shelley's poems. "Would you like to read aloud to me?"

"Of course." Taking the book from her, I asked casually, "Tell me, does anyone have rooms in the wing overlooking the garden door? It occurred to me that the view must be lovely in summer."

"No, that wing is seldom used—only when we have

guests other than members of the family. We don't entertain often. Hal's friends come, or used to. He seems to have lost interest in them of late. I'm just as glad. The fortunes that exchanged hands sometimes! Martin isn't the only one to wonder what my husband does with his money!"

We were soon lost in the beauty of "Adonais," and I found it soothing to put aside my fears for a little while.

Several days later I was in the hall alone, on my way to the breakfast room. The house was quiet, the servants busy with their meal and the family asleep or still in their bedchambers. I enjoyed this hour of the day and had made it a point since coming to Ravensholme to rise early to take my breakfast in a peaceful solitude that contrasted dramatically with our tense and often nerve-racking dinners.

As I crossed to the narrow passage on the right, my back was to the stairs, my thoughts sifting idly through plans for the day. The strange hissing sound had barely registered in my mind when something caught my arm from behind and threw me roughly against the far wall. Unsuspecting, unprepared, I cried out in alarm. A pain seared my arm near my left shoulder; I felt a sensation of being pinned to the wood, and a warmth spread in my sleeve.

Dazed, I turned my head and stared in shock at the short spear that had pierced the fabric of my gown and plunged deep into the carving, gashing my arm as it passed. There was blood now on the pale gray cloth, a rapidly growing dark circle. I pressed my forehead against the garlands of wooden roses for a moment, waiting for the upsurge of nausea to pass. Then, lifting my right hand, I touched the spear with trembling fingers. It was firmly embedded in the paneling. With infinite care I next moved my arm and heard the sleeve tear slightly as it came free. I smothered a gasp and stepped back, holding my arm awkwardly as if it were no longer a part of me.

The thing was indeed a spear, one of those from the collection in the library surely. Had it been meant for my *back*? I stumbled toward the stairs, stopped, and returned to grasp the handle with my right hand. Though I was lightheaded, I managed to pull firmly and somehow it came free, leaving only the scar in the carving to mark its place. I had no desire for this incident to become common knowledge, a subject of speculation. Terrified as I was, I was even more afraid of drawing attention to these threats and my own vulnerability.

Miraculously I managed to reach the safety of my room without meeting anyone on the stairs or in the passage, and for a minute or so I leaned against the bedchamber wall in weakness and relief. I locked the door, dropped the spear on the carpet, and began to unbutton my dress.

In the mirror the gash was ugly to see—a half-moon of discolored flesh after I had sponged away the blood. But not so deep or so serious that I needed to cause an uproar by summoning help. I found a soft old petticoat and forced myself to cut it into neat strips, though my left arm throbbed with each movement. There was a jar of unguent in my trunk that had proven effective with minor cuts and burns. In time I was able to clean and bind the wound, then clear away all signs of difficulty. Only the spear lay where I had dropped it, and I stepped over it to unlock my chamber door, putting off the moment when I must touch it again.

I was just congratulating myself on my resourcefulness when the room tilted crazily and everything went black.

I came to my senses to find Aunt Charlotte bending over me, Philip squatting on his heels beside her.

"My dear child, are you all right?" she demanded at once as I moved slightly beneath the quilt that covered me.

"I—I believe so," I began weakly and winced at the pain in my arm. It brought back a flood of images and I remembered what had happened. "It was nothing . . . a moment of dizziness."

"Slim as you are, you needn't lace yourself so tightly," she scolded. "Philip found you and came at once for me. You can't imagine how frightened I was, unable to see what was wrong or to know how to help!"

I was still in my petticoats and she must have thought I was dressing for breakfast. She had failed to notice the bandage as she had made me more comfortable, and I was glad. But Philip had seen it. His eyes were large as saucers, though he must have said nothing.

Aunt Charlotte sent for sweet tea and toast, for which I was very grateful, and promised to say nothing about my foolishness in putting vanity before proper breathing. After she had gone, reassured at last that I was sufficiently recovered to dress on my own, Philip scratched at my door.

He stared at me as I sat before the fire wearing a puffed-sleeve gown of dark blue merino.

"I hid the spear. I wasn't tall enough to put it back on the wall again. There was blood on your arm."

I bit my lip. There was no way I could hide the truth from him. If I tried, it might frighten him all the more. "Someone must have thrown the spear," I said at last. "But it cut my arm only a little. I fainted from fright."

"Was it the same person who dropped the slate?"

I laid my hands very gently on his slim shoulders and looked straight at him with an assurance I was far from feeling. "Someone was only trying to frighten me, Philip. It isn't anything for you to worry about. I promise."

He nodded gravely.

"You'll see, I'll be fine. Truly I will." I patted his shoulders and rose. "To prove it, we'll take advantage of this lovely day and walk down to Wastwater."

To my surprise he said quickly, "Not this morning, please. I—I can't."

"Well . . . perhaps it would be best for me to take care today." I smiled. "Tomorrow, then."

"Tomorrow," he promised, smiling briefly in return, and then was gone.

I leaned back in the chair and closed my eyes against the burning pain in my arm.

It was not until after luncheon that I could bring myself to enter the library and look at the ancient weapons on its walls. Philip had not told me where he had hidden the spear, but if it came from a conspicuous area I must somehow contrive to replace it. Even as I scanned the displays I remembered all too well Matthew's quiet voice telling me their history and then growing angry as he pleaded for the past to remain buried with its dead. Remembered Freya, her hands gripping my shoulders, shouting furiously at me. Had one of them come back for a spear, then waited patiently for me to cross the empty hall, my back to the gloomy stairs, day after day until the right moment came? I quivered at the thought of someone standing in the shadows watching, clutching the spear, feeling murder in his—or her—heart. Short as the haft was, even a woman could have hurled the old weapon.

But the circles were still perfect. Nothing was missing. Had the spear been found and replaced? Philip might not have hidden it well, or he might have been seen with it by someone watching for its reappearance. It was my fault if I failed the child and drew him into my own danger. Or had the spear come from somewhere other than these barbaric displays? Hal Langdale's father might have chosen only the best to hang upon his walls and left the rest to rust in the attics or cellars.

Confused and unhappy, I left the room and sought the safety and quiet of my bedchamber.

Because my gowns were demure, with long sleeves and high necks, no one appeared to notice the bandage about my arm. I had even managed to do my hair creditably, though not as severely as usual. There were curling tendrils clustering softly about my face rather than the smooth curves on either side of my head. There was no way for anyone to guess that the spear had done more than given me a bad fright.

I sat at the dinner table and looked covertly from one face to another.

Which of these people had tried once—possibly twice—to harm me? And why? Had these attacks been a warning or in deadly earnest? And would there be others because these had failed? The questions spun with the wine that seemed to fill my head with lightness.

Matthew spoke casually with my godmother, whose face was lifted to his as if she could look into his eyes in spite of her blindness. And Matthew had accused me of being a spy. So had Freya, who was quarreling desultorily with Martin over some event that had occurred on their visit to Cartmel. Martin believed I was concealing information he desperately wanted. Behind my chair Torver moved silently about his duties, an enigma in this house but unquestionably Hal Langdale's man. Langdale watched each of us in turn with those light, hooded eyes.

As his glance met mine, I looked quickly away. What was there in those pale depths? Something moved there, like black currents beneath cold golden ice.

With an effort I reminded myself that one of these people might have killed before. Charles Carrock had died on the sands of Morecambe Bay and so had Sam Hichen. The candles in the Venetian chandelier danced in the darkness overhead like fairy lights, blinding me with their brightness. The bay had been so black, so desolate. A fitting place for murder. As were the shadowed passageways and dimly lit rooms of Ravensholme. My murder.

I scarcely heard Martin's voice as he held the door for the ladies to retire. It was a mere whisper that reached my ears alone.

"You are incredibly beautiful tonight with your sparkling eyes and flushed cheeks, those curls falling so artlessly about your face. Neither Matthew nor Hal could keep his eyes off you. What became of the little Quaker maid who protested her innocence so vehemently?"

Before I could answer, the dining-room door swung closed and I felt the cool air of the passage fan my face and send icy fingers down my spine.

6

I was restless that night, by turns burning and shivering between the sheets. My arm throbbed with each beat of my heart; my lightheadedness had come from fever, not the dinner wine.

Twice I rose to splash what remained of the water in the ewer on my face and wrists, then huddled with chattering teeth under my blankets. My throat was dry, parched, but there was nothing in the room to drink. Finally, wretched and concerned, I thrust my feet into my slippers, pulled on my wrapper, and picked up the porcelain ewer. If I could keep the fever down *now*, perhaps it would go away before morning. Surely at this hour I could find my way safely to the kitchen!

Silence met me in the corridor as I closed my door and every nerve ending in my body was alert to the slightest sound or movement. The candle shook in my fingers as I made my way along the shadowy passages, down the twisting stairs, and into the kitchen.

Resembling a great barn with smoke-blackened beams and dark oak furnishings, the room swallowed the candle's glow and seemed full of lurking figures waiting to pounce. I found the water barrel beneath a shelf of dippers and pewter cups, filled the pitcher, and drank from its lip before topping it up again. The fire in my throat eased a little. The porcelain felt cool against my feverish arm as I started back the way I had come.

He was on the stairs, no candle lighting his way, and he waited there on the landing, watching me with those strange golden eyes. I didn't even see Hal until I was nearly upon him, for he was dressed in black. Only his hair and the front of his shirt were visible. I don't know what prevented me from crying out in terror or dropping the pitcher and racing back the way I had come. My heart seemed to stop.

For an instant we stood face to face. His glance slowly traveled over me, lingering on the tousled ringlets that lay about my shoulders, the plain blue wrapper tied at my waist, the worn toes of my slippers. I saw the heavy goblet between his hands, its rough-cut stones winking in the candle's gleam .

And then I brushed past him without a word, my feet flying up the stairs, my skirts swirling behind me. Weird shapes leaped and cavorted on the walls as the candle spluttered. Splotches of water from the ewer marked my wrapper. But he made no effort to follow me.

I reached my room and stumbled inside. The door was locked behind me almost as soon as it had closed. Setting the pitcher on the night table by the bed, I stood there gasping for breath, feeling the terror slowly subside as I forced myself to relax. After all, I was safe. He hadn't come after me. Nothing had happened. Yet there had been such an atmosphere of *evil* in that narrow landing . . .

Later, as I crawled into bed again, I wondered dizzily if he had really been there at all, or only a figment of my feverish brain, born of my fears and the relentless ache in my arm.

The next morning as a watery sunlight crept into the room, I felt a little better but very weak. The water had helped the fever, certainly, and my arm hurt less since I had cleaned and rebandaged it after dawn, but the wound was still badly inflamed. I had begun to wonder about the rusty head of that spear, and to worry.

My breakfast consisted of tea and toast, for I had no appetite. Afterward I walked in the gardens, hoping to take my mind off my discomfort, but the morning chill soon sent me indoors again.

Maggie, herding the girls before her, met me in the passage as I neared my room. " 'Twill be mist afore dinner," she said, shaking her head at me while Dora grinned and tugged at my hand. "The sun isn't strong enough to last."

"Gable was clear as I came in," I replied, smiling at Helen, who shyly peered from behind Maggie's skirts.

"Aye," the nursery maid said darkly, " 'tis a bad sign, that. I'd best take the little ones out whilst I may!"

My godmother found me hovering by the fire an hour later when she tapped at my door. I tried to seem cheerful and at ease, although it was an effort. She appeared not to notice. Freya occupied her thoughts.

"There's something on her mind, and Matthew *must* sense it, for he is not himself. I wish I knew—"

"Aunt Charlotte, do you suppose that . . . that Matthew might have been the man Sam Hichen saw with Charles Carrock, there in the bay? After all, he followed him that night, didn't he? There's only his own word that he didn't find Carrock, and Freya may fear he had something to do with Hichen's death because of it."

Her face was ashen. "Don't even suggest such a terrible thing! *Matthew?* He couldn't hurt anyone! No, I won't hear of it!" She was on her feet, poised to leave.

"I'm not trying to say anything against him," I told her hastily. "Only that Freya might *believe* the worst, even if it isn't true."

"If anyone killed Charles Carrock, it was his wife, not Matthew. Freya is strong, capable of anything in a rage. That's why I never understood when she accepted

Matthew. She didn't love him, and they are so entirely different!"

"But how could she have followed her husband? She had gone to fetch Philip."

"So *she* says. And where was Hal? Or Torver?"

"What earthly reason would they have had for harming Carrock?" I asked, wishing I had never brought up the subject, much less in the way I had.

"He had attacked Freya, hadn't he? Almost killed her? Hal's own sister?" Her hands were twining nervously, her brows drawn together in a frown.

Somehow I couldn't see Hal Langdale committing murder for anyone's sake but his own. "I'm sure Charles Carrock died accidentally," I said soothingly. "After all, Hichen was quite drunk. I merely wondered if Freya suspected Matthew, however unjustly."

"Or *he* suspected her . . ." she began in a low voice. Her hand felt for a chair and she sat down. "I told you not to become involved with us. Now I don't know where it will end, any of it."

She left soon after, that tiny frown still creasing her forehead in spite of my efforts to reassure her. I felt guilty for having been the cause of her concern. After all, she came to me to resolve her problems, not add to them.

Exhausted by her visit and yet too tightly strung to lie down, I couldn't bear the gloomy stillness of my room. I had no energy and no desire to make conversation with anyone who might wander into the morning room, and I didn't want to sit in the drawing room and stare at that golden goblet. I had last seen it in Hal's hands on the landing, and the very thought of that nightmarish meeting disturbed me. Instead I decided to walk in the fresh air until I felt drowsy enough to rest.

Wastwater was dark under the dim sky and Gable still reared his awesome head above the dale like the god he might have been—unmoving, untouched by human woes. My cloak's warmth was welcome in the damp air, though its weight on my left shoulder was uncomfortable. I could feel the fever rising in me again and the prospect of luncheon was nauseating.

The track up the shoulder of Gable beckoned. I walked along it while my mind tried to separate strands of fact and fancy into a sensible pattern of what was happening at Ravensholme. So much depended on whether Charles Carrock had drowned accidentally or had indeed been murdered. Always Charles Carrock, the man who had first tried to kill his wife and met his own death instead. What sort of man was he, Philip's dead father? I wished that I knew.

A shepherd, small and wiry and weathered, passed me as he followed his flock over the brow of the rise. He touched his cap and paused for a moment, leaving his black and white dog to tend his charges.

I smiled at the gambols of long-legged lambs and asked, remembering Freya's comment as we drove along Wastwater, "Are they Herdwick sheep?"

"Aye, and fine at that," he replied. "Hoggs and gimmers, wethers and twinters, ewes and tups." His lined face creased into a grin at my bewildered expression. "A lamb old enough to leave its ma is a hogg, and in the second spring a shearling, gimmer or wether shearling depending on whether it be female or male. After the second winter they both be twinters. A gimmer's not a ewe till she's had her own lamb. And a tup be a ram."

"That sounded like a rhyme," I said. " 'Hoggs and gimmers . . .' "

"Oh, as to rhymes, mistress, there be the old counting ways, so old I don't know who be the first to say it. Yan, tan, tether, mether, pimp, teezar, leezar, catterah, horna, dick. And on it goes to yan-dick, tan-dick, bumpit, yan-a-bumpit—they being eleven, twelve, fifteen, sixteen—till my granddaughter turns red with laughing and her ma scolds me for giving her hiccoughs." With a spark of mischief in his pale blue eyes, he touched his cap once more and set off after the flock. He had enjoyed the brief lighthearted contact with another human being during his solitary wanderings, and so had I.

Unaccountably cheered, I went on my way, and only then saw a man on the brow of Gable high above me. He was staring out over Wasdale from a jutting shelf of rock at the end of the track from the Sty, the narrow, twisting pass that runs steeply along Lingmell Beck's chattering course at the top of the ravine. A tiny figure, but something about him—the way he stood there, the black folds of his cloak catching the wind—reminded me of the man on the sands. His face was a dark blur against the sky, shadowed by the brim of his hat.

I had already come farther than Philip and I had ever ventured, but I never hesitated to go on. Stumbling in my haste, I ran along the track, skirting boulders, feeling first moss and then stones and then moss again beneath my thin shoes, trying to reach the top before he had disappeared. There was no way to know how long he had been standing there before I noticed him. If it was indeed George Askham, I wanted to speak with him, to tell him what nightmares his coming had brought in its wake. Whatever Freya and Aunt Charlotte might say about him, I couldn't believe that the man on the sands and in the hall of Abbot's Thorston was truly evil. I wanted to find out, if I could, why Freya was so terrified of him. I felt no fear, only the pressing need to hurry.

Minding my feet and the hem of my skirts, I failed to see him leave Gable. Nor had I realized that a wall of mist had settled over Scafell, spilling rapidly down the Screes toward the mere and sending long fingers to touch the dark shape of Ravensholme. My eyes had been turned elsewhere. Dizzy from exertion, all too mindful of the ache in my shoulder as I climbed, I quickly found myself regretting not having eaten all day. My knees trembled with weakness, soft yarn in the place of muscle and sinew. But I kept going, expecting at any moment to see him appear in the ravines ahead, climbing down to the dale.

Instead, the tall figure of Askham was outlined briefly on the track to Scafell beyond. Almost weeping with frustration, I sat down on the damp stone beside the track and tried to think what to do. There was no way I could catch up with him now. He was so *near* and yet might as well be on the moon for all I could do about it. Shouting to him wouldn't help. He had surely seen me from Gable and could easily have waited if he had had any wish to speak to *me*. Except for the occasional crunch of loose rock beneath his feet, borne on the light wind that drove the mist inexorably toward me, I could almost have convinced myself that he, like Hal Langdale last night, was imaginary. But no ghost walked with such firm, sure steps.

I admitted defeat then, resting my forehead against my arms for a few minutes before facing the descent. Below me the valley spread out like a half-finished quilt, the long shape of Wastwater only a faint darkness in the mist, the village and intake-fields vanishing house by house, Ravensholme floating in its shrouded gardens. The schoolmaster had warned me about being caught in the mists. Somewhere nearby a sheep bleated forlornly, answered by another. I started at the sound and got to my feet.

It had been a mistake to overexert. My head was spinning, the cloak seemed to smother me, and my arm ached abominably. I was still more feverish than I knew, that was all, I told myself resolutely as I plodded down the track. Before I was halfway to Ravensholme the mist engulfed me in its white blanket, shutting out the dale below, the fells, and the deep ravine that ran parallel to the route I had followed. Worried, I reached into my pocket for the compass Herr Raeder had given me. I had no desire to walk off Gable to my death. Even with the compass, there were pitfalls enough. Shivering in the clammy air I tried to remember exactly how I had come. But my mind had been concentrating on my footing, not the landmarks.

I picked myself up after a jolting fall on loose chipping that I was certain I hadn't crossed before. The compass was unbroken, thank God, and I kept it open before me as I set off again. A sheep's bell, tinkling behind me, made me jump, but I never saw the animal itself, only a blur in the whiteness. I was going in the correct direction, that much was certain, but was *this* the proper track to Ravensholme? Shouldn't the low shrubs along the garden's edge be somewhere to my right by now? Even the gurgling music of the beck had deserted me. I felt bewildered, uncertain which way to turn.

A dog barked shrilly, breaking the silence, and I tried to pinpoint the sound. Surely I hadn't *passed* Ravensholme? If I had reached the village, I'd have noticed the low stone walls, the gray shapes of the houses! I turned back, peering into the mist for something to guide me, came to a fork I hadn't remembered at all, and stood debating which branch to choose. The cold seemed to penetrate my cloak, touching my body with icy fingers. It was only late afternoon, yet darkness could not have been more blinding or so confusing. Every step I took might be leading me farther from Ravensholme, toward a precipice, a ravine, even another fell.

At last I chose the left fork and followed it for some hundred paces before stopping again, searching vainly for a familiar landmark, listening to the utter stillness that told me nothing. I walked another ten paces then tried again.

"What are you doing here?"

I whirled in alarm, staring blankly into the soft whiteness for the unexpected voice. Herr Raeder loomed from the mist behind me.

"I . . . I have lost my way," I began, gesturing about me.

"Lost?" he demanded sardonically. "I have heard you walking first this way and that, circling my house for the last quarter of an hour. What is it you want? What are you searching for?"

"The *cottage?*" I repeated in surprise. "Surely—"

"Surely I am not the fool you think me. Come inside." He took my left arm in a grip of iron and I cried out in pain as he led me firmly along the track and through the gate toward the cottage door. The green curtains had been drawn, or I might have seen the light for myself. I blinked in the brightness as he swung me to face him.

"So, Fräulein, I have spoken to Philip. Yes, he came to me yesterday, frightened by what he had seen. You are sowing the wind, and cannot see that you must surely reap the whirlwind! Leave Ravensholme at once. If you cannot, then stay out of affairs that in no way concern you. Before it is too late!"

Furiously angry, tired and wretched, unutterably relieved to know where I was, I couldn't stop the outburst that was partly reaction, partly temper.

"I have done nothing to those people! I haven't the faintest notion who is responsible for the two attacks on me. But *someone* believes I have knowledge I don't possess, and there is nothing I can do about it. And I can't possibly leave because I have nowhere to go!"

"You have interfered—"

"I have done nothing of the sort! Coincidence—not to speak of guilty consciences that won't listen to reason—pitched me into a situation I can't even understand, much less explain. And you are the worst of the lot, standing there passing judgment on *me* in a matter that is no more your concern than it is Bismarck's!"

"Nevertheless," he broke in sternly, "what you are doing is wrong. It will only serve to hurt Philip in the end, this stirring up of what is past. I have worked too long and too hard to let you thoughtlessly tear him apart. And I warn you—in any way I can, I shall stop you! Not for any other reason except to save him; but for that I shall go to whatever lengths I have to."

"Save him from what? From George Askham, who has some hold on his mother? From Matthew Ryland, who might have killed his father and the drunken freighter who saw it happen? From Martin, who doesn't care who is hurt if he can get his hands on the money he so desperately needs? Or are you afraid that Philip will learn the truth about Charles Carrock, who nearly killed Freya before Matthew came to her rescue? Why don't you tell me what danger Philip is in. Perhaps I could help as much or more than you! It does no good, Herr Raeder, to threaten me with vengeance for being in *your* way!"

"Vengeance belongs only to a man who is already dead," the schoolmaster said heavily. "And he would be the last to demand it. What matters is Philip's safety and welfare. In your ignorance you are the gravest threat to that."

Unwilling to listen to another word, I wheeled before he could prevent me and flung open the door. Outside a dog was barking wildly, closer this time, and Bismarck shot between my ankles into the sanctuary of the cottage. Ordinarily I might have kept my feet with ease in spite of being tripped up. Today I was in no condition to dodge the large yellow cat's precipitous entrance. As I stumbled, the schoolmaster's long fingers closed about my arm to steady me. This time they encircled not the swollen, sensitive flesh just above my elbow but the bandaged wound itself.

I screamed as splinters of fire seemed to explode in my shoulder. Strong hands caught me as a black curtain descended before my eyes, but I was beyond caring where or how I fell.

When I came to my senses I was lying on a narrow bed in a small unfamiliar room. A shielded candle burned on the rough table against one whitewashed wall. There was also a chest of brassbound wood, a plain battered wardrobe, and a chair occupied by a figure leaning back in the shadows polishing his glasses. It was the first time I had seen the schoolmaster without them, but the strong, clearcut face was blurred. As I tried to focus my eyes, he stood up, replacing the lenses.

His shadow arched swiftly across the low beamed ceiling as he came toward me. "So." There was satisfaction in Herr Raeder's voice. "You are awake. The child did not tell me the spear had cut so deeply."

The long full sleeve of my woolen gown had been unbuttoned and rolled to the shoulder, leaving my arm bare. The wound had been rebandaged and felt strangely cool. I struggled to sit up. "What have you been doing?"

"There is infection. I hope we have stopped it in time."

I thought again of the rusty, ill-kept weapon. Or had there been something else on the blade? All at once I remembered Aunt Charlotte's fear of being poisoned while her husband was away.

"In my years at sea," he went on quietly, "I have seen many such wounds treated. Not from spears, naturally, but knives. They are much the same."

"You were at sea?" I asked stupidly, my wits still scattered. "I thought you were a schoolmaster."

"So I am. But even a schoolmaster yearns for adventure in his youth."

I thought he was mocking me and began to ease my

cuff down over the bandage. "It was silly of me to faint again," I said stiffly. "You needn't have troubled. I can manage on my own."

"Can you indeed?" His eyes studied me from behind the dark glasses as he handed me a cup of steaming broth from the table. "Drink this, for you undoubtedly missed your luncheon and will miss your dinner as well."

I took the cup. The rich odor of barley and mutton was irresistable, and I had no desire to face the questions and suspicions of Ravensholme on an empty, nervous stomach. My fingers trembled as I lifted the broth to my lips, but some of the dizziness subsided as I drank.

"Much better." He nodded as if I were a recalcitrant pupil. "What is your Christian name? Elizabeth, I believe the child said?"

"Yes," I replied. There was no point in denying it. I set down the empty cup and got gingerly to my feet. They were, to my surprise, dependable, if a little stiff.

He followed me out of the room, ducking beneath the low lintel, and down the stone steps into the kitchen.

"Now, then. What were you doing out in that mist?"

"Trying to find someone, a man I had seen up on Gable. I wanted to speak to him," I answered defiantly. "Thank you for the soup and for attending to my arm, Herr Raeder. I shan't trouble you again!"

He chuckled and stood there staring down at me, exasperation vying with something else in his face. "Why do you quarrel with me whenever we meet?"

"Do I? As I recall, *you* were threatening *me* not half an hour ago for meddling. I have received a lecture from you every time I encounter you, and most of them are undeserved. I grant you that you have done wonders for Philip, but that doesn't mean *I* have to like you. I'm not a child of seven to be dazzled by birds' nests and a theatrical cat!"

"You are very young and very inexperienced," he replied quietly. "And unable to trust for fear of being hurt."

"If I am wary, it is because I have learned not to trust anyone connected with Ravensholme. For all I know, *you* might have dropped that slate upon us and thrown the spear at me. That house is such a rabbit's warren, I'm sure you could find a way in if you were determined enough! Good evening, Herr Raeder!" I snatched up my cloak from the chair by the fire and stalked to the door. As I pulled it open, something made me turn.

He stood there still, but his lips were set in a grim line and his dark brows were drawn together in annoyance. There was nothing of the schoolmaster about him then, only the arrogant, ruthlessly determined German officer. I was suddenly frightened without knowing why, and quickly closed the door. Though the mists still wreathed the dale, I found my way safely and swiftly to Ravensholme, though in the stillness my footsteps echoed strangely and I could have sworn someone was behind me nearly all the way.

The house was in an uproar, for Aunt Charlotte was insisting that search parties be sent out after me. Freya was torn between seeing the last of me and finding out what I had been up to. I heard them arguing as I stepped into the drawing room.

Matthew was the first to see me. "Here she is! Good God, have you given us a fright, wandering off without a word. Don't you know it is dangerous on these fells in a mist?"

"Elizabeth! Are you all right?" My godmother made her way across the room and stretched out her hand for reassurance.

Taking her cold fingers in mine, I said contritely, "I am very sorry I worried you. I didn't expect the mist to catch me on Gable, and I had trouble finding my way down again."

"What in heaven's name possessed you to climb Gable?" Freya demanded. "Have you no sense at all?"

"Apparently not," Martin said, coming in at that moment. "That is, if she really did go up there."

"Well? Did you?" Freya asked, staring at me from across the room.

"Yes. I met a shepherd and we talked for a few minutes and then I was concentrating on the track and didn't see the mist coming in until too late." Matthew, looking down at my scuffed shoes, shook his head. "I'm not very presentable," I said hastily. "If you will excuse me—"

"You ought to have climbing boots. Freya might have a pair to fit you," he said. "Hal must have an extra compass too."

I wondered how he could have tried to harm me if he felt such concern for me now. Or was it only an act?

"She has no business on the fells, not without a guide," Aunt Charlotte said quickly. "We've held dinner for you, my dear. If you will hurry, I'll tell Torver to serve in half an hour."

"Thank you," I said, pressing her fingers before releasing them. "It was very kind of you."

"I'll look for those boots," Freya said suddenly, coming after me.

I had expected her to take the opportunity to question me as we went up the stairs, just as she had done when she had found me hurrying in out of the gardens the day it rained. To my surprise she didn't speak of Askham at all but soon appeared at my bedchamber door with a pair of black leather half-boots.

"These ought to fit you," she said, eying my feet critically. "You may keep them while you are here. I've long since outgrown them and have no need of them."

"It's very kind of you," I replied, uncertain how to

accept her sudden generosity. "It is a pleasure to walk on the fells. But I shall be more careful in future. I'm sorry to have worried everyone and delayed dinner."

She smiled. "The fells dictate their own terms; it isn't really your fault. In time you'll come to know them better." And on that bewilderingly pleasant note she left me to finish dressing.

Dinner passed quietly enough, and I was forced to admit that Herr Raeder's care had been as wise as it was beneficial. My arm hurt far less than it had all day, and thanks to the broth I could face the meal without faintness or distress. But I did not want to be beholden to him for anything at all and was already regretting my angry denunciation just as I was leaving. It had occurred to me over dessert that it might even be true. Perhaps he resented my influence over Philip as a challenge to his own.

Martin had been staring thoughtfully at me throughout the evening, but he was unsuccessful in speaking to me alone, for I had pleaded weariness to leave the drawing room before coffee was served. He was still in the dining room with Matthew and Hal Langdale.

I slept surprisingly well that night, though I found it uncomfortable if I turned on my left arm. By morning the last remnants of fever were gone. I was still weak, however, and very stiff from my climb up Gable. Resolving to spend a quiet day reading, I chose a book from the library shelves and was on my way back to my own room when Martin pounced on me in the hall.

"I've been trying to catch you alone," he said in a low voice. "Come into the drawing room. We shouldn't be interrupted there."

"I have nothing to say to you," I replied, "that can't be said here."

"Well, I'm not about to let Hal find me talking to you here, so if you want any peace at all today, you had best agree."

With a sigh I followed him into the dimly lit room and opened the draperies myself to let in the sunshine. "What is it?"

"Where were you yesterday?"

"On Gable. Why should I lie about it?"

"Because I have reason to believe you were exploring the attics, and I'd like very much to know if you had any luck?"

I stared blankly at him. "Have you gone mad? Why on earth should I spend hours in the attics of Ravensholme? I've no business there!"

"Someone had been rooting around in a pile of old weapons. I could see the footprints and the changes in the dust patterns."

Was Martin trying to discover if I had been injured by that spear? I tried to keep my face expressionless. "There are dozens of old weapons in the library. Why should I look for more?"

"Yes, well, it didn't seem logical to me either," he answered, roaming aimlessly about the room. "But Hal goes *somewhere* at night. I thought at first it was a woman in the village, but after keeping watch on the road two nights running I'm almost certain he doesn't leave this house. I had hoped you might be onto something."

I had no intention of telling him that I had once met Hal Langdale on the stairs carrying that golden goblet. "What Mr. Langdale does in the night is none of my concern," I replied coldly.

Martin flung himself into a chair. "Listen to me," he said irritably. "I thought I had found something useful in that matter of the dead freighter. I've always believed somebody killed Carrock. God knows, he was bleeding badly when he left here, but he managed to reach the bay before one of them caught up with him and finished it. Hichen swore he saw a struggle, but he was so drunk that the constable couldn't trust his evidence. And now, after all these years, Hichen comes *back* and is murdered for his foolishness. Did you know I'd searched for him myself and never found a trace? A man doesn't disappear like that unless he's *afraid!*"

He had been—deathly afraid. But I held my tongue. "What do you mean, Carrock was bleeding? I thought he had attacked Freya."

"He nearly killed her, but she—or Matthew, or both—used that silver penknife on *him* before he got away. There was blood everywhere, and Freya just had cuts on her hands. It was a shambles. That's why I'm damned certain that it was murder. And Freya was with my dear brother when Hichen got in the way of the carriages. They knew who he was from the inquest. They both had an opportunity the night of the betrothal dinner to lure him out on the bay and kill him."

"You would believe such a thing of your own brother?" I demanded, shocked at his callous speculations.

"Why not? My brother, my very own brother, sat in this house and gambled away our money and our estates. I was a boy at the time, in his wardship, and he left me not a penny. Oh, he'll tell you he has repented, and he's lived an irreproachable life since he married Freya. But that doesn't provide me with an income from Ryland Hall or investments on the 'Change. He took care of himself, right enough, and nowadays deplores the way *I* live; but I'm expected to forgive and forget that he made me a pauper. He never felt he owed me *anything* in return!"

"No wonder you are bitter," I said slowly.

"Bitter doesn't begin to describe it! Well, I'd hoped to make something out of Hichen's death, but it hasn't quite worked that way. Little accidents—"

"Accidents?" I said before I could stop myself. "What accidents?"

He looked at me suspiciously. "For all I know, *you*

were behind them, trying to frighten me off the subject of Hichen. Be that as it may, I decided to leave well enough alone for the moment. But I'm curious about Hal, and wondering if there's some connection between his nocturnal disappearances and his refusal to play cards with me. What does he do with all his money? Is someone already blackmailing him?"

"Those are ridiculous suppositions!"

"Are they? He's strange, Hal is. In the last eight or ten years he has gotten worse. It might be lucrative to find out why." He frowned as he got to his feet. "I've searched the cellars, the empty rooms, the attics, everywhere I can think of. If we could pool our knowledge—"

I laughed. "You can't be serious! I'm not about to spy on Hal Langdale! The less I know about anyone the happier I am."

He shrugged. "Have it your way. Pretend to innocence and virtue if you like. I'm an honest scoundrel and admit it." Martin's finger traced the line of a ruby in the goblet on the mantelpiece. "This is the only thing Hal really cares about. If I had the nerve to hold it for ransom, I'd never want for anything in life again!"

Crossing to the door, I said coldly, "I want no part of your schemes. And I can assure you I have never set foot in the attics or the cellars of this house." With that I left him. In some ways Martin had a right to his bitterness, but not to his ruthless determination to be repaid for what he felt he had lost. And after his mention of accidents I had a lurking dread that his activities might somehow involve me in spite of all I could do to prevent it.

Two days later Freya announced over luncheon that she had decided to hold the ball at Abbot's Thorston as soon as possible rather than waiting until late May or early June.

"The weather is so unpredictable in April!" Aunt Charlotte protested. "The flowers won't be at their peak, the gardens will be too cold for use, there will very likely be rain—"

"Then I'll choose the first week in May," Freya replied thoughtfully. "But no later. The staff can begin to prepare, and I'll send out the invitations from here. I'm not planning to return to the house until just before the ball. And I shall expect you to attend, Miss Winton."

Surprised, I said awkwardly, "I don't know that I have a proper gown." The green silk for Parents' Day was not suitable for gala occasions.

"Charlotte will be happy to see that you have a gown," Freya said casually. "Something in blue, perhaps, to set off your fairness. I shall lend you my sapphires if you like."

Matthew toyed with his napkin ring. "Is there a particular reason for moving up the date?" he asked his wife.

"Not especially. I'd simply like to get it out of the way." But there was a gleam in her dark eyes that reminded me of her brother. She had no intention of telling anyone, not even Matthew, what was in her mind.

Hal Langdale said, "If you will have a list ready for me, I'll take it into Cartmel with me this afternoon. Wines, delicacies, ribbons. Old Birkby can attend to it for you. Beyond that, don't expect me to put myself out."

Freya agreed readily and the matter appeared to be settled. Hal left directly after luncheon, riding alone. Aunt Charlotte came with me to my bedchamber to discuss my meager wardrobe.

She was stunned at its inadequacies. "My dear child, you should have told me! I had no notion that you had come to these straits."

"I have everything I need," I replied stiffly. "It is only the ball gown that will be a problem. We did not require them at the Academy."

She smiled. "Pride, Elizabeth, is a poor substitute for good sense. It was to your mother's credit that her beauty—and her wealth until she married your father and was cut off—never went to her head."

"It isn't the same—"

"Isn't it? Pride in what one can do without is just as bad as pride in what one has. As for the gown, we shall see to it that you are as elegantly dressed as any woman there and you will enjoy the night immensely."

I had to smile, albeit ruefully. "How can I refuse without sounding ill-bred and petty?"

My godmother patted my shoulder reassuringly. I was glad she couldn't see me wince. Although the wound was healing well, it was still sensitive. "Never mind. You shall be wearing borrowed finery and I shall be blind. We can sit in a dim corner and weep into our champagne." And her high spirits made up, a little, for the difficulty of swallowing charity.

Late that night there was a frantic scratching at my door. I had begun to lock it upon retiring and hesitated even now to open it at this hour.

"Who's there?" I called, going to the door.

"Martin," came the wild whisper. "For God's sake, let me in!"

"No!"

"Elizabeth, in the name of mercy. Hurry!"

Frightened by his terror, I stood undecided for an instant longer, and then reluctantly unlocked the door.

He slipped through almost as it opened and locked it behind him. "Get into bed and pretend to be asleep! I'll climb into the wardrobe."

"You'll do nothing of the sort!" I whispered furiously.

"You are disgracefully drunk. Get out of here at once or I'll call your brother!"

His fingers, cold as ice, closed over my wrist. "Torver caught me! I don't think he actually *saw* me, but I can't take that chance. He knows someone was down there and he was coming up the stairs behind me. There wasn't time to reach my room, and I've got to hide."

Someone had quietly turned the knob on my door. Without a word I flew silently across the room and got into my bed. Martin moved with a swiftness and stealth that came from the instinct to survive. He was in the wardrobe as the key fell from my keyhole onto the carpet with a dull clink. I was feigning sleep, breathing as deeply and evenly as I could in my nervousness.

The door swung open, creaking only a little. After a moment, soft footfalls on the carpet told me that someone was approaching my bed. I clenched my fists and forced my eyelids to stay closed. Light spilled from a shielded candle and I let myself stir restlessly, as one might if one were truly asleep.

The breathing just above me told me that he was still there. Then darkness fell, the footfalls retreated, and the door closed. But I had played the same game with my students at the Academy when I took my turn as night monitor. I lay still, quietly breathing while he waited patiently.

After five minutes, which seemed like hours of unbearable tension, the door softly opened and closed. This time he had gone.

Martin had the good sense to wait another quarter of an hour before emerging from the wardrobe.

Even in the darkness I could see that he was white as a ghost. "Thank you," he said, barely above a breath. "It is safe to go now."

I caught his wrist. "But what happened? Where were you?"

"In the cellars. There's someone down there. Either a prisoner or a madman. I'm sure of it! Where he came from or where he went, I can't even guess. But he was there, and Torver was with him. And if they find out I was watching, they'll kill me!"

7

Stunned, I could only stare up at him.

Martin wrenched his arm free of my fingers and said furiously, "Don't you *believe* me?"

"I—I don't know" I replied, finding my voice at last.

"He was *there*, filthy and ragged, walking ahead of Torver one minute and gone the next. The only light came from a candle on one of the wine casks. I could barely see my own hand in the gloom. But I recognized Torver when he turned at the noise I made stumbling over those damned uneven stones. I tell you I ran for my life!"

"And led him *here*, to my bedchamber!" I exclaimed, picturing with a shudder the silent figure standing over my bed, watching me breathe. "How could you be so foolish!"

"He thought you were truly asleep, didn't he? That's all that matters." Concerned for himself, he gave no thought to the possible danger to others.

"Is it? I hope you are right. I want nothing to do with Hal Langdale or Torver or any secrets they may have!"

"It is too late," Martin said, contempt in his voice as he turned away. "You know what I know now."

With that he opened the door cautiously and slipped into the passage. I locked it carefully after him, this time leaving the key turned in the latch so that it couldn't be dislodged.

Wide awake, I lay in bed thinking over what Martin had said. A madman or a prisoner. Who could be locked in the cellars of Ravensholme?

Hal Langdale returned from Cartmel late the following evening as we were lingering over our after-dinner coffee. Martin, who had been trying desperately all day to appear normal and unconcerned, at once began to badger Langdale to play cards. I wondered sourly what he would have done if his host had agreed, for it was only pretense. Martin was terrified that Torver would betray him. And I was afraid that the servant might be led to believe that *I* had been spying on him in the cellars, not Martin.

Matthew had been sitting next to my godmother on one of the small sofas before the fire in the drawing room. He walked over to stand by my chair and inquire about my climbing.

"I haven't had the opportunity in the last day or so," I replied evasively. "Perhaps tomorrow."

"Freya gave you a compass?"

It was on the tip of my tongue to say I didn't need one. Instead I shook my head.

"I'll try to find one before you leave the house," he promised. Looking across at his wife, who was going over the list Hal had taken with him to Cartmel, he sighed. "This ball— Has Freya said anything more to you about it?"

"No. Only to ask if I had chosen my gown."

"I wish I could stop her. She is determined and the house is not mine to order as I please."

As I stared up at him, I wondered if he still loved Freya as my godmother said he once had. Did murder change such things? Had he killed Charles Carrock and Sam Hichen? Or was Charles Carrock the man in the cellars? Wasn't it Hal who had identified the battered wreck of a body that had washed ashore? The questions came unbidden, and I felt the blood drain from my face. Speaking hastily to cover my agitation, I said, "But the ball is a tradition, is it not? I understood there is one every spring."

He shrugged. "Not precisely tradition. But we can count on entertaining very infrequently in the winter because of the weather, though we ourselves often go to Kendal—even to Carlisle and Lancaster. The ball is an opportunity to return our social obligations. It is held in June, when the roses are at their best. Why she should insist on changing it like this is something of a mystery."

Something of a mystery, perhaps, but connected with Askham in a way only Freya understood. I dared not answer him.

The coffee tray was removed and Aunt Charlotte rose to leave. She rarely remained any longer than necessary in a room her husband entered. Glad of the excuse, I also said good night to Matthew and walked with her up the shadowed stairs. My godmother never carried a candle, and my own seemed to be no more than a pinprick of brightness as we turned down the dark passage.

"Come in, Elizabeth. I want to show you what I have found," she said as I paused before her door.

I followed her inside and waited while she fumbled in a chest for a bundle wrapped in tissue. "You must light the candles," she went on, holding the package until I had complied. And then she opened it, spilling shimmering blue silk across the bed. I stood there in speechless wonder watching the waterfall of color the same shade as my eyes.

"It is lovely, isn't it? You are pleased?" she asked anxiously.

"I— This is for *me?*"

She nodded. "It has been kept in camphor these

many years. I bought it in London and never had it made up. Dark blue does nothing for me, but I couldn't resist the marvelous color. It is all the way from China, you know."

"I couldn't possibly—"

"—let it rot, unused, in the chest? How considerate of you, my dear! If you will give me your best gown for size, I shall see that this is made up when the sempstress comes to sew for Freya." Aunt Charlotte was smiling.

My fingers lightly brushed the petal-soft silk. Pride warred with the very human desire to be beautiful once in my life, and then lost the battle. "Thank you!" I said fervently and began to gather up the lengths of blue for her.

"Elizabeth. If George Askham comes to this ball, you won't have anything to do with him, will you?" she asked tentatively.

My delight in the silk vanished before the suggestion of distrust in her question. Had the promise of a gown been no more than a bribe or even a form of reparation for her doubts of me? "No, why should I? I've never met the man. Is Mrs. Ryland inviting him?" My voice was colder than I had meant it to be.

She bit her lip. "I fear that she is, somehow. And I worry about why she is doing it. Matthew won't like it. He always hated Askham; he was jealous of anyone Freya cared for. You haven't told him about the man on the strand, have you?"

"I mentioned him in the course of my arrival, but it might have been anyone at all crossing the bay that night. I never told him more, and he never asked. Not even for a description of the intruder at Abbot's Thorston. For all I know, he still believes that it was Martin."

Aunt Charlotte took the silk from me and laid it carefully away in the chest. "If only something could prevent the ball!" she said in unconscious echo of Matthew's words. "Freya is so headstrong, impetuous. She will cause more trouble than she cures, mark my words!"

In my own room, I thought about my godmother's warning and wondered if she was right. But the main problem before me was Martin's revelation and my suspicions. On reflection, I couldn't believe that Philip's father was alive and in Hal's hands. Surely even Hal Langdale would never allow his sister to remarry and bear children if her first husband were *not* dead! He would have found ways to stop Matthew if not her. And there was no reason I could think of for secretly holding anyone captive for six years. While I wouldn't put anything past Martin, including making up such a tale, his terror at least had been very real. So was the person who entered my bedchamber and stood looking down at me to make certain I slept.

I checked again to see that my door was locked, the key sideways, then blew out my candle and slipped into bed. In my dreams I danced with the man from the East at Freya's ball, my lovely gown of cornflower blue silk sweeping the floor with a soft whisper as we whirled to the music.

Philip had been avoiding me since my injury from the spear. I suspected he felt guilty for having spoken of the incident to Herr Raeder, and I proved right. One morning as we walked through the village toward Wastwater, he asked anxiously, "Are you very angry with me?"

"No," I said truthfully. "I'm not. You shouldn't have talked about my affairs to the schoolmaster. But I understand. You trust him as a friend and turned to him because you were afraid. It was a natural thing to do."

Relieved, he skipped for a step or two. "I'm afraid something might happen to you," he said after a moment. "He said he would help protect you."

Touched by the child's concern as much as I was irritated by the schoolmaster's interference, I kept my eyes on the mere ahead. It was pale blue, reflecting the spring sky, and around it the fells had become pewter and red, plum and deep blue, as shadow filled the dips and sunlight explored the high places. "I don't know why these accidents happened, Philip," I said at last, measuring my words. "Perhaps I never shall. To be honest, I don't want to know."

He took my hand as we left the village behind and faced the length of narrow water. "If my father were alive, we'd be safe."

"Yes," I said gently, the thought of the man in the cellars rising unbidden. "We would all be safe."

We found the Ravensholme rowboat pulled up on the rocky strand near the head of the mere. Beside it lay a small battered canoe. Philip was all for taking the rowboat out into the still blue waters. I refused. I could handle oars well enough, but the presence of a volatile child in the boat was another matter. He could fall out all too easily, or tip us over. We were completely alone here; there was no one to see or hear if we ran into difficulty.

Disappointed, he clambered into the boat, fitted the oars in the well-oiled locks, and tired himself out rowing in the air. I sat on the overturned canoe, my face to the sun's warmth, and let him fight mock battles with Viking ships.

"They were fast, did you know that?" he demanded breathlessly. "Herr Raeder said they had sails and oars and could make fourteen knots when the wind was right. And the high prows with the dragons' heads not only frightened the enemy but also breasted the seas better than most ships. And they all had names."

All at once I felt as if I were being watched, and I looked uneasily around. The fells were empty except for the omnipresent sheep. Yet I had the distinct impression that somewhere someone could see us quite clearly.

Bored with his game at last, Philip replaced the oars in the bottom and swung himself out over the side. "Did you know I once owned a Viking burial mound? It's true, it was on part of my land. But it has been empty for hundreds of years." There was disappointment in his voice. No long ship, no treasure trove, no exciting glimpse of the past for him to discover. I smiled. "Uncle Harald bought the field from me to run *sheep* on. Mama said it was probably the tomb of an ancestor. *I* wouldn't run sheep there, no matter how much I could make from them!"

But Hal Langdale didn't have a boy's imagination. To him a field was an extra crop or a half-dozen more sheep, not a romantic site. Gold was his great passion, according to Martin, and he could never have enough.

The feeling of being watched was still there, and I shifted uncomfortably. Ravensholme stood out on its low shoulder, its windows blank and shining in the sun. The village sprawled between the mere and the house. Dozens of people might look our way and wonder what we were doing. There was no reason for the back of my neck to prickle so or the palms of my hands suddenly to become damp.

I stood up. "Shall we start back now?" I asked casually and he followed me without demur. By the time we reached the village he was skipping to keep pace with me and I forced myself to slow down to a more sedate walk. Feeling a little foolish at my inexplicable panic, I agreed readily enough when Philip asked if we might go back to Wastwater another day.

The schoolmaster was standing in the doorway of the square stone schoolhouse as we passed. Philip greeted him joyously, but I merely inclined my head silently in reply to his slight bow.

"I am glad to see you in good health, Fräulein," he said quietly.

"Indeed. Thank you," I said and called to Philip to come along. The child obeyed reluctantly and glanced once or twice over his shoulder as we went on up the narrow street.

The sunlight was short-lived. Rain fell steadily for several days, turning the dale slate gray and burnt umber. Philip begged to visit Herr Raeder, but I refused. My dislike of the schoolmaster had become, in a way, distrust. No, distrust was perhaps too strong a word. My feelings were more a wariness, an unwillingness to accept his interference and his presumption, a resistance to the forcefulness of his character. Scholarship might have ruined his eyesight, but it had not taught him such arrogance. Perhaps that was a legacy of his years at sea or his upbringing. Younger sons of aristocratic families were often as proud as they were penniless. I could explain none of this to Philip, however. Playing with his sisters in the nursery or listening to me read his favorite books soon palled, and he drifted about the house like a small ghost. My heart ached for him and I resolved to plan a picnic or a long walk as soon as the weather improved.

But when the skies cleared, the sempstress arrived from Cartmel and I was caught up in several days of consultations and fittings for my gown. My godmother sat quietly in the small drab sewing room as the plump little Miss Farrow measured and draped and murmured about me. Aunt Charlotte had a particular design in mind for the blue silk and this required a pattern to be made for the bodice before scissors touched the exquisite lengths. A reluctant excitement rose in me as the two women discussed in minute detail every step of the work. For Aunt Charlotte could not see what was being done except in her mind's eye. Bribe the gown might be, or a sop to a guilty conscience, but it would be mine for one night. At last Miss Farrow nodded her head and said she was satisfied with the results. I was dismissed until the gown was cut and basted.

Searching for Philip, I found Freya instead and was quickly set to work addressing the invitations. In my best copperplate I wrote out a hundred and twenty cards and their envelopes, then over the next few days I was given detailed lists to be copied and sent to Kendal and Lancaster for food and wines, instructions to be carried to Lithwaite and the staff at Abbot's Thorston, and finally a schedule to be kept by Freya herself.

Released at last from these duties, I asked Aunt Charlotte to order a small luncheon to be packed for two and—a week later than I had planned and full of apologies—hurried to the nursery to collect Philip.

Maggie was surprised to see me. "He left not half an hour ago, miss, wearing his cap and his coat. He's been waiting ever so patiently for you to be free and I thought you had spoken to him."

"No, I haven't seen him all morning. Perhaps he has gone to the gardens," I said and added to myself, Or to the schoolmaster's!

But Philip was not in the gardens and Herr Raeder's cottage was silent and empty. Freya, I knew, was taking her turn with the sempstress, Matthew and Hal had gone out soon after breakfast on their own errands, and Martin was nursing a chill in his bedchamber.

There was no need for alarm, I told myself firmly as I returned to the house. Three days with Miss Farrow, two in the library assisting Freya, following on the heels of the rainy weekend, all wore at a small boy's patience and he had gone out to play by himself. But where, asked an uneasy voice, where had he gone?

Torver was in the hall as I came in and I asked him if he had seen Philip.

"Indeed, miss, he said something about the mere just after you had bespoken the luncheon. I thought perhaps you were picnicking there. Has he gone ahead?"

I took the lunch basket he held out and went flying out the door. If Philip had indeed gone to Wastwater, surely he would have the good sense to wait for me, I thought anxiously, wasting no time in my haste. I was all but running as I left the village behind and searched the mereside for a small boy. There was no sign of him, but the rowboat rested on the strand, and I drew a sigh of relief. He hadn't tried to take it out alone. Thank God!

But my relief was short-lived. As I neared the boat, I noticed that the battered canoe was missing. Shading my eyes, I scanned the length of the mere but could see nothing on the cloud-dappled length. Except—

Running along the water's edge for ten yards or so, I stared at the object floating soggily some distance out. It looked like—it was—Philip's cap. I'd seen it numbers of times! And just beyond it, describing slow circles, was the broken paddle of the canoe.

As my breath caught in my throat, Freya's voice came back to me: "Wastwater must be the deepest lake in England. I find it cold even in summer." And Philip was such a small child . . .

There was no time to run all the way back to the village for help. It might be too late already. Without hesitating, I climbed into the rowboat, fitted the oars into the locks, and shoved it into the rippling water. While my mind concentrated on rowing out to the cap, I let my panic release itself in frantic cries for help in the desperate hope that someone, even a shepherd on the hillside, might hear and come.

There was no sign of Philip, no body floating near the surface, no bubbles floating up through the dark water. The oars were heavy and my arms ached with the effort as I guided the boat, moving in circles as I stared down into the empty depths. At last I thought I saw the canoe and hovered above it as the sun slipped out from behind the light puffy clouds to lance down through the currents I had created and touch the overturned side.

I don't know what I would have done if he had been submerged there, trapped and helpless. Alone and dressed in heavy skirts, petticoats, and walking boots, I was unable to swim very well, but I'd have tried. It would be partly my fault if Philip drowned and I couldn't have lived with myself if I hadn't tried. But there was no sign of him. Had he struggled and drifted out farther, where the bottom was invisible?

Rowing desperately, I moved on toward the floating paddle, hoping its direction would also mark Philip's. I had forgotten to shout, and tears were coursing down my cheeks. My eyes saw nothing but the mere. And so the bottom of the rowboat was well awash before I noticed that something was wrong.

Coming slowly at first and then with greater speed, water was gushing through a split seam between my feet. My skirts were already wet several inches up the hem, the soles of my shoes cold and damp. It seemed too much to bear that the winter-rotted caulking had separated just when I needed the boat so desperately. I stared at the planking in disbelief and frustration, knowing I must turn back or drown, myself, unwilling to make that impossible, heartbreaking choice. And then I saw the splinters along the seam and slowly, terrifyingly realized what had happened.

The canoe was gone, the broken paddle was drifting down the mere beside Philip's cap. But the boy was not lying in the black depths, drowned and accusing. Someone had led me out onto the water with carefully staged props after taking an axe to the bottom of the only boat I could have used. Knowing me, knowing my feelings for the child, they had cold-bloodedly calculated my reaction to the ghastly scene. I wouldn't have wasted precious minutes returning to the distant village, but instead have acted in the only way possible. And so I had.

Water weighted the boat now, making it respond clumsily to the oars. My arms, unaccustomed to such prolonged exercise, shoved the handles forward, dipped them, and brought them back with an effort that increased with every stroke. I hadn't thought of anything but reaching Philip and saving him if I could and I had come too far out to win the race with the rapidly swirling water. I knew it now but fought on in hopeless determination as cold trickles spilled down the tops of my shoes. My skirts felt heavy, pulling at me as I struggled with the oars.

So suddenly that I was caught unprepared, the boat sank beneath me, and I screamed as the water rushed up to meet me. Instead of paddling, I should have been tearing off my shoes, those useless petticoats that would now be my death.

The air in my skirts kept me afloat as I turned toward the shore and began to swim. For a moment or two I thought I might make it after all, and I blessed the terror that drove my weary arms to function almost of their own accord. But now my skirts acted as an anchor, sucking me back and down. I screamed again and this time someone answered.

"Don't struggle, Fräulein."

There was a splash and I saw over my shoulder that the schoolmaster had leapt into the mere and was even now swimming powerfully toward me. Water closed over my head, and I thrust with my feet to bring me up again. There was no time to take more than a gulp of precious air before the mere seemed to fill my throat. Hands grasped me as I choked and fought, my face rose above the surface, and something struck my chin with a sharp and painful blow. I thought I had somehow collided with the rowboat, and then I felt myself collapse helplessly into the water.

When I opened my eyes again, eager hands were lifting me from the schoolmaster's arms, and we were led out of the water to the rocky shore.

Dazed and shaking, I let them lay me on the ground and smooth the wet hair out of my face. My limbs seemed to have no will of their own. A woman clucked in concern above me and a man's voice asked, "Did she swallow much water?" He sounded like a villager.

"No," the schoolmaster replied breathlessly. "I think not." He was kneeling above me, dripping water over me and swearing savagely in German as he ran a finger across my chin.

I started to speak, choked, and then said for no reason I could think of, "Dora's boat—her beloved boat is gone." I felt like crying.

"Whatever possessed you to go out on the mere alone?" the schoolmaster demanded. "And where did this come from?" He held the waterlogged cap up so that I could see it.

"Someone left it there, in the mere, so that I would believe Philip—"

His hand closed over mine in a warning. "Don't talk. Your senses are wandering still."

I gingerly touched my throbbing chin. "I must have struck something, part of the boat . . ."

His glasses were back in place but a brief smile pulled at the corner of his mouth beneath the beard. "I hit you. You were fighting me. And . . . I saw the cap."

Sitting up, I glared at him but said nothing as the villagers expressed their concern and relief at my near drowning and rescue. Someone draped my cloak, which I'd left on the bank, about my shoulders, and I drew it gratefully around my shivering body. There was the sound of hoofbeats, and the villagers drew back to let Matthew, mounted on a nervous bay, into the circle. Scrambling to my feet in panic, I backed away.

The schoolmaster, after one puzzled glance in my

149

direction, stepped forward to greet Matthew. "There was a boating accident," he said. "Fräulein Winton is safe, but the rowboat has gone down in some ten feet of water."

Matthew's eyes went to the cap still in the schoolmaster's hand. "Philip?" he demanded sharply, turning to me.

"He isn't here," I began and wondered if I was telling the truth. Had I been right or wrong about someone trying to kill me?

Relieved, Matthew was already swinging out of the saddle and coming forward. "Thank God for that! I'll give you a hand up. The sooner you are out of those wet clothes the better."

"Ride your horse?" I asked hoarsely. "No, no! Please—"

He stopped short. "What is the matter?"

I swallowed against the dizziness that threatened to overwhelm me. "If you don't mind, I'll walk. If you would ask someone to draw a bath . . ."

Matthew frowned, ready to argue, but Herr Raeder said equably, "She is still dazed from striking her head. Walking may help."

For a moment I expected Matthew to insist, for he stared haughtily at the schoolmaster before turning back to me. Something in my face must have decided him, for he reached out to touch my hand before mounting and riding away.

Herr Raeder took my arm and we started briskly toward the village. He sent the chattering villagers ahead and when they were out of earshot he asked, "Why are you afraid of Herr Ryland?"

"I'm not," I said quickly. "It was the horse. I can't bear to be near horses." The wind was cold in my wet hair, but another sort of cold swept through me at the memory.

"What were you saying about Philip?" When I made

no reply, he said irritably, "This is no time for ridiculous stubbornness, Fräulein."

"The cap and the broken paddle made me think he was somewhere in the lake. When I took the rowboat out to look for him, I never noticed that the planks had been split. Someone knew I might drown."

His hand tightened on my arm. "So. One of the children heard you cry for help. He was playing truant, but this time I shall not punish him. Perhaps he can also tell me if someone else visited the mere this morning. The question remains. Who wishes to see you dead?"

We were coming through the village now, and there were people at the windows and doors, standing at their gates to watch us pass. "Dead? Or badly frightened? I wish I knew which."

"It makes no difference. Shall I take you to the cottage or to Ravensholme?"

"They will be waiting for me."

"If you are not ready to face them it does not matter."

In spite of myself I thought of the whitewashed walls of the cottage, the cheerful fire on the hearth, and the silence; and I knew I dreaded to enter the gloomy, watchful house and answer the questions of the people waiting for me there. One of them might have set that trap. Would he or she be glad or sorry to see me alive? But I had to discover if Philip was indeed safe, to put my mind at ease. I shook my head. "I must return to Ravensholme."

He said no more but accompanied me to the door of the house and saw me enveloped in Aunt Charlotte's tearful embrace before turning away. Only then did I remember that I had never thanked him for saving my life.

Because I had said nothing about the circumstances that led to my being out on the water alone, I was surprised to find that Matthew had already asked Freya about Philip's cap.

As I stepped into the dimly lit hall, she caught my shoulders and stared searchingly into my face. "Why was Philip's cap by the mere? Where is he?"

For an instant I wavered, still torn between my lingering fear for the boy and the growing certainty that the cap represented a cold-blooded trap. But Maggie, coming down the stairs at that moment, gave us both the answer to Freya's question.

"Master Philip? He was playing with those smelly sheep again, Mrs. Ryland! I was just going to the kitchen for the strong soap."

Freya wheeled, her copper skirts swinging about her. "He was on the fells? With one of *our* shepherds?"

"Oh, aye, with Dan Satterthwaite, who ought to know better than let Master Philip get himself into such a state," Maggie replied, her cheeks pink with indignation. "His clothes aren't fit to wash."

Philip's mother ignored her and turned back to me. "Then why did you have the child's cap at the mere?"

"I found it there," I replied defensively, my teeth chattering from my clammy gown and wet shoes. "I thought he might have lost it." There was no point in telling her more of the truth than that. Not in her present state. And I was strangely reluctant to admit to my danger in front of them all.

"You'll not take him near Wastwater again! Do you understand?" Freya demanded sharply.

"Freya, let her go upstairs! I told you Philip was safe," Aunt Charlotte said, taking my hand and leading me away from the open door so that Torver could close it.

Matthew, rather noticeably silent, stood watching my return. I wondered if he still felt irritated by my refusal to ride his horse or if he was weighing the outcome of a scheme to drown me. Freya seemed so genuinely concerned for her son, it was hard to imagine that she actually knew that I had been tricked into thinking him drowned. Or was it all a well-acted little scene to lull my suspicions? As I passed him I saw Matthew glance thoughtfully at his wife. Suspicion was an insidious thing—once implanted it grew by itself. The tension in the hall was almost visible, and not all of it was mine.

What if I had made too much of these accidents, and they were no more than that? I asked myself as we climbed the stairs.

Impossible, I answered almost at once. The slate may have fallen of its own accord, but the spear had been thrown. And someone had deliberately sunk the canoe, leaving the hat and paddle to float until I came. There was no other explanation.

Philip, his hair still damp from his bath, crept into my bedchamber an hour later to ask if someone had now tried to drown me.

"No," I said wryly. "There was no one at Wastwater except myself."

"But you even told *me* not to take the boat out alone," Philip pointed out reasonably. I had been ordered to bed for the remainder of the day with hot bricks and hotter tea to prevent an inflammation of the lungs.

"Even adults are sometimes foolish," I countered, and saw the fear deepen in his eyes rather than vanish.

"I can't protect you if you won't let me," he replied in a voice so low I could barely make out the words.

Impulsively I leaned forward and clasped him close for a moment, moved beyond speech by his concern. "Oh, Philip," I sniffed, at last sitting back and trying to stop my tears, "if love were armor, I'd be invulnerable!"

He blushed but seemed to be rather pleased in spite of his embarrassment.

"Tell me, what possessed you to go off with the shepherd?" I asked to change the subject.

"I was tired of playing in the gardens and you had promised for *days* to take me back to Wastwater. So when I saw Dan I thought it would be all right to accompany him. It wasn't as if I had wandered off alone or anything."

"But you should have let someone know. Your mother and I worried about you."

"I didn't think I'd be away quite so long," he said. "Next time I'll remember."

After he had gone I lay there thinking. No one had sent Philip off on a wild-goose chase. But someone had taken advantage of his absence to kill—or badly frighten—me. Perhaps he had been seen climbing the track at the shepherd's side or playing with the long-legged lambs. It was Torver who had mentioned the mere to me, but my *own* fears that had sent me flying after—so I thought—the child. I had walked willingly into that trap, and there was no way at all to determine who had set it so well.

Someone at Ravensholme was my enemy. Matthew? Had he come riding back in the expectation of finding me drowned? Or had Freya used my affection for her son to trick me? There was Hal, or even Torver, who might still suspect *me* of exploring the cellars that night when Martin had taken refuge in my room. It was difficult to believe that Herr Raeder had been involved, for he had pulled me out. But not until a village boy had spotted me in the water, I remembered suddenly. Even if he had intended only to frighten me away from Wasdale, the attempt had very nearly cost my life. And there was Martin, who saw in me a reflection of his own greed.

Someone at Ravensholme—but who was it? Only my godmother could have no earthly reason to threaten or harm me. And she was blind. Aunt Charlotte was the only person in this house besides Philip whom I dared to trust.

I contrived to talk to her that very afternoon, resolved to face my danger and go away before it was too late.

The next accident might actually succeed in killing me, whether that was its goal or not. Though I hated to leave, despising myself for being a coward and accusing myself of abandoning Philip, I knew I could do nothing for him dead.

Without preamble I said to my godmother as soon as she had laid her cool hand on my brow, "I must return to London. I've thought about it and this is the only sensible answer. Could you possibly lend me enough money to carry me through the summer? I promise you I shall repay it all, and with interest too." Unable to lie still, I sat up against my pillows.

She frowned and shook her head. "My dear, you can't leave. Not before the ball!"

"The ball!" I repeated in dismay. "I *can't* stay! Aunt Charlotte, I don't want to frighten you, but someone in this house— I have seen a number of indications that I am unwanted here. Did you know I found Philip's cap floating in Wastwater with the broken paddle from a canoe that had lain there on the strand only last week? Someone had sent it to the bottom and made me think Philip had taken it out alone and overturned. That is why I was in that rowboat—there was no time to find help. Only, the boards had been axed and it sank before I could reach the shore!"

Her face had turned very pale during my disjointed narrative. "Surely you must be mistaken!"

"It is the third accident that has happened to me, not the first. The next may be the last. Please, if you love me, help me to leave!" I pleaded desperately.

Biting her lip to hold back her tears, she shook her head. "I have told you, Elizabeth, I haven't a penny. Not even jewelry I could let you have to sell. Hal took everything, everything that wasn't entailed. Even his own mother's collection. And the heirlooms in the house are his. I dare not offer you any of them."

I reached out and touched her hand. "Could you ask

Freya or Matthew for money without telling them why you needed it?"

"No. They would wonder at it and demand an explanation. They might even speak to Hal. I have never borrowed from anyone. It would seem quite strange." She took a deep breath. "There *is* someone. He was a friend of my father's and is living now with his son-in-law in Carlisle. Old and rather irascible, but . . . but for your sake I could speak to him at the ball. We could think of a logical reason by that time. Surely you could wait that long?" she asked anxiously.

"Will my persecutors wait?" I asked, trying to keep the bitterness from my voice. "I don't know." My spirits wilted and I felt very tired. Much of it was undoubtedly from my exertion earlier, but depression can be exhausting too.

Aunt Charlotte's fingers tightened on mine. "Shall I speak to Matthew? In confidence? Tell him what is happening?"

"No!" I cried. "No, please. I . . . I prefer to tell no one. I— It may be only my imagination after all," I added quickly at the change in her expression. How could I make her understand that Matthew, for all his gentleness with her, might be driven to murder by greed or circumstances or even his own weakness? She would only be upset and even more reluctant to help me if I tried to explain.

"You are overtaxing yourself, my dear! It isn't wise after all you have been through today. Rest and try not to worry over what happened. And I promise I shall speak to Sir Edmund at the ball."

Like a good child scolded by its overwrought mother, I sighed and said meekly, "Yes, I'll rest."

She groped for the coverlet and drew it up to my chin. "Are the draperies closed? Good! And you shall have your dinner on a tray tonight. Tomorrow you will feel more yourself again."

"Thank you," I said, and watched her find her way out of the room, my last hope of escape going with her.

Whether I liked it or not, I would be at Freya Ryland's ball. If I lived long enough.

8

I insisted on dressing the next morning and taking my breakfast downstairs as usual. Aunt Charlotte, who had arrived in my room quite early to see if I had become feverish in the night, protested at first and then let me have my way when it was obvious that I had suffered nothing more than a few aching muscles as a result of my ordeal in the mere.

We met Hal Langdale in the doorway as we entered the breakfast room. I could sense the withdrawal on my godmother's part as he bade her a good morning, a touch of sarcasm in his voice. She relaxed almost at once as he went on to say that he intended to walk over to Borrowdale to speak to another landowner about a ram that was for sale.

"You will return in time for dinner?" she asked.

"I imagine I shall," he replied carelessly. His light eyes turned to me. "You appear to have recovered after yesterday's accident, Miss Winton. You must have pleased the gods of Wasdale. The mere is very deep and usually quite jealous of its victims."

"It was fortunate that help arrived in time," I said, suppressing the memory of that dark water enveloping me. "I am very sorry about the rowboat, however. Can it be salvaged?"

"Torver is sending several men down there to take a look today. The fault is mine for leaving the boat to the mercy of the weather. It should have been up on blocks over the winter." His glance flickered over me. "You are not as fragile as you seem. Matthew told me you tried to swim, although hampered by your skirts."

"Yes," I replied, wondering how Matthew knew. I couldn't recall mentioning it, and Herr Raeder had brought me ashore before Matthew arrived on the scene. Had he indeed watched me from afar, taking note of my struggles but doing nothing to save me? "I learned to swim as a child."

"What matters most is that you kept your head. Few women do in emergencies. I admire courage in anyone but see it rarely in females. I am very glad you came to Ravensholme."

With that he was gone, leaving us in shocked silence.

"I didn't know that he gave two pins for your visit," Aunt Charlotte said slowly, listening to his receding footsteps. "In fact, I had hoped that he hadn't."

Leading the way into the breakfast room, I said, "Does it matter?"

"Not in the way you think. My husband is strange, he isn't bound by the conventions you and I know. Your safety and mine lie in his indifference." She could say no more, for Torver entered through the servants' door with a plate of fresh eggs.

I helped myself to a bowl of porridge and cream, forcing myself to eat. My appetite had disappeared since my godmother's refusal to aid me. Fear had stalked the night and followed me today down the dim, drafty passages. My nerves felt tied in knots, so that every mouthful I swallowed seemed to struggle past the lump in my throat. But I could scarcely fast, and so after the porridge I spread a triangle of toast with strawberry preserves.

Aunt Charlotte, talking about her plans to add

pansies to the borders along the drive, paused to ask, "Have you the quince jam, my dear?"

It was one of my favorites and usually on the table. I looked across to the sideboard and answered, "No, it isn't out today. I have strawberry here— Oh, wait, I think I see the dish after all." Rising quickly, I went over to the cupboard where the extra cups and saucers were kept. As I passed the service door, I thought I heard a small muffled sound, as if someone had stepped hurriedly away from the entrance. Had Torver been listening? Did he usually eavesdrop on the family—or only on certain members of it? I could think of no excuse to fling open the door and verify my suspicion. Torver rather intimidated me at the best of times. The quince jam was indeed in the cupboard and I set it before my godmother, but my ears were still attuned to any movement from the service door.

"Thank you, my dear. The primroses seem to be doing very well this spring too. I can feel them poking up through the soil, and the first of the columbines are showing. This jam is rather bitter, have you noticed? I believe it was pressed through the sieve too long. I must speak to the cook." She made a face as she finished her toast.

"No," I replied absently, watching the door still. Had it moved a little, as if someone had laid his ear against the crack? "I hadn't noticed." Servants knew everything that happened in a household, probably from overhearing or listening to conversations that one supposed to be private. But why should Torver care what I said to my godmother over breakfast? Or she to me?

"The sempstress may have your gown basted for a last fitting this afternoon. Don't wander far if you go out. I do wish you would consider remaining in bed another day, but I shan't insist."

It was on the tip of my tongue to say that I felt very

well and intended to enjoy the pleasant weather while it lasted. In time I remembered the listener and replied instead, "I may indeed lie down again this morning." Aunt Charlotte smiled warmly and I felt a qualm of conscience for lying to her.

For her sake I did rest for an hour after breakfast, but Philip had other notions about what was best for me. "You must walk with me, please. Only a little way, and the air is very warm. You won't take a chill, I promise. Besides," he added confidingly, "Maggie is very angry with me for spoiling my clothes yesterday and says I may not go outside alone for the remainder of the week."

I laughed. "Very well, then, we shall take a turn in the gardens."

He glanced at me from beneath his lashes but said nothing more until I had fetched my cloak and followed him outside. Almost at once he begged to walk along the path toward the hyacinth beds, now wilted and no longer sweet. I knew it was only a matter of time before he tried to persuade me to visit the schoolmaster.

"Herr Raeder isn't at home this morning, Philip," I said. "Save your wiles for another day!"

"Oh, but he is," he said quickly, then blushed to the roots of his fair hair, his gray eyes staring up at me in anguish.

"You have already seen him this morning?" I asked sharply.

He nodded, then swallowed hard. "I saw him walking on the fells before breakfast. I only wanted to tell him you were all right. But Maggie caught me first, and then I overheard one of the parlor maids saying there was no school today because the villagers are decorating the schoolhouse for a celebration tonight. Long Tom, the Wasdale champion, just defeated the wrestler in Borrowdale and will be going to Keswick now."

Suddenly cross with the boy, though I had already guessed what was in his mind, I turned back toward the house. "I have no desire to visit Herr Raeder, Philip."

He trotted along beside me, protesting. "But he saved your life. My stepfather said so! You ought to thank him and let him see you haven't got lung inflammation, only the bruise there on your chin."

Remembering the cause of that bruise, I whirled on Philip and said furiously, "Perhaps I ought to thank him for *that*. It was his fault, after all!" As the wide gray eyes filled with shocked tears, I was overwhelmed with shame for lashing out at a defenseless child who truly believed that his friend had performed an act of heroism. In my fear and confusion I had been unjust, and I couldn't begin to explain the reasons why. Kneeling before Philip, I put my hands on his shoulders and said contritely, "I ask your forgiveness for behaving so badly. Yes, I ought to thank the schoolmaster. I was in no condition to do so yesterday."

He smiled through his tears, his hand reaching up awkwardly to pat mine. "I don't mind," he said generously, "if you feel cross. Very likely it is only your nerves. Ladies often suffer from them."

I laughed and got to my feet. "I dare say we do. All right, then, we shall discover if Herr Raeder is indeed at home this morning."

He was, and from the lack of surprise in his manner as he opened the door I could almost believe he had been expecting us.

"Good morning, Philip. I am glad to see you are none the worse for your ordeal, Fräulein. Please come inside."

We entered the cottage to be greeted by Bismarck, who entwined himself about our feet as if we were favored guests. Philip was allowed to offer the cat a dish of fresh cream, and the two soon had their heads together over the saucer.

162

"I have not thanked you properly," I began, but Herr Raeder cut me short.

"There is no need, Fräulein. One of the villagers would have helped you if I had not." All at once I was certain that there was a twinkle in the eyes hidden by the dark glasses. "Although there have been moments when I might have cheerfully advocated drowning you, when it came to the point, I discovered my conscience was unaccountably reluctant to take advantage of the circumstances."

I felt myself stiffen with hot anger over his amusement at my expense. But before I could form a suitable reply he went on in a more sober vein. "Please explain to me how the child's cap came to be in the mere."

"I don't know. Maggie said he was wearing his coat and hat when he left the nursery, ostensibly to join me for our long-postponed picnic. Torver thought he had seen Philip on his way to Wastwater. When I recognized the cap, I believed—" I broke off at the memory of that terrible moment when I realized the boy might be in the water.

He nodded. "So. It was indeed planned for you to drown. Philip."

The child looked up from the cat contentedly curled in his lap. "Yes, sir?"

"Your cap. Where did you lose it yesterday?"

"But I didn't lose it! When I saw the shepherd and asked permission to walk along with him, Dan said it would be very warm work keeping up with the flock. So I tossed my cap on the bayberry bushes by the garden wall. When I came home, Maggie had it and said I'd lost it in the *mere*, but truly I hadn't! I'm not allowed to go to Wastwater alone!"

"Never mind, then. Maggie was no doubt upset." He waited until Philip was once again absorbed in playing with Bismarck and said quietly, "You see. Anyone might have found the cap on the bushes. Why do you have an enemy in Ravensholme, Fräulein Winton?"

"I don't know. At least I'm not sure," I replied wretchedly.

"You must leave here, then. It is the only answer."

"But I can't!" I exclaimed, the warm blood rising infuriatingly up my face as he raised a skeptical eyebrow. "At least not until Mrs. Ryland's ball—on the seventh. I—I cannot possibly go before the ball."

"An evening's gaiety is worth the risk to your life?" he asked.

"No, no. Of course not!" There was no way to explain without admitting that I was nearly destitute, and my pride stubbornly refused to let me parade my personal affairs before a stranger. It had been difficult enough pleading with my godmother to lend me money.

His lips set in a grim line. "You are a fool, Fräulein. What must I do to make you see that you are in the gravest danger? And that you are a possible threat to Philip's safety as well? Surely his welfare comes before the pleasures of Frau Ryland's ball!"

I got to my feet, nearly overturning my chair in my haste. "You are impossible! I won't be tormented like this!"

He was standing now, facing me. "You don't like to be told you are selfish and stupid!" he said furiously. "Gott in Himmel, I thought you *cared* for the boy! But you are like all the others, using him as a pawn, paying no heed to what will happen to him in your blind concern for yourself."

It was unjust, every word of what he said, and I had never been so angry. Tears filled my eyes, but from wrath, not weakness. "And you? Playing at God, making your own use of his loneliness, sitting in judgment of those about him—" Words failed me and I caught up my cloak, completely forgetting Philip in my need to escape the cottage, to shut out the sight of the dark bitter face that looked at me with contempt and condemnation. I wanted to breathe the sharp air outside and stop the blood from pounding through my head like a red cloud.

He was at the door before me, his arm barring my way. "No, you shall not run from the truth this time! You shall listen to me, Elizabeth Winton, if I must hold you here by force!"

"Get out of my way!" I cried, beside myself now. "You are impertinent, arrogant, and opinionated. I won't stand for such rudeness."

"You *shall* hear me." He loomed above me, tall and menacing.

With all the force of my arm I slapped him, hard, across the face and then drew back in horror at what I had done. He was not a man to cross lightly, and yet fury had taken possession of both of us. Immediately his hands closed on my shoulders in a grip that nearly made me cry out. I was thrust against the whitewashed wall with a force that left me breathless. In a voice made even harsher by the clipped German consonants, Herr Raeder said through clenched teeth, "I have never known a woman as maddening as you. You would torment the devil and provoke a saint. I am neither of these, but I shall tame you to my hand—"

With a suddenness that caught me unawares he released me. It was all I could do to prevent myself from falling. Stepping back, his face as pale as it had been flushed before, he stared at me as if seeing me for the first time.

"Herr Gott, what have I done?" He drew a trembling hand over his eyes and then said with difficulty, "Sometimes I forget . . ."

The change in him was more frightening than his rage. He turned away and I let myself breathe again. Only then did I become aware of Philip, white and bewildered, clinging to my skirts. His eyes were great gray pools of pain and I touched his head lightly with my fingers.

"It— It's all right, Philip," I said shakily. "We were very angry."

"My mother and my father quarreled and then he went away," he said scarcely above a whisper. "Will Herr Raeder go away now?"

The schoolmaster's eyes met mine for an instant. "No," I said quickly. "He won't leave you. It is I who must go."

The child burst into tears, his shoulders shaking convulsively. I gestured helplessly, too drained by my own emotion to find the strength he so desperately needed. But Herr Raeder, his face set once more in the calm mask of the schoolmaster, knelt swiftly and drew the unresisting boy into his arms. He spoke softly, comforting and reassuring.

"You must understand, Fräulein Winton is not leaving because we have quarreled. She is a teacher and must return to her duties. You knew this when she came, did you not? As for the words we spoke to each other in anger, there is nothing in them to drive her from Ravensholme. Adults are not above squabbling as recklessly as your sisters in the nursery. It is difficult to be strong and wise and in the right all the time. There is sometimes great relief in behaving quite childishly."

Philip smiled and brushed away his tears. "You don't hate each other?"

Herr Raeder looked across at me. I still leaned against the wall for support but straightened quickly under his quizzical glance. "No. We do not hate each other," he said very quietly. "Whatever there is between us, it is not hate."

Unable to remain in the cottage for an instant longer, I turned and fled through the doorway and down the path, leaving them there together.

●   ●

As I stumbled down the garden walk toward Ravens-holme, still caught up in the turmoil of conflicting emotions I had not been able to leave behind me at the cottage, I met Martin on his way around from the stables.

"Well, I must say, you appear to be lost in reverie. I've said good morning twice. Or are you snubbing me?"

Forcing myself to think clearly, I replied, "No, I was indeed far away. I'm glad you are recovered from your chill."

"Are you?" He looked down at me, a slight sneer on his sulky mouth. "What were you searching for in the mere? Did you think Wastwater held secrets or treasures or perhaps even both?"

"I wasn't looking for anything," I said wearily, tired of his endless suspicions. "How could I? In the first place, Wastwater is too deep to show its secrets to someone in a leaky rowboat!"

"And in the second place, the Vikings always set the funeral long ships ablaze before sending them out to sea on their way to Valhalla or wherever the bloody barbarians went after death. I have spent my time in bed reading, you see." He was laughing at me now, and I cared for it no more than I had his suspicion. "They filled a dragon ship with the riches of the dead man, set it afire, and it all burned to ashes before it sank. If someone would kill Hal Langdale for us, Torver might do as much for him, even if Wastwater isn't really the sea. It is an idea that has its merits, I must say."

"I don't care for this talk of killing," I snapped and brushed past him. Over my shoulder I added, "Imagine the waste if Mr. Langdale's wealth did burn to the ground. It would do *you* very little good!"

"Very true, of course," he answered amiably. "By the bye, Torver has been very interested in you since my fiasco in the cellars. He watches you, did you know that? No, I didn't think you did. But it relieves *my* mind, I can tell you, *and* leaves me free to pursue my own plans."

I thought with a chill of the sound beyond the pantry door this morning at breakfast. How many other times had Torver been near, within sight and hearing? It was an uncomfortable, unsettling idea. Or was Martin only trying to frighten me?

He laughed again at the expression on my face, and before I could question him further walked away and left me standing there.

It lacked an hour to luncheon as I climbed the stairs on my way to my room, time enough for me to collect myself and forget that disturbing scene in the cottage. But before I could reach the sanctuary of my bedchamber, one of the upstairs maids met me in the passage.

"Oh, miss, we've looked everywhere for you! It's Mrs. Langdale."

I stopped short, my breath catching in my throat. The girl's pale, distressed face boded ill news. "What is it? What's wrong?"

"The gardeners found her lying in the primrose border not half an hour since. There was a terrible great cut on her head where she fell on one of the bricks in the edging, and blood everywhere. But 'twasn't the fall, 'twas a spell." Eager to repeat her tale to a new listener, she was stumbling over her own words, drawing out the suspense until I couldn't bear it any longer.

"Where is she? Can I go to her?" I demanded abruptly.

"They took her to her bedchamber. Mrs. Ryland is with her now. Such a job it was bringing the stretcher up yon stairs!"

"Has someone sent for a doctor?"

"Mr. Ryland himself went, paler than a china plate he was. Mr. Langdale isn't to home . . ."

Not waiting for her to finish, I hurried down the passage and tapped lightly on my godmother's door before opening it quietly.

The room was dark, the curtains drawn. Freya Ryland was bending over the still form on the bed and looked up as I entered. "Good. It is you," she said curtly. "That fool of a maid was no help at all. I finally sent her away. Where have you been all morning?" She came to meet me.

"Walking," I replied softly. "How is she? What is the matter with her?"

"Very weak, unfortunately. I don't know what is wrong. She tells me it is her heart, but it may very well be a fainting spell or even from the blow on the head. She must have been unconscious for some time before she was found, but her mind is quite clear at the moment."

As I crossed to the bed, my godmother's fine eyes, shadowed with tension, opened and turned toward me. "Elizabeth?"

I took her hand. It was cold, the pulse hard and irregular. The room already seemed to smell of sickness and fear. "Yes, I am here," I said gently. "Are you comfortable?" I tried not to look at the bandage on her bruised forehead.

"My head aches. I can scarcely hear you for the pounding."

With a glance at Freya I sat on the embroidered coverlet, still trying to warm the icy fingers in mine. "Is this better?"

"Much better. I am so giddy! It makes my stomach very queasy. And my heart seems to shake my body with every beat . . ."

"We ought to do *something*—keep her warm at least," I said to Freya. "Last year at school one of the children struck her head on the stove and the doctor warned us particularly not to allow her to be cold, to watch for nausea and dizziness, to avoid brandy but use spirits of ammonia and lots of black tea to keep her awake. Surely we should do the same?"

Freya nodded. "It can do no harm. If you will stand by here, I'll see to the rest." As she left the room, I found blankets in the chest by the windows and wrapped them about my godmother. She seemed like a child, so fragile and defenseless in the great bed.

"I knew eventually he would find a way," she said faintly, almost to herself. "I've been afraid for so long."

All at once I remembered the last time my godmother had been taken ill. The symptoms were very similar except for the blow on her head. And so were the circumstances. On that first occasion Hal Langdale had left to attend the betrothal dinner in Cartmel. And this morning he had made a point of telling us that he was on his way to Borrowdale, almost as if he wished to establish his whereabouts. But if he *had* devised a way to harm his wife, what could we do? If he had used poison, what antidote could we administer? If he had tried to strike her down, he had surely succeeded already in injuring her terribly. She was so weak! And the doctor was so long in coming!

"I'm sure you are mistaken," I said, chafing her cold hands. "You mustn't upset yourself. This can only make your head worse."

Aunt Charlotte smiled wanly but made no reply.

Freya came in, followed by maids carrying a steaming kettle, a tray bearing cups and spirits of ammonia in a glass vial, and a heated stone wrapped in flannel. She set about making strong tea as I tucked the stone against my godmother's chilled feet. The maids, blank-faced and clumsy, were quickly sent about their business and we soon coaxed Aunt Charlotte to drink down two cups of the nearly black, heavily sweetened brew. She was vilely sick afterward, and not for the first time, but was able to swallow more tea when the upheavals had passed.

"When is the doctor coming?" I asked Freya anxiously

as the kettle whistled on the hearth and we stood watching it. Hours seemed to have passed in the constant battle to keep my godmother from slipping away from us. Though terrifyingly weak, she was quite wide awake, and I thanked God for that. We had had to walk the child at the Academy. We could never have taken such measures to keep the sick woman awake. She simply hadn't the strength.

"Matthew must ride all the way to Cartmel—"

"*Cartmel!*" I cried. "Oh, but—"

"There is no doctor nearer to us," Freya answered, her voice low but firm. "We shall manage very well ourselves until he comes. I am not satisfied that the fall was the beginning of her illness. She says she felt dizzy *before* it and has no recollection of tripping. Blind people insist on their independence and often forget their vulnerability. What did she tell you?"

There was no way to explain about Hal Langdale without betraying my godmother's confidence. "Very little. Perhaps it *is* her heart. It is behaving quite peculiarly—beating violently as if struggling to work properly, while her pulse is erratic."

"Speculation will not serve her or us," Freya said, kneeling to pour the scalding water into the invalid's cup with its covered spout. "We must continue as we have begun. The important thing is to bring warmth back to her extremities."

The daylight faded early as storm clouds piled up over Scafell, but we knew only that the candles burned more brightly. Torver had brought a tray for our luncheon, but it remained untouched outside the door. Neither Freya nor I had any appetite.

In the late afternoon the doctor arrived, tired and irritable. He had been returning from an all-night accouchement and Matthew had met him on the road. Dragged to Ravensholme without a pause for rest or food, he strode into the bedchamber looking more like a thundercloud than a man of healing. But after he had seen my godmother, concern replaced his hostility.

As he made his examination, Freya briefly described what had happened and the measures we had taken.

The doctor nodded, his multiple chins bobbing. "Yes, yes. That was ideal. Hmmm. Yes, indeed." He straightened, pulled the coverlet about Aunt Charlotte, and glanced around the bedchamber. "Mr. Langdale? Is he here?"

"He walked to Borrowdale this morning. I have sent a groom to find him and bring him home," Freya replied.

"Then, Mrs. Ryland, I must talk with you. If you will step outside?"

"There is a warm repast waiting for you in the breakfast room, if you care to dine while we talk," she said, leading the way to the door.

"Thank you, perhaps later," he was saying as they disappeared into the passage.

"Hal will be angry with me for not dying more tidily," Aunt Charlotte said in a thread of a voice.

I turned back to the bed. "You aren't going to die!" I made my voice firm and steady. "That's nonsense!"

"It will be one way of preventing Freya's ball from taking place," she said lightly, as if she hadn't heard me. "Even she can't continue in the face of mourning. I hope Matthew will be happy . . ."

Her words made my blood run cold. Matthew had been so determined to stop his wife in any way he could, but surely not by causing Aunt Charlotte's death! Mine, perhaps—he might have already tried several times to kill me—but not hers! He was a weak man who might be driven to murder by the circumstances around him or his own terror of exposure, not a coldly calculating, vicious planner!

Unless he had meant to cause my death and his scheme had somehow backfired. He had set out after the doctor "paler than a china plate," according to the maid, and the doctor himself had grumbled about Matthew's cavalier treatment on the ride to Ravensholme. Aunt Charlotte had been his only consideration, but was it out of affection and worry or guilt? Yet how could he have mistaken her for me? We were as different as night and day!

The doctor returned, opened his case, and set about a more thorough examination. Freya came in shortly afterward, beckoning me to the relative privacy by the windows.

"It is more serious than we imagined," she said quietly. "It seems that the blow on the head is quite superficial—rather ugly in appearance but not sufficiently severe to explain Charlotte's illness. Indeed, the illness caused the fall, not the reverse. Somehow she had mistaken the drops she ordinarily takes for headaches—a result of her blindness—for those prepared years ago for an old servant's heart condition. They were sitting side by side in the cabinet where Charlotte keeps household medicines. How they came to be there together, only she can tell us! In effect, she has poisoned herself accidentally. I suppose it was inevitable. She does insist on managing for herself, and this is the consequence!"

"But she will be well again, won't she? It isn't fatal?" I tried to still the tremors in my hands by tidying the draperies.

"We won't know for a while yet. She appears to be over the worst of it. The doctor says the tea, if not the spirits of ammonia, was quite effective in counteracting some of the drug. The important thing is that she must not move or excite herself in any way! A sudden strain on her heart could be fatal until it has recovered its *tone,* or so the doctor told me. He said that these drops in excess quantities or even in accumulative amounts paralyze the heart if nothing is done to prevent it."

"Dear God!" I pretended to busy myself with unrolling the sleeves of my gown to hide the tears filling my eyes.

Freya noticed the stains of tea and illness on the brown muslin. "You must change and let the maids wash your gown. And you will feel much better yourself."

"I—I don't want to leave her yet."

"Then step behind the screen. I'll give you one of her dressing gowns to put on."

I did as I was told, replacing my gown with a rose silk wrapper. The rich spills of French lace at throat and cuffs felt strangely light and cool against my skin, a froth of palest pink. "Isn't there something plainer I could borrow?" I asked, uncomfortable in the frivolous color under the circumstances.

"Nonsense!" Freya said, her attention on the doctor. "Don't make a nuisance of yourself."

I said no more, but took a seat by the fire and concentrated on staying alert. My body ached with fatigue, my mind seemed numb. After a time Freya joined me, resting her head against the high back of the other winged chair. She looked as pale and drawn as I felt.

"It was a mercy that Mr. Ryland found the doctor so quickly," I said in a low voice. "Particularly since she didn't have a concussion after all."

"Matthew said he had never been so grateful to meet anyone in his life. He has always been quite fond of Charlotte, or perhaps it is only pity. Helpless women seem to bring out the protective instincts in a man." She stirred restlessly. "He has gone in search of Hal. He left as soon as I could tell him the results of Dr. Orton's examination."

Would Hal Langdale be pleased? Set free at last, able to marry again and father the son he wanted so desperately. Even if he was guiltless of planning Aunt

Charlotte's death, he would never inquire too closely into the cause of it, I felt sure. That man took his advantages where he found them and could cold-bloodedly rejoice if someone else's ineptness brought him what he desired. Well, if I could help it, my godmother would not die!

Freya moved again, bringing me out of my thoughts. "If you wish, I can call you when Dr. Orton needs you," I said diffidently. "Meanwhile, you might be able to sleep a little."

"Thank you," she replied absently. "But I shall stay here for the present. She appears to be easier, do you think?"

I looked across toward the bed. There seemed to be very little change. My godmother's eyes were closed, but that could be exhaustion. "Perhaps," I replied doubtfully.

The hours vanished somehow. Dr. Orton, after satisfying himself that the laudanum he had administered had taken effect, agreed to join Freya for a late dinner. I asked for a tray of soup and tea, unable to swallow more, and ate it quickly in the passage for fear of disturbing the patient. Hal came in just after dinner, but the bedchamber was lit only by the fire and a single candle near the bed. I don't think he even saw me standing in the darkness by the windows.

"She is very still. Are you certain . . . ?"

The doctor lifted his heavy shoulders in a shrug. "We must let nature work, sir. The damage to the muscle must heal, and only rest can achieve that. If she is as strong physically as she appears, that is to our advantage. I have done what I can for the moment."

Hal Langdale's features were too shadowed for me to read their expression. After a moment he straightened. "I am merely in the way here. If she asks for me, I shall be in my bedchamber."

"Yes, I shall call you at once. Or if there is any change

in her condition." He followed Hal to the door. "A very tragic situation, Mr. Langdale, very tragic. While one must encourage the blind person to develop a certain independence for his or her own sake, one cannot always foresee the dangers a false sense of self-reliance brings in its wake."

"Indeed," Hal replied noncommittally. "Charlotte has never been one to enjoy invalidism. I can't blame her for that."

My godmother continued to rest quietly. Freya went to her own bed for a few hours' respite after the doctor added his persuasions to mine, and then he, almost ill from lack of sleep, gave me instructions and left for a guest bedchamber that awaited him.

Aunt Charlotte slept, I thought, her breathing much less irregular, and I had to walk the floor to keep my own eyes open. Once Matthew knocked lightly to inquire after her, but there was little new to tell him. In the flickering glow of his candle he looked haggard.

When Freya, refreshed by her rest, returned to the sickroom, I made little protest over leaving. My mind was clogged with fatigue and the thought of my bed, cool and beckoning, was almost more than I could bear.

"You will call me if there is *any* change?" I pleaded, lingering by the door.

"Of course. Sleep as long as you can, for *I* shall need to be relieved by morning, and the doctor expects to have you alert and capable. You will do yourself no good if you lie awake worrying and possibly do Charlotte a great deal of harm if you fail to nurse her properly because of it!"

"I doubt if I could keep my eyes open another quarter of an hour," I told her ruefully. "Good night."

Too tired to do more than wash my face and hands, I tumbled into bed, wrapper and all. My mind, filled with a confusion of images, tried to relax but found it difficult. How strange to think that scarcely a day ago, at breakfast, Aunt Charlotte had been concerned for *me,* fearful that I might contract a lung inflammation from my accident in the mere!

Breakfast! I sat up in bed, startled wide awake. The quince preserves that I hadn't found on the table but in the cupboard. The quince preserves that *I* was known to be so fond of! Usually *I* was one of the first down to breakfast. Ordinarily my godmother would not have risen until nine, but she had been concerned about me. And she had eaten the preserves and called them "bitter." Had she really mixed up the bottles of drops, taking the heart remedy by error, or had she gotten the preserves laced with a poison meant for *me?*

Scrambling out of bed, I felt for my shoes and quickly put them on. If I could only find that dish of preserves and be sure! Of what? Attempted murder? By whom? Meant for whom? I didn't know the answers yet, but if my godmother died I would have *something* to offer the authorities besides mere speculation or feminine intuition!

Shielding my candle carefully, I hurried down to the breakfast room. In the silent house my own heartbeats sounded loud as I opened the cupboard and took out the dish of quince preserves, dipped the end of my finger into the golden contents, and gingerly tasted it.

There was nothing bitter about it, only the sharp, sweet flavor of quince. I tried again, fearful but determined. How much must one eat to feel the effects of the poisoning? But the second dab was no different from the first. Had someone forestalled me and long since emptied the tainted preserves into the shrubbery or under a rock? Why had it taken me so *long* to remember! But of course this would have been the first thought in a murderer's mind, this dish of his own making that could quickly become the instrument of his betrayal. I had come on a fool's errand.

Dejected, I replaced the dish where I had found it,

closed the cupboard, and started back the way I had come, twice as tired from sheer disappointment and frustration.

He took the candle from my hand before I knew that he was there in the hall, his golden eyes dancing in the golden light. "I want to talk to you," he said. "Come into the drawing room."

"I—I must return to the sickroom. Freya sent me on an errand," I said quickly.

"She sent you to bed." Hal led me into the long dark room and closed the door. "I want to make a bargain with you."

"What . . . sort of bargain?" My breath was coming with difficulty, the thuds of my heart nearly choking me.

"She will die, I know the look of death when I see it. Marry me and give me a son. You will be rewarded beyond your fairest dreams and free to go wherever you choose. Give me an heir and I shall show you what gratitude means."

I gasped. "I—I can't marry you."

"You can and you will. Time is running out. I'm nearly forty, and I can't waste time in courtship and fine promises. I must have a son *now*, within a year or at most two, if I am to see him grow to manhood, train him as I want him to be trained. I shall, even so, be sixty when he is twenty. A man cannot count on living much longer than that, not with his health and his mind unimpaired. I want to finish what I start, see that he marries as he ought and learns to manage Ravensholme and love it as I have. I want to see my grandsons if I can. It is nearly too late for that. If Charlotte dies, and she will, we shall be married by special license. I shall give you a month if you must have it, but not a day longer."

Listening in growing shock and astonishment, I could only shake my head in disbelief. "No! I couldn't possibly marry you!" I nearly blurted out that I was frightened to death of him. "She isn't going to die, and even if she did I couldn't."

His fingers untied the ribbon that held my hair in place. "You are fair, like a Viking princess in the old legends my father used to tell me. Strong, healthy, young. I don't give a damn whether you care for me or not. Love doesn't enter into it. But give me a son and you will never regret your choice."

His hands smoothed the curling strands about my face and I shivered in spite of my resolve to remain calm. "Such lovely hair . . . our children will be tall and splendid, with eyes the blue of the sea like yours. It was in the lap of the gods to choose my next bride. I made no demands, and they have chosen well." His voice was low, mesmerizing. I simply stood there like a victim charmed by its own death, unable to escape my captor any more than a robin could escape Bismarck's predatory claws.

But then he stooped and laid his cold lips on mine. The spell broke, and I sent the candle flying with the back of my wrist. It fell to snuff itself out on the hearth. And in the darkness I fled, with only one thought in my mind: Whatever happened, I must not disturb my godmother or she would die.

9

Caught completely off guard, Hal Langdale lost precious seconds searching for me in the drawing room. I took advantage of them, racing headlong into the hall and pulling at the heavy front door. It had been barred for the night, and the key had been turned in the great locks. There was no way out, not here.

I turned and started for the long dark passage leading to the garden door. Unlike my full skirts and petticoats, the silk wrapper allowed me to run as freely as a boy.

There was no sanctuary in this house. Wherever I went, Hal Langdale could find me. As master of Ravensholme, he had keys to every lock. I dared not seek Matthew or even the doctor, for any uproar might reach my godmother's ears and precipitate her death. Perhaps that was exactly what he hoped would happen! My safety rested in her hands as surely as if she held a pistol at my breast; as long as she lived, I was useless to Harald Langdale and to Ravensholme. After all, an illegitimate son could inherit nothing. Still, I was driven by a blind, unreasoning panic at the thought of his touch and an overwhelming desire to escape the oppressive shadow-haunted atmosphere of this house. Even the open fells would be preferable until the crisis had passed and Aunt Charlotte was pronounced out of danger.

My footsteps rang on the flagstones of the passage, but his rang louder. I could hear him closing the distance between us, and a sob rose in my throat at the thought of being cornered here in the darkness or by the door at the far end. But he never called my name or demanded that I stop—whether from shame or pride I would never know. I stumbled once on the uneven stones, grazed my hand as I flung it out to save myself, and hardly noticed the sting.

The door was locked, but by some miracle the key was still there. I turned it as soon as my fingers touched it and threw open the door. For an instant I was outlined against the overcast sky, and behind me he laughed like some exultant beast.

I prayed feverishly that I would not twist my ankle as I plunged down the almost invisible garden path. He was nearer now, confident of his ability to overtake me at will, enjoying the chase. I never turned back to look, but ran on, letting my feet find their own way as I stared ahead, alert for any obstacle that might cause me to fall.

A bird flew up from a shrub by the walk, crying out in alarm as we disturbed its sleep. I was so startled that I lost the path for a moment, sinking deep into the soft tilled earth of the newly sown beds. And then I was back on firm ground where I belonged, though my lungs were bursting as if fear had closed them off. I never even realized that I had left the gardens behind until the loose chippings beneath my feet laid traps for my thin-soled shoes. It was more terrifying to know that he was playing with me, taunting me, able to catch me at any moment he chose, than to hear him coming nearer and ever nearer.

My shins struck the low-lying wall that surrounded the schoolmaster's cottage, bruising them painfully and sending me headfirst over the rocks and sprawling into the dried stalks of last year's Michaelmas daisies. Scratched and winded, I struggled to my knees and then got to my feet. The house was only yards away, and surely help waited inside. I found a fresh spurt of speed in that new hope and raced across the hummocks of the old garden to the cottage porch. Hal had come leisurely to the gate and was moving up the path toward me as I pounded frantically on the door.

No one answered and I cried out in terror, calling to Herr Raeder as my hand fumbled for the latch. The door opened. Throwing myself inside, I tried to shut it in Langdale's face, but he laughed a second time and shoved it wide with a force that nearly hurled me into the wall. He halted briefly, as if at a disadvantage in the pitch black, unfamiliar room. I ducked under the stairs, found the archway to the tiny dairy, and half crawled inside, using the last ounce of my strength to collapse against the wide stone ledge of the cream shelf. Surely the schoolmaster had heard the commotion and would come down to investigate!

But the cottage was as silent as a church, only the sound of my breathing, labored and ragged, and *his*, still fraught with laughter.

"You have performed your little charade of maidenly reluctance. Now come out of there and be sensible. This is as private a place as any to settle the matter between us. Frankly I would much prefer your compliance. But carry you to the altar I shall, willing or not."

I said nothing. My tongue couldn't have formed words even if I had had the breath to speak them.

He waited impatiently for a moment and then added, "Very well. Have it your way." And he crossed the threshold after me.

I was standing to meet him, my pride refusing to let me cower like a craven against the wall, helpless and at his mercy. But I was no match for his strength. In the end he dragged me, still struggling, into the kitchen.

And as he did he trod upon Bismarck's tail. The outraged cat uttered a fiendish shriek, and Langdale's tight grip loosened momentarily. I broke free just as a figure darkened the open doorway. With a cry of unspeakable relief I threw myself into the schoolmaster's outstretched arms.

They closed about me like iron bars. From the pounding of his heart beneath my cheek I realized that he had been running. His voice was breathless as he spoke. "What is it, Elizabeth? What has frightened you?"

Before I could answer coherently, Hal Langdale said from the darkness near the stairs, "*I* frightened her. Stand aside, schoolmaster. This is not your affair." There was menace in the cold voice.

"You have entered my house and that makes it very much my affair," Herr Raeder said quietly. "You will leave at once, Herr Langdale. Alone."

"Get out of here or I shall break every bone in your body," Hal replied contemptuously. "You are no match for me, schoolmaster."

"No? We shall not break up the furnishings or annoy the cat, if you please. But outside I shall be delighted to teach you a lesson in correct behavior as well as self-defense." Still holding me firmly by his side, Herr Raeder stepped into the kitchen and waited for Langdale to move. I could sense the crackling tension between the two men. Herr Raeder's body was taut and ready.

Langdale hestitated only an instant before launching himself with a growl. The schoolmaster put me aside, whispering swiftly, "Bar the door!" And then he gave way before the onslaught, taking Hal with him into the yard. I slammed the heavy oak door and dropped the bar into place—as I had been told—before flying to the small window.

"I don't brook interference from those beneath me," Hal was saying as they struggled on the path near the porch. "Your misplaced chivalry will cost you dearly."

Strong, heavily built, raging, he lashed out with his fists, but in two swift movements the schoolmaster had him flat on his back. Hal lurched to his feet again almost immediately, only to find himself pinned once more to the ground. Yet I could have sworn that Herr Raeder had not laid a hand upon him.

"I have not walked the streets of Hamburg and Shanghai for nothing, Herr Langdale. The sea also teaches a man many things." He loosened his grip. "In his cups even a gentleman sometimes forgets what is due a lady. The Fräulein is under your wife's protection, and therefore yours."

"My wife is dead. Or nearly so," Hal answered thickly.

"Then you will return to Ravensholme and leave Fräulein Winton here." Herr Raeder got up and stepped back, allowing Langdale to rise. I cried out as he sprang, but the German was prepared. With three short blows he sent Hal backward into the gate. After two more, Hal crashed to the ground, fumbled to his knees, and then fell heavily on his face. The schoolmaster moved to stand over him, but he never stirred.

Torver loomed out of the darkness.

"Take your master home," Herr Raeder ordered curtly. "I tried to let him save face but he would have none of it. He brought this on himself." And he turned on his heel, leaving the fallen man and the silent servant there by the gate.

I unbarred the door and let him in. As it swung shut behind him, he gathered me into his arms and held me close against him. I rested my head on his chest and knew I had found sanctuary at last.

When Torver had gone, taking his master with him, Herr Raeder led me to a chair and lit the candles. Bismarck, hiding behind the stacks of peat by the hearth, stalked out, his eyes yellow slits in the sudden brightness. Herr Raeder poured a glass of wine and brought it to me. As I drank it down, I took stock of myself. The wrapper was stained with dirt, its fine lace torn and bloody from the scratches on my face and hands. My knees felt bruised and stiff. But most of all a great exhaustion seemed to suffocate me.

As he took the glass from me, he held my hands in his and looked first at the long scrape on one palm, then at the bleeding scratches from my tumble into the dried stalks by the low wall. "I should have killed him!" The savagery in his voice shocked me awake.

"It . . . it wasn't what you think," I said quickly.

"No? I had made a belated appearance at the village celebration and was on my way home again when I heard you cry out. You were terrified."

"My godmother is very ill. He said she couldn't live and then asked me to marry him within the month." I shuddered at the memory of Hal Langdale's cold lips on mine. "He frightened me and I fled. I don't even know what brought me here, but there was no one in the house I could trust."

"Then you must leave Ravensholme. Tomorrow. For your own sake." His firm mouth was grim, unrelenting.

"But how?" I took a deep breath. "I am *penniless.* That's why I came to Ravensholme in the first place! My mother was cut off without a farthing for marrying a younger son with no prospects, only a small heavily mortgaged estate. Even that was wrested from me when my father died. I was taken on charity as a teacher at the academy I had attended, and then summarily dismissed this spring. I have scarcely enough money to see me to London again, and no prospect for a position, though I have tried every possible avenue. Except for my god-mother I am completely alone in the world." Tears filled my eyes in spite of all I could do, and I angrily brushed them away. *"Where am I to turn?"*

He knelt beside my chair and took my hands again,

kissing the fingertips one by one. "So. I begin to understand," he said gently. "And it is intolerable to know I can do nothing! My circumstances never seemed to matter before you came. Elizabeth, I can't protect you, I haven't even the right to tell you how I feel. But I *can* make it possible for you to leave here. Will you permit me to offer that much?"

I stood up hastily, inexplicably hurt. "I was not asking for pity or charity or . . . or anything else from you! Besides, I couldn't possibly leave my godmother alone in that house, not until she has recovered. I haven't told you—she was poisoned. Whether by design or accident or mistake, I can't tell you. I'm not even certain who might be responsible. Any one of them might have a good reason for murder. Someone has certainly tried to kill me. For a while I even wondered if it might be you!"

"I!" he repeated, thunderstruck, standing to face me. "In God's name, *why?*"

"Because you threatened me and wanted me to leave."

He turned his back to me, staring down at the white ashes of last night's fire. His voice was low when he spoke at last. "Elizabeth, my heart, go upstairs and sleep. You have endured enough. We shall talk tomorrow. I shall stay down here, in the event Herr Langdale returns."

"He won't," I said wearily, pausing by the stairs. "He is too proud. And I shall be safe enough if my godmother lives. I am useless to him and to Ravensholme without marriage lines. But you will have to leave Wasdale now. He'll see to that. You will need your savings for yourself."

He smiled bleakly, only his profile visible. "The villagers will be glad, I think, to see me go. A foreigner stretched their tolerance to its limits." The smile vanished as quickly as it had come. "Good night."

I climbed the stairs and closed the door of the little room. Though my scratches hurt, I only bathed my face and hands, plaited my tumbled hair, and crawled into the neat, narrow little bed. Tears, coming unbidden, soaked into the pillow, his pillow. I told myself it was only my exhaustion, that I was not—couldn't be—crying for the loss of something I had never had. Only my loneliness had magnified my feelings and his into more than they could ever be.

Herr Raeder was gone the next morning when I came down. Breakfast waited for me on the table, and in the dawn's pale glow I saw the note by my plate:

Elizabeth,

I must set the schoolhouse to rights before the pupils arrive. Wait for me, please. We have matters to discuss.

Kurt.

There was nothing more to say to him. I ate my breakfast hurriedly, sharing part of it with Bismarck, who begged shamelessly. Then I resolutely set out for Ravensholme, borrowing the schoolmaster's cloak to cover the ruined dressing gown. There was no one about when I entered the garden door and climbed the stairs to my bedchamber. The house seemed quiet and dark, as if waiting for something to happen.

As soon as I had bathed and changed into a plain blue gown, my hair once again in its accustomed knot, I made my way to my godmother's room and, after the briefest hesitation, entered. Was she alive or dead?

She lay on the bed, a single blanket replacing the heaps we had piled about her last night. Blue smudges encircled the closed eyes. But her breathing was easy, quite regular, as if she slept.

Freya glanced up as the door closed. "So you have

come back. Very well, then, you may spell me here. I am nearly asleep where I stand."

"How is she?"

"Comfortable enough. Dr. Orton has advised her to stay in bed for a week. After that she should be completely recovered."

"Thank God!" I said weakly, grasping the bedpost for support. "I was so afraid—"

"Afraid of what? Of giving her too much—or too *little*—of that dangerous drug?" Freya asked derisively. "Hal has told me how you threw yourself at him last night. Oh, she is full of laudanum, she can't hear us! Eager to become the next mistress of Ravensholme, are you?"

"That's untrue!" I cried.

"Oh, spare me your protests," she said contemptuously. "As long as you stay away from George Askham, I don't care what you do. As for Charlotte's illness, for all I know she might have poisoned herself. I wouldn't put it past her to try to prevent the ball."

"What a horrible thing to say! She nearly died!"

"Did she? Only Dr. Orton knows the truth of that. You little fool, you are just like Matthew, lost in pity for poor, blind Charlotte! Well, she brought it on herself, taunting Hal for never fathering a child."

"She didn't!" I broke in, outraged. "*He* called her barren. She told me so herself!"

"Naturally. It is her pathetic tale, and all a pack of lies. She is in love with Matthew and thinks no one sees. He objects to the idea of the ball for some reason, and it would be just like her to try anything to prevent me from seeing Askham. Did George tell you—that's where we first met? A ball at Abbot's Thorston. I was only eighteen and just out, but Hal and my father wanted me to marry Charles Carrock even then. George was visiting a family in Carlisle and came with them. He won't be able to resist the irony of that, not George.

He'll be there, mark my words, and neither you nor anyone else will stop me from talking with him!" She left the room, all but slamming the door behind her.

After a cautious peek at my godmother to be certain she slept still, I took one of the chairs to the hearth and sat staring into the low flames that licked at the red coals. What Freya had told me about Aunt Charlotte was unbelievable. Perhaps now that the crisis was over she was only trying to throw suspicion away from her husband or her brother. Or herself! If only I knew whether the drug had been meant for me or for my godmother!

The tangled webs of deception and suspicion in this house involved every one of them. Lies and guilt hedged them all. Freya feared for her son and went in angry terror of Askham. Matthew might have killed Charles Carrock and Sam Hichen. Martin wanted some sort of restitution for his lost inheritance and suspected me of standing in his way. My godmother and Hal Langdale were caught up in a hateful, barren marriage from which there was no escape, short of death. Torver guarded a prisoner in the cellars, yet everyone accepted Carrock's death, for Freya had remarried openly.

And I held the key to their obsessions. I had dealt with Hichen, met Askham on the sands and had seen him in Abbot's Thorston as well as on the fells of Wasdale. I had inadvertently placed suspicion on Martin as the intruder, only to be mistaken for *him* as he explored the Ravensholme cellars. I had even made my godmother doubt me because she couldn't prove either my identity or my honesty in the face of so much evidence to the contrary. Indeed, their own guilt made mine seem more certain in their eyes, and someone had taken steps again and again to frighten me away or kill me.

Where would it all end? I couldn't even accept the schoolmaster's offer of help. Because of me, he too would be sent away. Philip would lose both his friends, just as Herr Raeder had feared, a defenseless child, a haunted child left to the mercies of those who hated his father, who might even have murdered him. No wonder, I thought sadly, Kurt Raeder could reject the growing attraction between us. I had brought nothing but trouble in my wake.

I thought of him as I had seen him last. Tall, his dark hair falling over his forehead, his face stern behind the dark glasses, his knuckles bruised and scraped from his encounter with Hal Langdale. A foreigner, some ten years my senior, a man who had been to sea and taught school, but who had the long slender hands and cultured voice of an aristocrat, the bearing of a German officer. Whose world was so different from mine and yet so similar, for we both understood what it was to earn our way, to forget our ancestry and leave our homes, to forge a new life in place of the old. He had touched my heart almost without my knowledge and against my will, a Pied Piper who had no place for me in his life. Perhaps there was someone in Germany waiting for him, perhaps I had only filled the loneliness but not the emptiness in his heart.

Unable to bear the company of my thoughts, I rose quickly and crossed to the bed. To my surprise I saw that my godmother's eyes were open.

"Elizabeth?" she said tentatively. "My dear, I haven't kept you from your bed all night, have I?"

"Yes, I'm here, but it is morning and I—slept—last night. Would you like anything?"

"A sip of water, if I could have it. I feel so dry."

I gave her cool water in an invalid's cup, barely lifting her head from the pillow. She lay back and smiled. "Lovely! I'm as weak as a babe, though. My head spins just from that small effort."

"You must rest. Dr. Orton says it is what you need most."

She nodded drowsily. "But I shall be going to the ball. I shan't miss it after all." And she drifted into sleep again.

For the next week I never left my godmother's bedchamber more than a few minutes at a time. A trundle bed was brought in for me and I took over nursing duties from Freya, who seemed to be glad to turn them over to me. In the long hours of the night I found myself wondering if she had been so concerned for my godmother's life because she had poisoned her by mistake or feared someone else had. Once Aunt Charlotte was out of danger and Dr. Orton had departed, Freya showed no more interest in her.

I managed to send Herr Raeder's cloak back by Philip, reluctant to entrust it to a servant and arouse speculation about how I came by it.

The child was curious enough, but I gave him no answer.

"What shall I tell him?" he asked, frowning in bewilderment.

"Only 'Thank you.' And that I shall be occupied in caring for my godmother until the time comes for me to leave. We won't meet again."

"Yes," he said after a moment's hesitation when I finished. "But he won't like it. I know he won't! You are his friend; he said so."

"Yes, I am his friend," I replied softly. "But you see, I must go away soon; and now that Aunt Charlotte is ill, I ought to do all I can to help her before I go. She has been very good to me."

"I suppose," he replied, torn between his loyalties. "I wish—" But he never finished the sentence. Tucking the bundle of cloak under his arm, he gave me a smile and turned toward my bedchamber door.

"Philip," I called before I could stop myself. "Does—

Has Herr Raeder ever talked to you about his home in Germany?"

The smile deepened, filling his gray eyes. "Oh, yes, very often. All about Hans and his pony, about Ilse, who is as beautiful as Rapunzel in the fairy tale, with long fair hair and a governess like a witch, even to the big nose and bigger feet, and about the ships that their father owned which go to *every* corner of the earth . . ."

My heart turned over at the description of Ilse, and I heard no more. As beautiful as the princess in the fairy tale. Was it Ilse who held his heart in thrall? Was I only her pale shadow?

". . . and Herr Raeder himself has seen the Great Wall of China, which is ever so much bigger and longer than our Roman Wall! And the Pyramids too, because his ship put into Alexandria after a storm took the topmast—"

"How exciting," I said quickly to stem the tide. "It must seem very tame to be a schoolmaster now."

"I expect it is," he said wisely. "But Hans is a man now, or almost, and old enough to manage on his own. And Ilse is betrothed to a prince, a *real* one, so Herr Raeder isn't needed there any more. Just as you weren't needed by your school. He came to England to seek his fortune, he says."

Or to forget? Was he a younger son, like my own father, with no prospects to offer the fairy tale princess? "You must hurry or Maggie will be calling you," I chided. As he left, closing the door behind him, I sternly reminded myself that I had foolishly mistaken infatuation for something more, and I resolutely determined to put the schoolmaster out of my thoughts. Completely.

And it was surprisingly easy, for I spent my every waking moment too busy to think. I amused, fed, tended, and watched over my godmother, until I was too tired to keep my eyes open at night. She was not always a perfect patient, accustomed as she was to a great deal of activity in spite of her blindness. We never spoke of her illness or what had caused it, but read or played quiet games or talked about her childhood. Sometimes she told me tales of my mother, several years older than she was but the idol of her school years. Wherever Mama led, Aunt Charlotte followed or tried to, even into mischief.

"She was so lovely, no one had the heart to discipline her too harshly. As the ugly duckling, I was not so fortunate," she said ruefully, "and bore the brunt of the headmistresses' wrath. They told me it was good for my character, and no doubt it was! Still, I bore your mother no grudge, and she always did what she could to alleviate my sufferings. Once when I was denied my dinner she slipped me a gooseberry pie. I ate the whole but was *dreadfully* ill afterward and dared not tell any of them why!"

I laughed. "And so she made you godmother to her only child."

"After promising not to revenge myself on the hapless babe! I look back on those years at school as among the happiest of my life. Only, the ugly duckling never became a swan, merely a woman of character." She laughed to remove any sting of criticism from the words, but I realized that there was a grain of truth in her last remark. She had indeed hoped to grow up to be beautiful, as many awkward, plain girls do. And the sorrow of that lost dream still echoed in her heart.

Matthew came to visit her at that moment and I was glad. He always left her cheerful. I looked at his face and wondered if he had lived with the fear of bringing about her death in place of mine. But nothing showed except his concern. That was genuine.

Hal made no pretense of visiting once the doctor had departed. If he sulked over his wife's recovery, I had no

193

way of knowing. I made every effort to avoid him and succeeded. Freya was fully occupied with arrangements for the ball, now only a fortnight away.

Twice Philip brought me messages from Herr Raeder, but I steadfastly refused to see him. And so the messages ceased. I wanted desperately to know if Hal had dismissed him from his post as schoolmaster, but there was no one I could ask, not even Philip. It appeared that Hal had blamed me for the bruises he had suffered at the schoolmaster's hands, just as he had covered my absence by hinting that I had thrown myself at his head. Martin had angrily accused me of using my feminine wiles to curry Hal's favor. I hadn't dignified the charge with an answer, merely hurrying past him in the corridor and closing my godmother's door in his face.

But I was afraid that Hal would have his revenge on the schoolmaster in one way if not another. He need only wait until no one thought to connect Herr Raeder's fate with mine. I thought of the man Martin claimed to have seen in the cellars. I had never had the courage to investigate for myself, but sometimes in my dreams I saw myself being forced into a dark, evil-smelling cell with a ragged creature who might be a raging madman or only another wretched prisoner of Hal's spite, and left to Torver's mercy.

My godmother insisted that she was well enough after a week in bed to travel with us to Abbot's Thorston. Freya made only cursory objections. And so the maids set about packing our baggage. I planned to take all my belongings with me, for if Sir Edmund, my godmother's friend, could make me a loan I would never again set foot in Ravensholme.

The elegant ball gowns were carefully laid between sheets of tissue in a separate trunk. I had no desire to look at them, much less try mine for a final fitting. The sempstress knew my measurements. And if the gown didn't fall properly or required extra tucks at the waist, what did it matter? My pleasure in the exquisite silk had vanished in fear and worry. A little voice reminded me sometimes as I read aloud to my godmother or lay on the borders of sleep that I should have accepted the schoolmaster's offer of aid rather than pin all my hopes on the turn of events at the ball, only adding to my misery.

But I answered myself quite logically, forcing myself to believe that I had taken nothing because Kurt Raeder himself would have need of all his resources. He would be dismissed, under suspicion or without recommendations, as soon as Hal felt free to act. I could feel it, like a premonition, dampening my spirits night and day.

In my secretmost heart I knew there was more to my refusal—an unwillingness to be beholden to the schoolmaster, a question of my pride and my hurt. I would serve as a scullion in London or beg on the streets while I tried to put him out of my thoughts, rather than swallow my daily bread and remember painfully that he had provided it. He had made the offer after I had wept over my plight, not before.

It was tempting to walk off my mood on the fells, to tramp the gullies and high places where only the wind and the bleat of the flocks distracted me from my concentration on the track. But I was too vulnerable there—to Hal Langdale's importunities, to another attack by whoever hated me or feared me, to a meeting with the schoolmaster. Instead I moved quickly between my godmother's bedchamber and my own, hemmed in and wretched, tormented by thoughts I couldn't completely put aside.

Martin sneered and asked me if I expected to be remembered in Aunt Charlotte's will, but I ignored him. And then he forgot me in an excitement of his own.

It was apparent on the last evening we spent at

Ravensholme before the ball. He came to the drawing room just after I had entered, and his pale blue eyes sparkled with what I took to be wine at first.

"Well, well. A dowdy green silk to replace the dowdy muslin gowns," he said. "You haven't made your fortune yet, have you?"

"I didn't come here to make it. Only to visit my godmother."

"And when she failed to line your pockets, your fancy turned to her husband. But Hal isn't interested in a mistress, is he? Only an heir, and *you* can't give him that."

I started toward the door, angry and disgusted, but he blocked my way. "You thought you were a step ahead of everyone. You knew Hichen, you knew Askham, you had done your homework well. And you got nowhere with that little scheme either. Frankly, I'm surprised it was Charlotte, not you, who nearly died, because you were treading dangerous ground. Someone," he said with a mocking grin, "must have slipped up."

"What do you mean?" I asked quickly, wondering if he was indirectly taking credit for the accidents I had had.

His brows lifted in amusement. "Only what I said, nothing more. And no one has paid you in pounds either. Matthew hasn't got any money, Freya is keeping hers for her son, and Charlotte wants you to stay here and distract her beloved husband. The less she sees of him the better. Hal knows how to look after his own." He laughed. "Yes, he does! Of course, you can't see the jest in that, can you?"

"I'm not interested."

"Everyone is interested in money. How much would make *you* happy? Ten thousand pounds? Twenty-five?"

"Fifty pounds," I said bitterly. "Even thirty."

He stared at me in disbelief. "You can't be serious! Freya spends that much on a gown! Charlotte mayn't have her fortune any longer, but she could hand over that little sum from her household accounts. I don't know about Matthew. Everything is tied up in Philip's name, and my brother won't say what he is given to live on. Certainly he dresses well enough and doesn't owe his tailor. They won't make *me* loans any more because they know I try to double them at the gaming tables instead of paying my debts, but *you* could have been bought off very cheaply at fifty pounds! And they'd have done it in a flash!"

"Would they?" I asked, unable to keep the anger out of my voice. "I don't think so. Just like you, they all believe I want more, far more."

"It is human nature, isn't it, to be greedy?" He laughed, pleased with himself. "As I shall be. Be kind to me, my fair beauty. I may soon toss you fifty pounds as a mark of favor."

Freya entered with Matthew, followed by my godmother, and spared me the necessity of answering Martin's foolishness. Hal joined us just as Torver announced dinner.

It was my first encounter with Hal Langdale since he had chased me to the schoolmaster's cottage and dragged me from the dairy. I found it hard to meet his glance, almost as if I had been in the wrong, not he. But with all my resolution I managed to greet him politely when he spoke to me at the drawing room door. And all through dinner I was conscious of his eyes gazing down the table toward me, golden brown and strangely patient.

It was an uncomfortable meal. At first I believed it was only a reflection of my own state of mind. But it soon became apparent to me that Matthew was stiff and silent, unlike himself. My godmother toyed with her food as if she pondered over the secret contents of every morsel. Freya, her color high, snapped at Martin twice, as though taking her frustration and anger out on the handiest object. It occurred to me that Freya and Matthew might have quarreled, very likely over the ball.

Martin, holding in his excitement, baited everyone, showing the years of privation and hurt pride in the darts he hurled at us. At length, full of wine—for he drank heavily of the claret that accompanied the saddle of lamb and hothouse asparagus—and his wrongs, he became insulting. I saw Hal glance once at Torver, one eyebrow slightly raised, and the bottle was not passed again.

Hal was silent, sitting in his place at the head of the table brooding, just as Great Gable sat at the head of Wastwater and stared out across the dale in godly contemplation. I remembered my first impression of Hal—a cruel man with a cruel face. And a chill traveled down my spine at the thought of marrying him and living in this house forever. But if my godmother had died, I would have been forced to his will somehow. He was as implacable and as unchangeable as Gable. She had told me once, my godmother, that I had nothing to fear from Hal Langdale unless I posed a threat or was of use to Ravensholme. I would much rather have aroused his hatred than his desire.

A mousse was served with almond cakes, and then we were free to escape the dining room. No one lingered over coffee. The journey on the morrow provided an excuse. I accompanied my godmother upstairs and quickly locked the door of my bedchamber as soon as I had reached it.

Later, in the passage, I heard Martin quarreling furiously with someone, his voice raised once to a shout.

"I don't have to leave here. You can't *force* me into the carriage! I shall do as I please!" And then, "Oh, yes, I have never mattered, have I? I never had anything to gamble away, so it is wrong for me to try to make *my* fortune at cards. It isn't proper for me to turn Charles

Carrock's death to *my* advantage, though everyone else has. Or to stoop to trickery to take what by rights was mine. You play your games, don't you? I *know* what you pretend and why. Well, by God, I shall play mine!"

And his footsteps passed my door, but I could not judge where he had been standing or to whom he had spoken so savagely. It had nothing to do with me, after all.

Morning came, and with it gray clouds that sifted down the brow of Scafell and obscured Gable before pausing to spill a cold drizzle over the village. I was dressed and ready for departure before I joined my godmother in the breakfast room. Quince preserves in their silver-rimmed dish sat before my plate, but I took none of them and I helped myself only from dishes preferred by others, leaving the porridge and coddled eggs I was known to like.

To my surprise, Philip was coming with us, though his sisters would remain in Maggie's care at Ravensholme. And Martin, spurs on his riding boots, clumped morosely to the long buffet where the hot dishes waited. But Hal was to remain behind; I heard him promising his sister to join the family early next Saturday morning, in good time for the arrival of the first guests. I drew a sigh of relief, then realized that Aunt Charlotte had done exactly the same as he made his plans known to her.

The baggage had left at dawn, and we set out shortly after nine. Philip, riding in our carriage, had taken the seat between mine and the window, pressing his face against the glass as the coachman called to the horses.

I had no desire to see Ravensholme for a last time. Instead I faced Freya and my godmother across the sea of robes and hot stones, wondering what lay behind their calm façades, if worry and tension tore at them as they did at me. My only consolation was a small one—that perhaps my features were as serene and expressionless as theirs, no matter what lay beneath the surface.

Martin had ridden ahead as we approached the village, and Matthew was keeping pace on the far side of the carriage. I felt Philip grow rigid beside me and recognized the schoolhouse just beyond. Herr Raeder, the wind stirring the dark hair on his forehead, stood in the doorway to watch us pass.

Sudden tears filled my eyes and I glanced swiftly away, staring down at my hands folded quietly in my lap. He had come to say farewell to Philip. It was natural for him to reassure himself that all was well with the child as we took our departure, I told myself firmly. He would be standing there in the rain whether I rode in the carriage or not!

Philip, ignoring his mother's displeasure, waved to his friend. I could see his arm moving in a rapid semaphore. His other hand nudged me, but I kept my eyes on my lap, refusing to look up.

And then the village was behind us. Philip settled in his corner, a sigh escaping him as he pulled the robes higher.

"Well," said Freya with a certain vicious satisfaction, "Hal has at last come around to my way of thinking in one matter. He told me this morning that there had been complaints from the villagers about the schoolmaster—he didn't say what—and that he must reconsider letting the man go. The position is yours, Miss Winton, if you still want it after the ball."

I stared at her in astonishment, scarcely aware that Philip was sobbing brokenly at my side. But she closed her eyes as if preparing to sleep, cutting off any questions or denials. There was a cruel little smile about her lips, making her look unpleasantly like her brother.

Putting my arms about the boy, I looked blindly down the rain-swept mere, fighting the urge to call to the coachman and bid him stop the carriage. Such an exhibition on my part could only make matters worse for the schoolmaster. But I had done wrong, burying myself in my own selfish hurt and thinking of my silly pride when I ought to have gone to Herr Raeder and warned him. He didn't know Hal Langdale as I did or realize that he would never be satisfied until he had repaid his humiliation tenfold, that a man who held another prisoner in the cellars, who might have poisoned his own wife, who would have forced me into a loveless marriage, was not beyond a savage retaliation.

And that, of course, was why Hal had stayed behind! Why his eyes had held such patience last evening. In my relief at being spared his company, I hadn't considered the reason. Why had I sent no warning, made no effort to put Herr Raeder on his guard! Now it was too late.

As the wheels turned monotonously, Philip cried himself to restless sleep, but I could find no such escape. I could only sit there wide awake and terror-stricken as the miles relentlessly separated us.

10

A brilliant golden sunlight bathed the stark gray house and silhouetted the Old Man as we turned into the drive and halted by the door.

It was a great relief to enter the bright elegance of Abbot's Thorston again after the depressing gloom of Ravensholme. The twisting narrow passages and dimly lit rooms had oppressed my spirits as much as the fear that had haunted me there. Though I was no safer in this house—for my enemies had come with me—at least I could breathe more freely. And Torver could no longer spy on me, softly following me or noiselessly creeping to listen at keyholes.

Lithwaite welcomed us formally and, in answer to Freya's queries, replied that preparations for the ball were proceeding according to schedule.

"The wine merchant comes tomorrow, and we expect the lobsters by Thursday, no later. I have arranged for the palms and other flowers to be brought by easy stages so as not to damage them," he was saying as I ushered Philip upstairs.

The child was exhausted, his eyes puffy from crying. I was afraid he might have made himself ill. He clung to my hand as the maid came to bear him off to the nursery and so I went with them.

"My father will have to come back now," he said softly as I unlaced his shoes and the maid went to fetch a fresh nightshirt. "You are going, and Herr Raeder—" Tears filled his eyes and he broke off. "Why is Mama so cruel? Just because I love him she doesn't like him. And she hates you. I heard her tell Uncle Harald so. She says I must love *him*—my stepfather—but I *can't!*"

"Don't worry about it," I said soothingly, smoothing back his soft fair hair, "until it happens. I am still here, and for all you know, Herr Raeder will still be at Ravensholme when you return!" But I couldn't make my voice convincing, though I tried desperately.

Philip shook his head. "They'll not let him stay. They won't even let me write to him. But when I am a man, like Hans in Germany, I'll find him. Wait and see!"

I pulled him into my arms to hide my own tears, then said as briskly as I could, "Shall I read you a story after your dinner?"

He agreed listlessly and I left him to his bath, feeling that I had failed him somehow.

I was given the same small faded bedchamber as before and smiled to myself as the maid hurriedly explained that the other rooms were prepared for guests who would stay the weekend at Abbot's Thorston. It was as good an excuse as any for keeping me in my place.

As soon as I had washed away the dirt of travel, I sat down at the table and wrote a note, only to toss it into the fire along with the next two attempts. At last I said simply, without superscription:

Steps are already being taken against you, but you may be in more danger than you expect. For Philip's sake, take care.

E.W.

There was no way to send it tonight, but the first thing in the morning I would walk into the village and find someone who would deliver it by hand. Until then I slipped the folded paper into my reticule.

I felt a little better as I began to dress for dinner.

Walking down the stairs later, I paused to look at the portraits of the Carrock family. I understood now why Maggie had said they annoyed Freya. These were not her people or Matthew's but the ancestors of her dead husband, a constant reminder perhaps that he had tried to kill her. What did the paintings remind Matthew of? Murder? Or the bitter fact that he was a pensioner in another man's house. And it was here in this very hall that I had seen George Askham—so long ago, it seemed now—lifting those silver candlesticks from the table by the hearth. I had once felt strangely attracted to him, sometimes even dreamed of him. A gambler who had played with Freya's affections and then deserted her, who had embezzled regimental funds to pay his gaming debts, who had returned to the Lake District to frighten a woman he had once—supposedly!—loved. A man I had never met. Yet something drew me to him, whether for good or ill. But then I had found myself falling in love with the schoolmaster. Two such different men, yet sharing one compelling trait that had reached out to my loneliness—the quiet strength of self-command. Surely love, the deepest bond between a man and a woman, should be based on more than that!

"Good, it is you," Matthew said, coming down the passage beyond the library door. "I had hoped you might be the first one down. I'd like to speak to you alone."

I followed him into the drawing room, took the glass of sherry he poured out, and waited for him to begin.

"Freya is expecting Askham to appear at the ball, isn't she?" It was more of a statement than a question. "You made out the invitations. Where did you send his?"

"I didn't. Or perhaps it is more accurate to say there

was no invitation listed for him. If Mrs. Ryland sent one, she wrote it herself."

He watched me thoughtfully, as if weighing my words. "I see," he said at last and walked toward the windows overlooking Thorston Water. "But he *is* coming, isn't he?"

"I believe she expects him," I replied carefully.

He said nothing for a time, continuing to stare out the windows. "I wish I knew what you wanted. Why you came north. We had made our peace with the past. You have meddled in our affairs, stirred up what is best forgotten." Matthew wheeled to face me. "Wherever I turn, I find you in my way. But let me tell you this. If Carrock's relatives arrive Saturday evening and create trouble for Freya, I'll hold you responsible! Do you understand me?"

"I have told no one about the ball! No one! I don't even *know* Charles Carrock's family. How could I invite them here? Why are all of you afraid of shadows—"

"Shadows be damned! Someone finally convinced Hichen to talk—you or one of the others. Why else would he come out of hiding and drive you here? *Because he thought he had nothing more to fear!* You know too much, young woman, to be as innocent as you claim. And it will be the death of you yet, mark my words!"

I flinched in the face of his savage denunciation, spilling a drop of sherry on the arm of my chair. As the golden stain spread, I stared helplessly at it. What had Hichen feared on the sands—that the dead might walk again and accuse him of not bringing a murderer to justice? Had he truly seen Matthew struggling with Charles Carrock? No wonder he had died, stabbed in the back, when it was discovered that he had returned to Cartmel. Matthew had all but confessed just now—because he thought I already knew—that Carrock's heirs had at last found proof that would send him to the gallows and mark Freya as an unfit mother and guardian of her son! And if he discovered that there was no connection between me and Carrock's family, he would have all the more reason to rid himself of the only person who could possibly betray him: me.

Forcing myself to meet his eyes, I said as steadily as I could, "You are wrong about me. I intend to leave here as soon as possible. And if I can help it, I shall bring no harm to anyone between now and then."

But I never discovered what reaction my reply might have provoked, for Aunt Charlotte came in, her fingers lightly running over the furniture as she found her way into the center of the drawing room.

"You are quarreling, aren't you?" she asked. "I could hear your voices before I reached the door."

"No, not quarreling," Matthew said evenly, his eyes warning me not to distress her. "More a difference of opinion. But I imagine that Miss Winton has come around to my way of thinking."

"Yes," I said in my turn. "Mr. Ryland understands my position now."

Aunt Charlotte stood between us, her head turning from one to the other of us as if she somehow sensed the tension in the air. "All is truly well between you?"

I crossed the room and led her to the chair I had vacated. "Of course. You'll take sherry, won't you?"

As Matthew poured the glass half full as he always did for her, Freya came in, her green watered silk sweeping the floor with a soft whisper. "Philip is impossible. I even suggested that he dine with us this evening, but he prefers to mope in his room."

"I thought he would be glad of being home again," my godmother said, accepting her glass from Matthew. "Or is it still the schoolmaster?"

"I suppose it is," she answered, standing by the hearth and running her fingertips restlessly along the carving of the mantel. "You will have to amuse him, Miss

Winton, or I shall never manage. But you are not to take him beyond the gardens, do you understand?"

"Perfectly," I replied.

"Everything is moving as it should be for Saturday, though the cook insists she will need three more girls from the village if she must spend all her time on the pastries. I dare say we shall be fed cabbage and boiled ham for the rest of the week if I don't let her have her way."

Matthew laughed, making it sound almost natural. "Then by all means hire the village girls. Every room in the house will reek if you don't."

Martin joined us as we entered the dining room half an hour later. He was sulky, but everyone ignored him, and the excellent meal of roast chicken with oyster stuffing passed without incident. Tired and over-wrought, I was glad of the excuse of reading to Philip to slip away early.

He was already in bed, his gray eyes almost hollow with exhaustion. Though I chose his favorite book of stories, Malory's *Morte d'Arthur,* he seemed to lose track of the tale at times, forgetting to smile or cheer as he sometimes did. At length I tucked him in, kissed him good night, and snuffed out the candle. Rest, at this point, was what he needed most. Indeed, I thought he was glad to see me go.

I myself fell asleep almost at once, but my dreams were far from peaceful and I roused from time to time or tossed uncomfortably. At length a sound brought me fully awake. Someone had tried my chamber door. It was locked as usual, but the latch had been tested twice.

Sitting up, I stared at the door, waiting for a further sign, but none came. Had I imagined it? Surely not. The handle had turned.

I wrapped a comforter about my shoulders against the chill and waited for a few minutes longer, but nothing happened. Who had tried to come in and why?

Perhaps my godmother had been unable to sleep or felt ill. Or Matthew had hoped to find me at his mercy. Freya might have wished to make certain that I had indeed gone to bed. I wouldn't put it past Martin to try to frighten me.

Nonsense, I told myself sternly. The sound was undoubtedly a part of my dream, an outgrowth of my worry. Settling the comforter again, I lay down and closed my eyes, only to have them fly wide as I thought of Philip. He hadn't been himself tonight. Why?

I was fumbling for my wrapper almost before the question had formed in my mind. As I unlocked my door and swung it open, a scrap of something white fluttered to the floor. A piece of paper jammed into the crack. I lit a candle with trembling fingers, held out the torn sheet, and read, "I'm going to leave with him, so don't worry, but please don't tell. I will miss you, love, Philip."

The laborious printing was smudged and hasty but legible—all too legible. My heart turned over at the words. How could one small tired boy find his way to Wasdale alone, especially at night? It was unthinkable! Unless he went over the fells, as the crow flies. But of course. It was a shorter route, no one would see him except the sheep and an occasional shepherd. He wouldn't consider the dangers of falling, of losing his way, or being caught in a mist. Dear God!

Wasting no more time, I dressed in my warmest gown, pulled on my walking boots, found my cloak and gloves and a light blanket. My compass was in the pocket of my cloak, two of them in fact. One was the gift of the schoolmaster, the other a spare one that Matthew had left on the breakfast table for me after that dreadful evening when I had been lost in the mists on Gable. I found my way down the passage, took the stairs carefully in the darkness, and let myself out by the great front door.

My conscience worried me that I hadn't gone to Freya or at least to my godmother, but I hoped to find Philip quickly before anyone else discovered his foolish scheme. Both the child and the schoolmaster would suffer severely for this escapade, if it became known.

There was moonlight, though broken clouds promised difficulty before the night was over. Skirting the gardens and the stables, I headed in the direction of the Old Man, expecting at any moment to see the child on the slopes above me. I found a path almost at once, which made walking much easier, but the climb was not as simple as it looked.

I toiled upward, uncertain which of the many branching tracks to follow. Some were no more than a sheep's trail, others had served the miners and quarrymen who had once worked the face of the Old Man. In the strange light the mine shafts and huts and rock workings were dark scars on the surface, ugly and man-made in contrast to the slashes of gully and humps of loose stone carved by weather. My only hope was that I could spot the small figure ahead of me once I reached higher ground. Philip must have raced and scrambled over the loose scree in a frantic effort to put as much distance as possible between himself and Abbot's Thorston before his absence was detected. I lifted my skirts and plodded on, trying to judge my direction by the fells ahead and the gleaming finger of Thorston Water below. The manor house, set in its grove of trees, was dark and silent, its inhabitants asleep. I could only hope they remained so until I had returned Philip safely to his bed.

The question began nagging at me after three quarters of an hour had passed without a sign of the child: Had he come this way or taken the highroad? Was he asleep in his little room, already having discovered the hopelessness of his plan? I should have looked in before I left. I should have thought of it. For all I knew, I had been lured out here into the darkness under false pretenses. Someone other than Philip might have scrawled that note. These black mine shafts and old unguarded quarries were ideal places for murder to be done. My body might never be found, or if it was, who could say exactly how I had met my death? A stumble in the dark while trying to walk off a headache, a sudden mood of suicidal depression at being unable to find a position, any plausible excuse.

Worried and uncomfortably vulnerable, I glanced behind me down the track, but nothing stirred in the scrubby heather-fell, not even a flock of sheep. Had someone already frightened them away? Ahead the track was empty also. I fought down an overwhelming urge to run somewhere, anywhere away from this open fell where I could be seen all too easily, where someone might lie in wait behind a pile of rubble or in the shadow of a ruined hut.

Resolute in spite of my growing anxiety, I crested a slight rise and looked about before taking the right fork of the track, bearing northwest toward Ravensholme rather than southwest toward Eskdale. Surely Philip would be in sight by now? I cast a worried glance at the sky, wondering if it was only my imagination that the clouds were thicker, scudding toward the moon twice as rapidly as before.

It was only by chance that I saw him at all. A dried branch of some shrub had caught in my skirts and I paused to disentangle it. As I tossed it to one side, I noticed the gray slab of rock some ten yards away, a blacker shadow along its base.

I found Philip huddled in the shelter of it, a bundle of his belongings pillowing his head. The iron will of his spirit had foundered on the limitations of his seven-year-old body. Exhaustion had caught up with him and demanded its due. There were tear streaks on the upturned face, but his breathing was deep and even. My heart went out to him as I knelt to wrap him in the folds of the blanket and then cradled him in my lap.

Let him sleep a little, I told myself, before he has to make the tiring descent. Before I have to face the unpleasant task of telling him he can't go on to Wasdale. Freya would like nothing better than reporting the schoolmaster for "kidnapping" the heir to Abbot's Thorston. Like her brother, she would savor such petty revenge.

The moon cast its pale light over the fells, marking the hollows with deep shadows and the high places with eerie brightness. I could see a tarn in the distance, a black diamond in the gray rock, and from somewhere came the lonely tinkle of a ewe's bell. Stars filled the sky like tiny flowers embroidered on sable brocade, a spark of blue-green here, a pinpoint of red there, white scattered in random patterns. I had meant to sit there for only a quarter of an hour, time enough to catch my breath and take the edge off Philip's fatigue. I had not reckoned with my own, and woke with a start some time later.

The moon and stars had vanished as if they had never been. Dark clouds scudded across the sky, heavy with rain. How long had I slept? I stared about me, but the familiar landmarks were obscured now, the high fells lost in murky darkness.

Waking the boy was difficult. He mumbled and turned away from the hand on his shoulder, squirming down under the blanket's folds again. I had to speak his name sharply several times. He blinked in bewilderment as he sat up, then realized where he was—and why.

"You aren't taking me home!" he cried, scrambling to his knees and preparing to run. "I won't go!"

"I must! Philip, you can't go anywhere you like. Not until you are a man—or at least as old as Ilse's brother Hans! Trying will only cause more trouble. You must think of Herr Raeder, not yourself. Your parents will be very angry. They will even say that the schoolmaster was to blame for your decision to leave your mother and your responsibilities here. That you are the heir to three estates, not an ordinary child free to make friends where he pleases. How can Herr Raeder live if no one will allow him to teach again? Oh, Philip, I understand, truly I do, but it can't be!"

His fingers touched my face gently. "It will be all right if we *both* go, won't it? You can tell everyone, make them see," he pleaded desperately.

I couldn't speak for the pain in my throat. Tears fell unheeded as I shook my head.

Philip stared at me, his face crumpling. But he didn't cry. The spirit simply went out of him and he picked up his bundle without a word, waiting for me to collect the wrinkled blanket.

As I drew the compass out of my cloak pocket, my fingers felt the ornate pattern of lines and whorls that encircled the initials *KHR*. I couldn't bear the reminder, not now. Dropping it like a hot stone into my pocket again, I found the plain steel case Matthew had set out for me at Ravensholme.

I handed it to Philip and said, "Can you guide us home?" in the hope of distracting him.

Without a word he opened the lid, bent his head over the dial, and set out, not waiting to see if I followed. I sighed, knowing I might have lost his friendship forever and yet unable to see any other choice but the one I had already made. Perhaps as he grew older he would come to understand why I had brought him home.

It was not until we had covered some two hundred yards down a narrow track that Philip said in disgust, "This is wrong. You have broken it. The way to Abbot's Thorston is over *there*. I know where we are, for I've climbed this far before. Many times."

"Are you sure?" I asked doubtfully, wondering if he

was telling me the truth. In the darkness everything seemed unfamiliar to my eyes.

"Of course I am! Look, the needle is pointing the wrong way. *That's* north, I could show you the Pole Star and prove it if the clouds weren't there. But the needle is jammed. We'd find ourselves in the Duddon Valley if we followed your compass!" He closed the case with a snap and stuffed it into his coat pocket.

We made our way back to the original track and began the descent in silence. My mind was as busy as my feet. Matthew must have wrecked the compass before he gave it to me. He had been so insistent on providing one, asking on several occasions if I planned to walk on the fells soon. He had even arranged for Freya to lend me a pair of sturdy shoes. Had he hoped I might walk off Gable or fall into a ravine while caught out in a mist, or simply lose myself so thoroughly that I died of exposure before the search parties could find me? No wonder Philip couldn't bear to call such a man *father*! Weak he might be, but he had shown himself capable of murder. I had proof now, and no one to whom I could take it.

We tramped on, concentrating on keeping to the track. Philip's shoulders stooped with fatigue and unhappiness. I longed to comfort him, but what was there to say to a small boy whose world had turned upside down? If only I could somehow make Freya agree to send him away to school where he would be too busy to brood! Nothing would persuade her to allow the schoolmaster to return, even if Hal had no grudge against him, but surely she cared enough for her son to help him forget his wretchedness.

They met us just a quarter of a mile from Abbot's Thorston, their torches flickering wildly in the windy darkness. Matthew grasped my arm and said furiously, "Where do you think you are taking the boy?"

"Nowhere," I replied, pulling away from him as the three grooms stared curiously at me.

Philip, his gray eyes wide with alarm, said quickly, "I was wandering again." His cold fingers found mine and pressed them urgently. "Miss Winton came after me, that's all."

"With a blanket on her arm and a bundle of your belongings in her hand?" Matthew asked derisively. "Take the boy home," he told one of the grooms. "I'll follow shortly."

I wanted no part of staying behind in the darkness with a man who had tried to kill me. "No! We'll go together." And I broke free to plunge down the track ahead of them. Matthew caught up with me at once but was clearly unprepared to make a scene before the startled grooms.

We found Freya waiting where the path met the gardens. Dressed in her riding habit, her crop tapping angrily against the palm of her right hand, she dismissed the grooms with a nod and turned on Philip.

"I told you she was not to be trusted! Stealing you from your bed, dragging you God knows where—" She broke off and brought her temper under control with visible effort. "I'd like to take a whip to you, Miss Winton. You deserve it, believe me!" she told me between clenched teeth. "But not yet. There's more at stake than your folly."

With a hand on Philip's shoulder she marched him toward the house, leaving me to Matthew's mercy. He gave me a slight push and I went after them, angry and frightened.

Philip was locked in his mother's bedchamber and I was taken to mine. "Here you are," Freya said, opening the door wide. "And here you shall stay until the night of the ball. Food will be brought to you, and if you are sensible you will pretend to an indisposition. I have no desire to parade my private affairs before the servants, but if I must I shall tell them that you came to Abbot's Thorston expressly to kidnap my son." She began to light the candles over the mantel.

"And what of the ball? Shall I be made a spectacle there?" I asked, thinking of Sir Edmund and the loan that might set me free of this hateful place.

Freya smiled, her dark eyes lighting momentarily. "Oh, no. Merely an honored guest, if you behave yourself."

There was nowhere I could go, nothing I could do between now and Saturday. The ball had become as important to me as it had to Freya.

"I'll cause you no more trouble," I promised, taking my cloak off and folding it over the back of a chair.

She turned to Matthew. "Perhaps you ought to let Charlotte know that all is well. She will be worried."

"You won't take long here?" he asked, his face still grim.

"No. Tell her I shall come directly."

He left reluctantly, I thought, and Freya watched him until he was out of sight before saying to me, "If necessary, your door will be locked. My concern is to prevent you from leaving here with Philip or sending any more of these."

She held out a square of·paper. It was the note I had written to Kurt Raeder and planned to send in the morning. "There is no name, of course, but then I don't need to be told for whom it is intended. Oh, yes, you recognize it, don't you? Your warning to George. I found it in your reticule when I came here looking for Philip."

"You don't understand—"

"Don't I?" Her hand closed over the riding crop until the knuckles turned white. In spite of myself I took a step backward. "I know that I came to my son's room—by chance, purely by chance!—and found his bed empty. And yours. It is half past three in the morning, Miss Winton. Were you taking your daily exercise at that hour? Climbing to enjoy the famous view? Searching for the cairn on the summit of the Old Man? What am I supposed to believe except that you have tried to take my son away from me!"

"I heard Philip pass my door," I said earnestly, telling most of the truth if not the whole of it. "And I found him on the fells, asleep. I was bringing him home when Mr. Ryland met us."

She laughed, a bitter and sarcastic sound in the stillness of the house. "Whatever he may do in daylight, my son has never wandered at night. You are a liar, Miss Winton. And you won't prevent George Askham from coming here, I'll make certain of that. People who use children as weapons to hurt their parents are despicable. I could gladly see you dead!"

And she left the room before I could say another word in my own defense. Frightened by her vehemence, I made no effort to call her back. She was in no mood to listen to reason. I pulled off my shoes and began slowly to undress, wondering what punishment would be meted out to Philip. Even if he told his mother what he had done, she wouldn't listen. At best she would believe it was all a trick of some sort to make him leave home with me. At the worst she would suspect him of lying to protect me.

I should have gone to his mother the instant I discovered Philip's note, though she might not have recognized the truth even then.

I blew out the candles and soon fell into an uneasy sleep, too wretched to face any more problems that night.

Whatever excuse Freya gave the household for confining me to my bedchamber, it was obviously acceptable. She herself brought my meals on a tray, busy though she was with the final arrangements for the ball.

216

I could hear furniture being moved, bedchambers turned out, and the rattle of delivery carts on the drive.

My godmother came shortly after breakfast, upset and bewildered by what I had supposedly done.

My first thought was of Philip, but she assured me that he had returned to the nursery last night with one of the underhousemaids to watch over him.

"To take the child on the fells in the dark!" she chided. "The quarries and mining operations have made the whole face of the Old Man incredibly dangerous for someone who doesn't know the proper track. Surely you must have realized that!"

"But I didn't take him!" I cried, hurt by her readiness to listen to Matthew's or Freya's version of what had happened. "I went after Philip—"

"He never goes wandering after dark!" she said, just as Freya had done. "I can't believe he would *ever* venture on the fells alone at night."

"He was deeply concerned about the schoolmaster's dismissal," I said, trying to make her understand. I dared not explain her own husband's reasons for punishing Herr Raeder. It might frighten and worry her even more than she was already. But there was nothing to prevent me from speaking of Freya's attitude. "Mrs. Ryland should never have mentioned the matter in his hearing! Could you talk to her? The man has only given Philip the sympathy and attention he so desperately needs just now. Rightly or wrongly, the child is searching for his father—"

"All the more reason for him to accept Matthew! No, I agree with Freya, the sooner that man leaves the sooner Philip will come to his senses. And you are wrong to encourage the boy this way! Last night was foolish, dangerous even."

"Oh, Aunt Charlotte, please try to believe me," I implored. "No one will listen to me!"

"I may be blind," she said, a new reserve in her voice,

"but I see a great deal more than anyone gives me credit for. You don't like Matthew, I can hear it when you speak of him. Freya never really loved him. Lately I've begun to wonder if she didn't marry him as a bulwark against George Askham's return. But he is a good man, kind and *caring*. I'm glad the schoolmaster is leaving, and I hope that George will have the sense to stay away too. Then we can go on as we were before. I warned you not to let yourself be drawn into our problems, but you wouldn't heed me. If the trouble you have stirred up isn't to your liking, then you have no one to blame but yourself." And she felt her way to the door, leaving me to the unpleasant companionship of my thoughts.

Restless and unhappy, I paced my room by the hour, turning over and over in my mind all that had occurred since the stage had lost its wheel outside Lancaster. I could not have chosen a worse moment to arrive on a visit to my godmother. Pitched into a maelstrom of hate and fear and guilt, I had never been given a chance to prove my innocence. No wonder Hal Langdale thought I would be willing to step into my godmother's place. If even half of what the Rylands believed of me was true, I'd have leapt at the chance to become mistress of Ravensholme!

My only other visitor was Matthew, who brought my luncheon tray on Saturday. Freya was already busy entertaining her early guests. I had watched them arrive, laughing and calling to one another. Martin had been pressed into service to entertain the younger visitors, for he had strolled toward the mere with them not a quarter of an hour ago. Hal Langdale had kept his promise, riding in at ten o'clock. I longed to ask if he had said anything about the schoolmaster, but dared not. Matthew's face was too stern.

As he set my tray on the table by the window, he said coldly, "I've done my best to provide a fitting home for the boy. Spies are beneath contempt, Miss Winton. And so are the excuses they offer for their vicious activities. Remember that before you do anything rash this evening!"

I ate what I could, my stomach in nervous knots, and listened to the bustle and excited laughter filling the house and spilling over into the gardens. The day was gloriously warm, one of those special spring days when the sky is blue and cloudless, the wind mild and soft. I longed to escape to a quiet place, to walk off the growing tension that filled me. What would happen tonight? What terrible confrontation or scene would be laid at my door? If only it were over and I in the carriage on my way to Kendal! Nothing would persuade me to cross the sands again—nothing on earth!

At last Freya came for me. She was wearing an exquisite creation of cream silk embroidered with peach and sea green, her dark red hair piled in curls on the back of her head and falling gracefully from an emerald clasp that matched the emerald chain she wore at her throat. I had never seen her so lovely or so cold. She had been named for the Norse goddess of love and beauty. Never had it seemed a more fitting choice than now.

She cast an eye over my gown and the borrowed sapphires that she had insisted I wear to complete my toilette. I had not cared for them, but the square-cut neck of my gown required more than the thin gold chain that had belonged to my mother. She nodded with approval. "You'll do. See that you behave as you look. Frankly, I'm astonished that Charlotte gave you that silk. It is vastly becoming."

I followed her from the room and down the passage. "Why shouldn't she wish me to look my best?" I asked, puzzled.

Her eyebrows rose as she turned to me. "Haven't you guessed yet? She was always bitterly jealous of your mother. I was surprised that she would even allow you to come north. She must have had a very good reason."

I refused to believe her, though the words echoed something I had heard before.

Dinner was a confusion of faces and laughter. I remember Martin trying to catch my eye and Hal Langdale watching me beyond the dancing flames of the massive silver candelabra. Both Matthew and Freya were aware of every move I made, every word I spoke to my table partners. I swallowed the food mechanically—salmon and roast duck, endless dishes of asparagus Hollandaise, veal in cream, peaches in brandied sauce, jellies, and conserves. They came and went on my plate, a tasteless blur that I scarcely noticed. At last a strawberry Chantilly, and then we were rising to leave the dining room. The gentlemen were not permitted to linger over their wine. The room must be prepared for the midnight supper, and new guests were already rumbling up the drive in their heavy carriages.

A year ago I had listened to the older girls at the Academy excitedly talking of their debuts into Society, of the parties and picnics and balls they expected to attend, of the dozens of young men they hoped would sign their dance programs or send them flowers. My heart had ached then, not so much from envy as from sorrow that I had never had such a dream of my own. And tonight, as I stood at the head of the staircase beside my godmother and Freya Ryland, the dream had come true—only it was a nightmare.

As Lithwaite formally announced each guest, Freya and Matthew greeted them warmly before passing them to my godmother, who presented me. And in my deep blue China silk, cut in the latest fashion with a low bodice framing Freya's sapphires, my hair carefully arranged, no one could have guessed that I was not what I appeared to be—a wealthy young woman visiting in the home of friends. I smiled and bowed and replied to the polite comments of strangers, fervently wishing myself back in my small silent room.

We stood there interminably, or so it seemed. Freya hissed once, "He hasn't come!" and glared at me. But what could I answer that she would believe? She was so certain, that any denial on my part would only serve to anger her more.

At last we were free to enter the ballroom. The orchestra, surrounded by palms, was playing softly in the background as ladies in an array of colorful gowns and gentlemen in distinguished black evening clothes conversed with friends. The long columned room blazed with light from the exquisite Venetian chandeliers and matching sconces between tall mirrors. The ornate coffered ceiling in gilt and cream echoed with voices and violins. Gold brocade draperies, pulled back with heavy cream cords, framed the long windows at the far end, and the gentle stir of air wafted the fragrance from graceful baskets of scarlet carnations. My hands were cold with tension.

Martin had asked for the first dance. I had reluctantly agreed, and as Hal led Freya onto the floor followed by Matthew and my godmother, I found him at my side. To my surprise, he danced exceedingly well. We had nothing to say to each other at first, but when other couples began to fill the dance floor, he said in a low voice, "I need your help."

"I don't want to become involved in your schemes. I'm already in enough trouble of my own!"

"Help me and I'll give you a hundred pounds!" he said, ignoring my refusal. "Twice what you asked for."

"I don't want your money."

"You may not want it but you need it. There is something I must do tonight. They won't like it, but I've got to make money somehow." He paused as Freya and her brother swept by. "If you must know, I'm going to Cartmel," he went on hurriedly.

"What on earth for? Not to gamble!" I demanded.

"Yes. Exactly. The greatest chance of my life," he said

excitedly. "I can't miss this opportunity. You've got to help me. Tell them if they start looking for me that I'm here, that you saw me dancing not a moment ago, or stepping into the cardroom—anything. I need *time*—time to reach my destination before they even realize I have gone. Will you do it? You must! I'll give you two hundred pounds!"

"If you win it!" I replied derisively. "Keep your money. I won't have any part of this deception. No, wait." I didn't like what he was asking of me, I didn't want to be paid with his ill-gotten riches. But there *was* something I wanted desperately to know. I could leave here tomorrow with an easier mind if I could only discover what Hal had done about the schoolmaster. And there was no one else I dared to ask. For a moment longer I was torn between refusing him outright and making a bargain. At last I said, "I want you to find out whether Hal Langdale dismissed the German school-master as Freya said he would. If you can do that, I'll promise not to betray you."

"You drive a cheap bargain, don't you?" he sneered. "I already know the answer to that one. Hal has sworn out a warrant for his arrest. Seems the fool tried to steal the goblet—the 'Honour of Ravensholme'—and Torver caught him at it."

"Dear God!" I lost track of the music then, stumbling over his feet.

"Don't look like that!" he said hastily. "Everyone will stare. You are as white as death! It isn't as bad as it sounds. Someone must have warned him in time. He was gone when the constable arrived. I overheard Hal telling Freya just before dinner. They haven't found a trace of him. He just quietly disappeared."

11

I managed to concentrate on the final loop down the ballroom by shutting my mind to every other consideration.

"Smile, damn it!" Martin hissed, his lips frozen in a wide grin.

Somehow I did as I was told, staring blindly up at him, a smile pinned in place by sheer will.

As the dance came mercifully to an end, he squeezed my hand in a grip that hurt. "Don't forget! You made your bargain!" And then he was bowing over my aching fingers in mock gallantry.

He left me then and I moved quickly toward the nearest column, hoping to step behind it until I could think clearly again. But Hal Langdale was standing before me asking for the next waltz, his golden eyes alight with an inner fire. As the music began, he slipped his arm about my waist before I could protest or turn away. We were in the middle of the ballroom before my scattered wits realized what he was about, and then it was too late to escape him without making a scene.

"Relax!" he ordered as I stiffly followed his lead, cold to the heart in his close embrace.

"I can't."

"Oh, but you can. I watched you dance with Martin.

You were very graceful—until he said something you didn't care for. What was it?"

I dared not tell the truth. He mustn't suspect I cared a fig for the schoolmaster's fate, or he might find his revenge all the sweeter. It was also a two-edged weapon that could be turned on me. "Martin is always insulting," I managed to say. "I refuse to repeat it."

He nodded. "I shall see that Freya sends him packing."

Afraid to say more, I fell silent. We circled the ballroom, but my eyes saw nothing, only a haze of light and color and swirling faces. I felt dizzy, half sick, but I held my head high and smiled. Anything to shorten my ordeal, to keep him away from me again.

"That's better," he said after a moment, and was content to watch me with those strange eyes.

The interminable waltz finally ended. Hal led me over to the gilt chairs where my godmother sat but walked away without speaking to her.

Trembling, I made some excuse about catching my heel in the hem of my gown and slipped out the tall windows before Aunt Charlotte could reply.

The cool air struck my face like a slap and I shivered, more in reaction than from the cold. Lifting my skirts, I hurried through the immaculate gardens until I found Philip's favorite oak. Though the music was as clear here as it had been on the ballroom terrace, I was completely alone, hidden from view by the wide rough trunk of the great tree.

I dared not give way to my feelings. Freya might send someone after me at any moment, and I had no desire to be caught off guard. But I leaned against the tree and breathed deeply to ease the constriction in my throat.

Kurt Raeder had never so much as touched the Ravensholme Goblet. I doubted if he even knew it existed. But Hal couldn't have found a more certain way to blacken his character. It was a vicious, despicable lie, meant to damage the schoolmaster's reputation and prevent him from finding another position in England. He would have no choice now but to return to Germany.

If he was free. If he had indeed escaped before the constable arrived. The terrible memory of the man Martin had seen in the cellars came to mind. Surely Hal would never—

But what had Martin said? Torver caught the schoolmaster stealing the cup. Afterward the man had vanished without a trace! Torver, Hal's silent, faithful servant, who guarded the cellars—and their contents—for his master. What if Kurt Raeder was imprisoned in them? Who would know? Who would even care?

And if Freya told such a lie about the schoolmaster to her son, what would it do to the impressionable child?

I lost track of time as I stood there so deeply disturbed that I could think of nothing else but Martin's news. I would have to find out for myself. I would have to return to Ravensholme long enough to discover what had become of Kurt Raeder. It was impossible to turn my back on him. He had incurred Hal's wrath because he had tried to help me!

There was a sound behind the tree, a step on the lawn, and I whirled with a startled gasp to face a man standing some ten feet away from me. To my utter relief he was no one I knew, only one of the guests out for a breath of air. His evening attire was impeccable, his handsome face chiseled by moonlight, his manner commanding. I thought I recalled seeing him in the receiving line, though his name escaped me.

"I'm sorry if I startled you," he said pleasantly. "They are going in to supper shortly. May I have this dance? That is, if you are not waiting for the return of a partner with a glass of champagne punch!"

I smiled but shook my head. "Thank you, but I'd rather not return to the ballroom yet. The . . . heat has given me a headache," I finished mendaciously.

"It is a shame to waste such music. If you care to dance, we shall do very well here on the grass."

There was nothing I could say without appearing rude. He held me lightly but firmly, guiding me about the smooth lawn beneath the spreading branches of the oak as easily as if we danced on the polished ballroom floor.

It was indeed a lovely waltz. I felt myself relaxing in the circle of his arm, seeming to float in a spell cast by moonlight, my problems suspended by a moment of magic. Here was the ball as it was meant to be—a tall man smiling down at me, my silk gown and borrowed sapphires making me seem elegant and desirable, my rebellious hair for once arranged in proper ringlets, with two long fair curls falling on one side of my throat. Time stood still and I wished we might go on dancing forever, with no past and no future waiting for me at the end of the music.

The violins fell silent. My partner bowed gracefully to me and I suddenly knew who he was, why I *thought* I had met him in the receiving line.

"Shall we walk a little?" he asked. "I shall be happy to lend you my coat if you find the night too chill."

With my heart thudding against my ribs, I placed my hand lightly on his proffered arm and we strolled through the shadows to the gardens.

"I have wanted that dance for a very long time," he said softly as we passed the beds of roses, thick with leaves and unopened buds. "Ever since I saw your face in a carriage window. Do you remember?"

"Yes. Yes, I remember." After a deep breath, I took a chance and added, "I also saw you in the hall at Abbot's Thorston . . . and standing on Gable above Ravensholme. And I know your name. George Askham."

The muscles beneath my hand became rigid. *"How* do you know?"

"Because Freya Ryland is deathly afraid of you and yet very angry that you have come north so secretly. I don't understand why, except that you left her long ago and she married a man she didn't love. She is expecting you tonight."

He paused before an ornate bench set in a bower of climbing roses. "Why?"

I took the seat he indicated and said earnestly, "I can't answer that. She has suspected me of being involved somehow with you, and when you never contacted her directly she said she could be certain of seeing you at this ball. Will you talk with her?"

"Yes, all in good time." He smiled. "Most of all I wanted to dance with you. You may not believe that later, but it is true."

"Will you be careful? I don't know what is happening. I'm terrified! I can't even be certain how much I should tell you—how far *I* can trust you."

He shook his head and seated himself beside me. "You have nothing to fear from me, I promise you. The past doesn't touch you in any way."

"But it has! Don't you see, they all suspect me of something, searching for their own guilt in me. An innocent man has already suffered on my account. I don't know where it will end!"

His fingers brushed my lips. "Shhh. Trust me. I shall deal with it now. That's why I came back. Once I believed that matters were best left alone. Now I have realized that evil spreads if it isn't stopped. Leave this affair to me." He lifted my chin so that moonlight filtered through the young shoots of the climbers and fell on my face. "You are very beautiful, Elizabeth, a beauty that comes from within. Oh, yes, I know your name. You see, I've fallen in love with you. I hadn't meant to, but your face has haunted my dreams since that night on the sands. When this is over and I am free to pick up the threads of my life again, will you marry me?"

Too astonished to speak, I could only stare at the shadowed face. He bent his head and kissed me, his lips warm and light on mine. "I've wanted to do that for a very long time," he said softly. "Could you love me, my dear?"

I looked away, startled by my own reaction to the kiss and yet uncertain. "I can't tell you the answer to that, not now."

"No. It is too soon. I understand." He rose. "I must leave you. It is nearly finished, Elizabeth. When I come back, will you hear all I have to say before you judge me? I won't deceive you about the past. You have the right to know everything."

I recalled his gaming debts and the embezzlement from the regiment. That was seven or eight years ago, when he was young and under Hal Langdale's influence. I couldn't reconcile all I had heard with the quiet, controlled man before me. Surely he had changed, and for the better. "I'll listen," I promised. The words seemed drawn from me in spite of myself. What spell had he and the softly scented night woven about me?

For a moment I thought he would kiss me again, but he drew back reluctantly. "I must be patient a little longer," he said wryly. "Though it won't be easy." He moved away, then turned for a last look at me. As the light breeze stirred the trees beyond the gardens, moonlight caught the side of his face.

My heart stood still. "Oh, God! Oh, dear God!" I whispered, too shocked to hold back the words. I knew why he had seemed so familiar to me and yet was a stranger. Why Freya feared him so. The likeness was not pronounced—a fleeting expression about the eyes and the well-chiseled line of the cheek and jaw. But it was there, in the bone if not in the coloring. George

Askham, not Charles Carrock, was Philip's real father!

"What is it? What do you see?" He came back and took my cold hands in his warm ones. "In God's name, Elizabeth! Don't look at me like that!"

"I understand now why Freya is afraid. You are Philip's father, aren't you?"

"What do you mean?" His hands were hard on my shoulders now, his eyes—hazel, not gray—blazing in the darkness of the bower. "What are you saying?"

"I couldn't understand—yet the resemblance is there! When you turned just now I saw it clearly. Though your hair and eyes are darker than his, Philip must be your child! That is why Freya was so deeply hurt when you left her and she had to marry Charles Carrock! It explains so much. No wonder she never loved him, no wonder he tried to kill her the night he died! If she told him the truth—and it has to be the truth—he must have hated her for it!"

"I never saw a resemblance between the boy and myself," he said harshly. "And I made the opportunity to look for it. I even examined the Carrock portraits, expecting to find a stronger likeness there."

"So that's what brought you to Abbot's Thorston that night! I believed Freya fainted because I said you picked up those silver candlesticks. But it was what I had told her about the portraits! She *knew* what you were after. That's why she was so desperate to keep the boy away from 'strangers.'"

He was barely listening. "Elizabeth, it is incredibly important. *Can you be certain that I am Philip's father?*"

"He is so fair a child that the likeness isn't noticeable at first. It's in the bones of the face, you see, not the coloring. I can't explain, but I could try to show you in a mirror."

He sat heavily on the bench beside me, staring down at his clasped hands, lost in his own thoughts.

"You won't tell Philip?" I asked, suddenly frightened

by the implications of my discovery. "He isn't ready for such a blow, not yet. He loves the memory of his father—Charles Carrock, that is—and is deeply attached to Abbot's Thorston. You mustn't take them away from him until he can understand *why*."

Askham smiled then and took my hand again. "I promise you not to hurt Philip if I can help it. Rest easy! But this news alters my plans."

The music had begun once more, softly spreading through the night. "One last waltz, Elizabeth?"

I followed him to the oak tree, and when the melody ended on a tremulous chord that lingered in the darkness, he disappeared into the shadows.

I never returned to the ballroom. I found my way to the servants' entrance, slipped upstairs and to my bedchamber, and locked my door behind me. Sitting by the window in the darkness, I stared down at the pale outline of Thorston Water.

Had I stumbled on the secret behind Charles Carrock's death?

Everyone agreed that he and Freya had quarreled bitterly that night. In the heat of the moment, had she lost her head, flinging Philip's true parentage into her husband's face? Matthew had arrived in time to prevent Carrock from harming Freya, but I had no way of knowing how much he overheard before he opened that door. And Carrock had left the house. The accepted story was that he had fled after trying to kill his wife. In reality he might well have been trying to escape from Ravensholme before he himself was murdered. Freya must have been in a frenzy when she realized what she had said. And Matthew was in love with her even then.

There was surely no question now that Hichen *had* seen someone struggling with Carrock. Only he hadn't been able to prove his story and had taken to his heels in fear. Perhaps the freighter had eventually tired of running or thought it safe to return. Perhaps only his drunken nightmares had forced him to drive me across the bay when I had so foolishly demanded to be taken to Abbot's Thorston by the shortest way. Who knows what, after all these years, he really dreaded most—the living or the dead. But he had been too badly frightened by losing the track to go back the way he had come. And so the Rylands had seen him in Cartmel. One of them must have killed him.

No wonder Matthew dreaded the appearance of Carrock's distant relatives from Gloucestershire! If they even suspected that the boy who had inherited Abbot's Thorston wasn't Charles's son, much less that murder had been done—

Freya was more afraid of Askham. Back from India at last, he might have asked awkward questions or even have seen the likeness for himself. There was also the matter of those embezzled regimental funds. If Hal had wanted his sister to marry Carrock, he might well have engineered that disgraceful affair in full expectation of the young officer's exile to India. George Askham could have come north bent on revenge for that and completely unaware that the perfect weapon was waiting for him.

I stirred restlessly. Possibly the man he had once been would have stooped to such tricks, but the years had changed him. Freya couldn't have depended on that. She could only judge him as he once was.

It was easier now to understand why Matthew had tried to drive me away, why Freya would go to any lengths to see Askham tonight. I had unwittingly threatened their possession of Abbot's Thorston and its income. Matthew had nothing of his own and Freya was determined that her son should have a name and all that came with it.

The ball was breaking up. Those who planned to

travel home tonight were already saying their farewells. Had I been wrong to tell George Askham about Philip? How ironic that the child was waiting for his father to return, completely ignorant of the fact that he had!

But what had happened downstairs when Askham appeared? Soon I would have to face Freya and I wished I knew what had been said between them. There had been no commotion, no angry shouts or loud voices. Perhaps for Philip's sake he had sought her out privately or made arrangements for another meeting. For a moment I pictured the tall handsome man dancing under those Venetian chandeliers with the beautiful cold-hearted woman who was the mother of his child. Somehow it depressed me to think of them together.

I took the borrowed sapphires from my throat and laid them carefully on the table. As I began to unhook the silk gown there was laughter from somewhere below, a voice raised in the passage. The younger people would dance on, but the older couples were retiring now. The evening had been quite a social success, if that mattered at all.

There was a tap at my door and when I hesitated over answering, dreading to face anyone, my godmother called, "Elizabeth? Are you inside?"

"Yes. A moment, if you please." I found the faded blue wrapper and drew it on, then hastily lighted the candles before opening the door to her. "Come in. I was just undressing for bed."

"It has been a long evening for all of us." She sighed. "Elizabeth, Sir Edmund didn't come. He has been ill."

"Ill? Oh, but— What shall I do?" My heart sank. Why wouldn't they let me go?

"We'll contrive something, my dear, I promise you! By the bye, Matthew is looking for his brother. Can you tell me where he is?"

"He was in the ballroom when I saw him last," I said

evasively but quite honestly. "Something was said about cards." There. My debt to Martin was fully paid.

"No matter, then. He probably took a walk to clear his head. Go to bed, Elizabeth. You sound very tired. The future will work itself out. Wait and see."

For an instant I wondered if she was taunting me, but there was nothing in her face to indicate it. She smiled in my direction and found her way out of the room.

I sat down before the empty hearth too weary to think. Behind my closed lids I saw Philip's face, so different from and yet so like Askham's, and then the schoolmaster lying on a cot in a cold and hidden cellar. I must help both of them somehow. I couldn't live with myself otherwise.

Afterward I realized that I must have fallen asleep where I sat. Suddenly Freya was in the room with me, her face white with rage, her eyes blazing.

"Well? Where is he? You'll have to tell me now. I'll make you tell me!"

Dazed and utterly confused, I struggled to my feet. "I don't know where he is. Believe it or not as you like."

Her hands were gripping my shoulders, shaking me furiously. *"Where is he?"*

Jarred fully awake by her roughness, I realized that Askham hadn't come to the ball after all. Except to see me, and Freya must never guess that. "I don't know!" I repeated, breaking away. Certainly he had been dressed to come. Why had he changed his mind? Because I had so foolishly blurted out the truth? "I have no way of knowing."

She paced to the window, the cream satin gown swaying with her angry strides. "We're leaving for Ravensholme on Monday. I can't trust these servants, but Torver will do as he is told. And if I must, I shall lock you in your room until you tell me precisely what I want to know." She came back to face me. "If you are sensible, you will cooperate. That man will betray you as quickly as he betrayed me. Beneath his charm and his promises there is only treachery. One day you will realize that I am right!"

And she was gone, taking the key with her and locking the door from the outside. I tumbled into bed thinking only that at Ravensholme I might be able to discover what had become of Kurt Raeder.

The last of the overnight guests left the next morning shortly after nine o'clock, their carriages rattling down the drive in the spring sunlight. I couldn't see from my window who had come to bid them farewell, but the departures were quiet, almost sedate. It was a marked contrast to the laughter and gaiety with which they had arrived.

The maids set about turning out the bedchambers and putting the house to rights again. But no one came to my door. It was locked. I had tested it as soon as I had risen and again in midmorning. No one brought a tray or inquired after my welfare. Abbot's Thorston seemed strangely deserted except for the servants. By noon I was very hungry and beginning to wonder if Freya had deliberately left me alone this way to frighten me. Surely my godmother wouldn't allow such treatment, assuming she even knew of it! And what of the servants?

I paced the floor, restless and worried, then sat by the window in the sun's warmth wondering what might have happened last night after I went to bed. There must be a *reasonable* explanation for leaving me like this. I refused to let myself panic or give way to wild imaginings. Perhaps Freya had been called away to attend one of her daughters, taken suddenly ill. Or something might be wrong with Aunt Charlotte. It could even be a problem with Philip, running away while we were occupied with the ball or fretting himself into a fever over the schoolmaster's dismissal. But surely someone would have come to tell me!

The hours crept by, and my head ached from tension and lack of food. Fear as much as pride kept me from pounding on the door and calling for Freya or anyone who would answer. There must be a reason, I told myself over and over again, a good reason for being forgotten. Yet the house seemed so dreadfully empty except for the servants moving about downstairs.

What if it was a deliberate test? Freya had threatened me with the consequences of refusing to tell her where to find George Askham. What if he had come back after all last night and Freya had lied to him, saying I had left? For all I knew, he might be with Freya at this very moment, unaware of my predicament. Would he believe whatever she told him or demand to see for himself that I was not in Abbot's Thorston? How could he have fallen in love with me after we had spoken so briefly on the sands when Hichen's carriage was stranded? In the light of day, cold and sensible, it seemed absurd. Somehow I still believed him. Stranger things had happened. I desperately needed someone who cared what became of me. And Kurt Raeder's rejection had left an aching wound in my heart. But Freya's last words gnawed at my confidence, reminding me that she knew Askham very well: "That man will betray you as quickly as he betrayed me." I had been ready to believe him because he reminded me of Philip. My deep affection for the child had touched the man.

Poor Philip! I thought of him in his little room, despondent and alone, unable to understand why the people about him hurt him so. Was he still completely unaware that he had become a pawn between his mother and his real father?

By teatime I felt lightheaded and weak, but no one knocked at my door, no key turned in the lock. Surely the plan was still for us to travel on to Ravensholme tomorrow. They must let me out then! What lies were being told about me? Why weren't Lithwaite and the servants concerned about what had happened to me?

The questions circled endlessly until my head throbbed. Still no one came and at last I decided that Freya was only proving her power over me. If she could keep me locked *here* all day, without arousing sympathy or objections, what might she do at Ravensholme? That had been her best weapon against me: fear. I shuddered to think of it. Matthew wouldn't care what became of me, and my godmother had already shown herself all too easily convinced that he was right and I was wrong. Indeed, blind and dependent as she was, how would she know they were lying to her? If Freya or her husband *said* that I had packed my cases and fled, how could she prove I hadn't? Like Kurt Raeder, I could vanish without a trace, disappear under a cloud of suspicion. Aunt Charlotte knew I was penniless. Why shouldn't *I* want to steal that golden goblet? It was as likely for me to try as it was for the schoolmaster!

I heard the stable clock chime midnight before I fell asleep. I had vowed that I would not be found huddled in my bed in the morning, moaning over my treatment. If Freya had planned to frighten me, she had succeeded. But there was no power on earth that would make me admit to it before any of them!

I was standing defiantly when my door was unlocked the next morning, though relief mixed with uncertainty at the sound of the key turning. My hands were pressed into the folds of my green gown to hide their trembling as I waited to see who was outside. Whether my giddiness was from hunger or fear I refused to consider.

Freya stood there in the opening door, dressed for travel. Her face was very pale, and I held my breath as I waited for her to speak.

She said only, "Are your belongings packed?"

"Yes," I replied steadily. "I have only to change my gown."

She hesitated, about to say more, then stood aside to let me pass. We walked in silence down the stairs and into the dining room, together and yet worlds apart. My godmother and Hal Langdale were already seated at one end of the table, and Matthew occupied his chair opposite Freya's.

All four of them looked haggard, as if they had not slept for several nights. Beyond a brief greeting as I entered, no one spoke to me. I took my place and accepted the dish of eggs and Cumberland ham that Lithwaite set before me. My stomach twisted at the sight, threatening to betray me. But I took my knife and fork in a firm grip to prevent them from clattering against my plate and forced myself to eat as naturally as possible. After a few minutes the food and the hot tea gave me much-needed strength in spite of my difficulty in swallowing even a morsel.

I soon began to feel better and to notice that the silence in the breakfast room was absolute. Only the clink of china and cutlery, the soft movements of the butler as he passed from the servants' door to the buffet or table disturbed the stillness.

No one seemed to think my appearance among them strange or unusual. No mention was made of yesterday. It might never have been. I found myself wondering uncomfortably if my door had only been jammed, not locked, if my absence had seemed no more than a fit of the sullens or even an admission of some wrongdoing. Yet I knew I had heard the turn of the key in my lock this morning. Surely I had! It couldn't have been a figment of my lightheaded imagination!

Everyone seemed to be utterly absorbed in his or her own thoughts, depressed or burdened by them. I glanced surreptitiously from face to face, trying to consider how much their moodiness might have to do with me and how much with problems of their own. I was beginning to feel guilty when there was nothing at all to account for it. Uncertainty could do that, the odd sensation of having misplaced a whole day which no one else had lost.

Hal was finishing his coffee, his expression grim and forbidding. Where was Kurt Raeder? In his power or safely on his way home to Germany? Was Langdale considering what to do with his victim or angry over the lost opportunity to humiliate the schoolmaster completely?

My godmother was crumbling a corner of toast in her plate, her fine eyes clouded with worry as she stared straight and unseeingly before her. Was she trying to think of a way of keeping me here or setting me free?

Freya was tense, her motions sharp and nervous as she folded her napkin. Matthew frowned down at his plate, his face bitter. The ball had brought no joy to either of the Rylands. I could almost see the marriage falling apart before my eyes. How much did Matthew know about George Askham? Or guess?

Freya was the first to push back her chair. "We leave in three quarters of an hour," she said to the table at large. "I have ordered the carriage for nine-thirty."

I excused myself and hurried upstairs to change my gown. My trunk had been taken away. Only my satchel remained, waiting for the gown I was wearing and the items on my dressing table.

When I was ready there was nothing to keep me in my chamber. I walked down the stairs into the hall, looking at the portraits on the walls and wondering if Charles Carrock had had his painted before he died. Most of the faces peering out at me were in clothes a generation or more too old for the man who was called Philip's father.

Before I could search too far, Philip himself came down. He was very subdued, but there was color in his cheekbones. He looked at me quickly and then away, as if afraid of what I might see in his eyes. I felt like gathering him in my arms and keeping him away from

Ravensholme, where the last flickering ray of hope would be extinguished. He was trying his best to hide it from all of us, but he was expecting the schoolmaster to be there, in the door of the schoolhouse or in the cottage. But he wouldn't be. I could feel it like a cold weight on my heart.

My satchel was loaded into the boot of the carriage, and then Freya was bringing my godmother downstairs, talking to her in a low voice. I walked out the door past Lithwaite and down the steps to take my seat. Looking back at Abbot's Thorston for an instant, I wondered why I had ever thought it severe or forbidding. The gray stone—dark green and wine red in the sunlight—had a certain strength and grace. Tears came to my eyes when I remembered that Philip might never inherit his beloved home. Very likely I myself would never see it again, but that was because of Freya and her husband and all they represented. Abbot's Thorston itself had never threatened me as Ravensholme had.

I brushed a hand across my eyes as Philip climbed in beside me and then my godmother took the seat opposite. Freya joined her after a last word to the butler. Hal and Matthew were mounting restless horses, waiting for the signal to the coachman. And then we were rumbling down the drive toward the sunlit mere.

The journey was long and tedious. Freya and my godmother rarely spoke either to me or to each other. Philip sat stiffly by the window, almost counting the revolutions of the wheels. The hours must have dragged unbearably for him, but he shook his head when I suggested a game to pass the time.

There was much to think about on my own. I was almost grateful for not having to make polite conversation. Freya and I no longer had anything to say to each other, and Aunt Charlotte seemed withdrawn, as if she were full of doubts about me. Outside the carriage Hal and Matthew rode in a silence of their own. They had little in common these days, since Matthew had become respectable and a settled married man. I had the feeling that they had never really liked each other.

I found myself wishing that I had told George Askham more about what was happening, even though it was not actually his affair. I wanted someone to know what was happening to me, a virtual prisoner. As I looked from Freya's face to her husband's, I had no illusions about my safety. Perhaps if Askham knew the danger in which I stood, if he really cared, he would explain to Freya that I was no part of a plot against her or her son. Or was I? Had I told Askham the very secret she was trying to keep from him?

At last we turned up the road running along Wastwater. Philip had become increasingly restless for the past several miles, fidgeting in his seat until his mother had spoken sharply to him. He settled back, chastened, and waited for the village to come into view at the head of Wasdale. What would he say, what would he do, when he learned of the accusation against Herr Raeder? It might break his spirit entirely. Surely his mother could see that!

I watched the ripple of wind across the mere, disturbing the dark patterns of the fells reflected there. How could Philip begin to understand the interactions among the people surrounding him? Much less come to terms with them! I wished for the hundredth time that I hadn't spoken so impetuously to George Askham about his resemblance to the boy. It might have repercussions I couldn't begin to foresee.

Something floating on the mere reminded me unpleasantly of that day I had found Philip's cap and the broken paddle of the missing canoe. I glanced away, my eyes turning toward Great Gable, then found myself looking back, drawn by the terrible memory.

Someone had tossed a bundle of rags into the water. They stirred with the wind. Black rags, shapeless and heavy with wet just as my skirts had been. I shuddered.

No, it wasn't a bundle of rags. It was a man. A tall man wearing a black suit of clothes. Kurt Raeder! They had killed him, somehow they had found him and killed him!

I screamed, calling to the coachman to stop, pulling frantically at the carriage door, heedless of Freya's sharp voice and my godmother's frightened hands groping for my arm. The carriage jerked to a halt, almost pitching me headlong through the opening door. I ignored Hal, coming around the boot toward me. I didn't even wait for the steps or for the groom to scramble down and help me. I flung myself out in a tangle of lap rugs and nearly stumbled over my skirts as I started to run. Matthew, his horse rearing nervously, was out of the saddle and after me. I plunged into the cold water, crying out again in horrified disbelief as the body rocked gently in the wind. No bundle of rags— only a dead man could float like that. All at once I felt myself being pulled roughly back to shore.

"It is deep along here. Wait," Matthew was saying.

I jerked free of his grasp, but Freya had left the carriage and caught my other arm. "Stop it! Do you hear? He is dead. You can do nothing, nothing at all!"

She was right. I stood there for an instant longer, my skirts clinging wetly to my ankles as I forced myself to accept a nightmare. And then, covering my face with my hands to shut out the sight, I let her lead me back to the carriage.

Ten long, endless minutes later they dragged the pathetic figure to the shore and laid him gently on the rocky strand above the waterline. I could hear them talking and splashing as they worked, but I never turned around. Philip, white and shaking, was clasped in Aunt Charlotte's arms, and she stared desperately into the darkness trying to comprehend what was happening all about her. I didn't have the strength to comfort either of them. My bones seemed to be made of jelly, refusing to support me. Somewhere behind me I could hear whispers, as if the coachman and the groom were afraid to speak out, then other voices, low and urgent.

Something inside me had ceased to function. Emptiness spread through me like a cold wind, chilling my heart and numbing my mind. I could find no way to come to terms with my horror and my loss. I had loved him. I loved him still . . .

Matthew crossed to the carriage and I steeled myself for what he had to say. He took my godmother's hand and spoke with what reassurance he could muster in the face of such a death, such a lonely death.

"It is Martin," he told her. "He has drowned in Wastwater."

The world seemed to spin wildly and I leaned weakly against the high wheel. My breath came in painful gasps as I turned slowly to look toward the shore. Martin. Not the schoolmaster after all. The dark clothes—my first thought had naturally turned to Kurt Raeder. He had vanished without a trace, or so I had been told, and Wastwater, dark and deep, often kept its secrets.

Poor Martin, with his vicious, bitter tongue, his dreams of wealth and security. I had not liked him, but I could not wish such a death on any man.

12

Martin's body was wrapped in his brother's cloak and laid across his vacated saddle. While the groom stayed behind to lead the horse to Ravensholme, Matthew joined us in the carriage, his face wan and tight.

It was a silent ride until he said almost at random, "He was still wearing his evening clothes. He must have come here directly from the ball."

"For heaven's sake, how did he come to be in the mere? Unless he was too drunk to heed where he was going," Freya added.

I asked myself what he was doing in Wasdale at all, unless he had lied to me about going to Cartmel. He might well have. Martin trusted no one. Had he *expected* me to betray him? If I had been the sort of person he believed I was, I might have taken malicious pleasure in giving him away at the first opportunity.

We were approaching the village. The schoolhouse door was closed, a look of emptiness about the gray stone walls and the blank windows. Philip's eyes lifted in anguish to mine before he leaned back against the squabs. Thank God, I told myself fervently, he hadn't understood my moment of terror when I thought I had recognized the body in Wastwater! It was terrible enough for the dead man to be Martin.

Aunt Charlotte was saying, "How could he have reached Wasdale, Matthew? I thought you said there were no horses missing from the stables at Abbot's Thorston?"

Matthew shrugged wearily. "He might have arranged for a horse from the village or somewhere along the way. Though from the state of his clothes, I'd say he came over the fells. It is far more direct."

"Yes, but the note the boy brought before breakfast this morning indicated he was on his way to London. We were even asked to pack his belongings and send them on to his lodgings there!"

"He wrote you a note?" I asked in surprise, drawn out of my own thoughts.

"Yes, Lithwaite gave it to Matthew as we came down to the dining room," she said, turning to me. "You hadn't joined us, had you? It was rather nasty in tone. I shan't repeat it here. Enough to say that he was angry with us for showing so little sympathy toward his situation. I expect he was full of brandy and self-pity, poor boy. Freya said she could barely decipher half of it." Her eyes filled with tears. "That's when he must have decided to put a period—"

Matthew stirred uncomfortably and my godmother broke off. But I couldn't accept the suggestion of suicide. Martin had been so certain of success on the night of the ball. His fortune was made, he was already offering me two hundred pounds with an offhandedness that grew out of complete self-confidence. The excitement in him had been almost tangible. Or had the bubble burst, leaving him prey to black despair? We might never know the answer to that question.

Torver met us at the door of Ravensholme, and Matthew gave him brief instructions for attending to

Martin's body. The servant was visibly shocked, his well-trained reserve slipping a little at the news.

"A sad thing, sir, very sad. May I offer my condolences?" I heard Torver saying quietly as I watched Philip racing up the stairs. "Mr. Martin was so young."

Aunt Charlotte took my arm and I reluctantly went with her to her bedchamber, wishing myself anywhere but inside this house again.

As soon as I had helped her remove her cloak and bonnet, she said uneasily, "Elizabeth, why were you so distraught over Martin's death? There was nothing between the two of you, was there?"

"Of course not. No."

"You seemed somehow bereft."

Remembering that she was blind and couldn't have known what was happening, I said briefly, "There appeared to be a bundle or something in the water. Suddenly I realized that it was actually a man." To forestall further questions I added mendaciously, "I suppose I was reminded too vividly of my own experience when the rowboat sank under me."

"I understand," she said quietly. "Did Martin confide in you before he left Abbot's Thorston? Had he possibly met Askham that night?"

Surprised, I said, "I really don't know." Martin had spoken of the greatest chance of his life. But I couldn't believe he was referring to George Askham's arrival. How could it have benefited him? Unless he had made the same astounding discovery I had and decided to blackmail Freya or his brother! Still, that wouldn't explain why he drowned in Wastwater.

She absently smoothed the embroidered satin coverlet of her bed. "Well, we shall never know, I suppose. You won't speak of this to Freya or Matthew, will you? I'd rather not add to their distress. Poor Matthew! He had practically raised Martin after their parents died. It must have been horrid for him to discover that the drowning victim was his own brother!"

"Yes, I'm sure it was," I agreed. "But about that note, Aunt Charlotte. What did Martin write?"

"That the wild life he had chosen to lead was better than the pious pretenses we made at godliness, because it was at least honest. That he alone was not plagued by a guilty conscience. There was something about our callousness in refusing to help him when he had needed it so desperately, though this part was rather garbled. Then he said he had found a way to leave and was taking it—which Matthew believed to be a reference to traveling south with one of the parties returning home that night—and wanted his luggage sent on to London as soon as we could arrange it."

It sounded very much like Martin. I could almost hear his sneering voice as he said the words. Was the note another red herring? Or completely counterfeit? How had Martin come to be in Wastwater?

"You said a boy brought it?"

"Yes. According to Lithwaite, the boy said a man in evening dress had paid him a shilling to deliver the note to Abbot's Thorston early on Monday morning. He could remember nothing more about the man, only that he appeared either very excited or very intoxicated." She sighed. "We failed Martin, I'm afraid."

"Put it out of your mind and rest for a while," I said gently. Closing the door, I turned toward my room, greeting Maggie as she passed me in the corridor.

"Such a shame about Mr. Martin," she said, shaking her head. "I'm that glad the little ones are too young to know. Master Philip will be having nightmares, mark my words. I've never seen him so upset."

Though I knew that Martin's death was only a small part of Philip's distress, I agreed and went on to open my door.

There by the hearth stood Philip, his face anxious and tear-streaked, his arms clutching the squirming form of Bismarck. "He's not at the cottage! They did send him away. But why did Uncle Hal leave my cat to starve? He should have taken it to someone in the village, or brought it here!"

From the looks of Bismarck he had not been helpless to forage for himself. Taking the animal from the child, I said gently, "Perhaps Bismarck didn't care for his new home and went back to the cottage to live."

Philip's face brightened. "Yes, I expect he did! It was just finding him there by the porch, so lonely and unhappy, that made me cry. I couldn't bear to think him forsaken and hungry."

But it was the boy who had felt forsaken. "I think it might be unnecessary to tell anyone whose cat Bismarck used to be," I said, watching the animal smooth down the fur that Philip had ruffled in smuggling him into Ravensholme. "Perhaps if you ask nicely, your aunt will allow you to keep him as a pet."

"And then when Herr Raeder comes back, he'll find us both waiting for him!"

"Yes, my love, he will." I tried to sound hopeful.

Philip flung his arms about my neck, nearly pushing me over as I knelt there by the empty grate. I resolved to find my way to the cellars this very night, while Martin's death distracted everyone's attention from me. I had to know the answer to what had become of the schoolmaster. I couldn't stand another shock like the one I had had this afternoon.

Disentangling myself from boy and cat, I smiled. "If you run down and ask the cook for a glass of milk, we can offer Bismarck a treat."

Philip was gone at once, and I looked down at the animal stretching itself so smugly on the hearthstone. "If only you could talk!" I said softly. "If only you could tell me what I shall find—or if I am risking everything on a wild-goose chase!"

Two of the old women came from the village to look after Martin. We ate our dinner in an atmosphere of depression, still shocked by what had happened. The vicar called and discussed funeral arrangements with Matthew after expressing his sympathy. The death was spoken of as a tragic accident. Why Martin had come to Wasdale, and in evening dress, was never questioned.

Freya seemed to have forgotten about me, and I was allowed to join the family as a matter of course. But I dreaded the possibility that she would remember and at least lock me in that night. How then could I make my search? But with the servants busily going about their duties, I dared not try anything that might arouse undue suspicion.

And so we finished our meal, drank our coffee afterward, and listened to a simple speech of condolence from a deputation of villagers. The evening hours seemed to drag by. My courage began to falter. What if I met Hal Langdale or Torver somewhere in the dark passages? How could I explain to Freya or Matthew why I was wandering about the cellars of Ravensholme, especially tonight? But they would be sitting with Martin, surely.

I went up the stairs. It was shortly after ten and I looked in on Philip for a moment before going to my bedchamber. He was asleep, his soft fair hair fanned across the pillow, his long lashes shielding his sad eyes. Something stirred beneath the blanket as my candle's pale glow spread over the bed, and then Bismarck blinked at me from the edge of the fringe. I touched the top of his head lightly and tiptoed from the room.

Although I had undressed and slipped between the sheets as if I had retired for the night, I lay wide awake, my heart pounding. At every sound I jumped, fully expecting to hear the key turn in my door or someone enter my room. It would have been more bearable if I had not extinguished the candles. My eyes seemed to play tricks with the darkness. But no one came near me.

In spite of myself, my thoughts turned to Martin. What was the great gamble he had spoken of? Surely that much of what he said was true. And it wasn't a game of cards, whatever I had believed at the time. He had been boastful, excited, utterly alive and certain of success. Had he written that note? But if he hadn't, who had? Every man at the ball had worn evening dress. Who had wanted us to think that Martin had left for London to sulk? I recalled the quarrel I had overheard that last night at Ravensholme. If Wastwater had kept its secrets this time, we might never have known where Martin Ryland had gone or why. Who could have had a reason to kill him? And if no one had, what had he been searching for that had taken him into the mere? What had he known or seen or found? Had everyone been shocked—or had one of them been relieved—that he had died? Because I had been so deathly afraid that it was Kurt Raeder in the water, I hadn't taken note of anyone else's reaction. Murder, accident, suicide—which might it have been?

I should have asked my godmother where Matthew and Freya and even Hal were yesterday, I thought, rolling over uneasily. Would Matthew have killed his own *brother*? Oh, God, how I wished I knew some of the answers before venturing into the cellars!

But the time had come. It was nearly one and the house was as silent as a tomb. Martin's tomb, I thought nervously. And perhaps mine.

I dressed quickly in a brown woolen gown, walking shoes, and a darker brown shawl. Then I found extra matches and stuffed them into my pocket. Too craven to walk about this house in total darkness, I lit the nightstick.

My heart was thudding as I turned the knob and found my door still unlocked. Had Freya forgotten—or intentionally left it so? It took almost more courage than I possessed to step into the passage and begin my slow journey. Down the corridor. Down the stairs and into the silent, shadowed hall. Down the passage toward the garden door and the archway that led to the cellars.

My footsteps seemed to echo hollowly in the stillness, my breathing to suffocate me. Three times I faltered, ready to fly back to the comparative safety of my room. But I had a debt to pay. I could not live with myself if I made no effort at all to help the schoolmaster. He would haunt me my whole life long if I shut my eyes and turned my back on what had been done to him because of me.

All the same I prayed that I was wrong, that Martin had seen no one imprisoned here, that Kurt Raeder was well on his way back to Germany.

Even through the soles of my shoes I could feel the coldness growing as I neared the cellars. The dampness was penetrating, as if the foundations had been carved from living rock. Pulling my shawl closer, I held the candle high as I turned right into the twisting stairs and crept forward a step at a time. The stone walls seemed to close in, gray-green and sinister, curving downward in an endless spiral. And then I reached the bottom.

There were open storage rooms and bins, great kegs of beer and wine, shelves of preserves and jams and jellies, rows of crocks and sacks and bags of every description, hams and cheeses and twists of herbs, and, at the far end of the long high-ceilinged chamber, a small wooden door that appeared to be rusting on its hinges.

Surely nothing could be hidden where the servants

were free to come and go as they pleased. Yet an army might be secreted here, behind those great barrels and in the gloomy cobwebbed corners, screened by the long rows of shelves or stacks of provisions. I stared warily about, swallowing to ease the constriction in my throat. Who was here now, watching me, gloating over my foolishness, waiting to spring? My spine crawled with horror as the nightstick trembled in my fingers and sent shadows leaping down the length of the cellars like madmen dancing.

Walking down the great cavern, I put out my hand to touch the door at the far end; I expected it to screech as I pulled it open. But it only creaked a very little, though the noise seemed to deafen me. I stood rooted where I was, watching for any sign of movement beyond the door or from the cellars at my back. At last I took courage, stepped through the narrow opening and into a stairwell that disappeared from sight. I followed it, remembering what Freya had once said about the oldest portion of Ravensholme having been built by the first Harald, who had come to the dale from Iceland. Indeed, the passage was lined with great wide stones that must have been hand-cut and piled here long before the Norman Conquest. The archway ahead, crude and low, led past a stout oak door into a single long chamber, stone-paved and rectangular. At the far end was an iron-bound chair drawn up before a table with dragon-claw feet. There were no other furnishings except for long benches or shelves that ran around the walls, and no cells where a man might be kept prisoner.

But there was a pickaxe and a shovel in one corner next to a pile of new chains, and on the table was the Ravensholme Goblet. The goblet that Kurt Raeder had supposedly tried to steal. Next to it was a scrap of paper. I held it up to the candle's light, for it was smudged with earth and streaks of what might have been blood or mud. At first it made no sense, and then I was able to decipher figures, measurements. Scrawled beneath them was a rough diagram, rectangular and bearing the ominous notation in one corner of it, "Grave One," and beyond it, "Grave Two." For a moment I stared at it, puzzled.

Hadn't Philip spoken of a Viking burial mound on grazing land that his uncle had purchased from him—somewhere on the fells above Wastwater? What better place to hide the dead than in a place of the dead?

The paper fluttered from my nerveless fingers. The prisoners kept in this cold, frightening cellar were gone. Had they been killed? When? While we prepared for that dreadful ball? Or sometime yesterday? Had Martin died because he had witnessed too much?

The cellar door, the one with the rusty hinges, creaked in the stillness. I caught my breath in stark terror. Some instinct of self-preservation moved my fingers to snuff the candle I carried, but the sudden plunge into darkness was far, far worse than whatever was moving quietly, surely toward me.

I was trapped, at his mercy, for there was no other way out of here. My mind seemed petrified, but my feet slipped toward the wall almost by their own volition. As the cold stone met my outstretched hand, I heard someone step into the chamber and pause. Neither of us moved, but I could smell the hot wax from my candle, and whoever was standing there carried none. A banner proclaiming my presence would not have been more of a betrayal.

"Elizabeth?" a voice whispered. The strange echo of the stone warped it beyond all recognition.

My heart was beating so heavily that I couldn't breathe. It seemed to fill my throat. I made no answer. I doubt if I could have if I had tried to.

Whoever was there walked forward after a moment

until he—or she—came up against the table. I felt my way toward the stairs, knowing only that I was cornered here and stood some chance if I could somehow reach the cellars above. There were myriad places to hide among the barrels and provisions, but none at all in this chamber.

A match scraped but misfired. Panic filled me at the thought of being found here with that incriminating scrap of paper. I felt for the low arch leading to the stairs and miraculously found it just as the voice repeated, "Elizabeth! Stop!"

But I was running, my hands tracing the twisting tunnel of steps as my feet stumbled up the worn stone treads. Blundering through the door at the top, I made straight for the row of wine barrels. My memory hadn't played me false. My left hand touched the heavy oak surfaces just beyond where I had expected to find them, and I dodged down the narrow space between the first two. Cobwebs brushed my face, almost causing me to cry out in revulsion, but I was hidden in a niche formed by barrel and wall as the glow of a candle spread into the chamber.

Grateful that I had not foolishly tried to find my way out of the cellars in the darkness, I covered my face with my brown shawl and anxiously huddled against the wood. With any luck a single candle could never pick me out here, not with so many shadows and cul-de-sacs to choose from. The shawl hid my telltale fair hair, and my simple brown woolen gown would never reflect the light.

But I could see nothing. Only a yellow brightness penetrated the knit mask over my eyes, lifting high or swooping through the darkness as he made his way through the alcoves and storerooms, searching. Yet it was a strangely cursory search, as if he was in a great hurry or had reason to believe I had not stopped here.

At last the light winked out, his footsteps receded into silence, and I was—hoped I was—alone.

Leaning weakly against the smoke- and wine-scented wood, I let my heart resume its normal beat before venturing out of my sanctuary. Though I had matches with me, I couldn't bring myself to risk lighting the candle until I was certain I hadn't walked into a trap. Using my hands as I had seen my godmother use hers, I shuffled slowly, cautiously in the direction of the stairs leading up to the garden passage.

Stumbling over sacks of meal or flour, coming up against the sharp corner of a shelf or the rounded edge of a wall or a barrel, I made my careful way down the central aisle to the foot of the stairs. By some miracle, in spite of my erratic course, I had made a minimum of noise, though the fear of knocking over a crock or jar had kept pace with me all the way. With my hands still stretched before me, I started up the winding stone steps.

I think if I had touched the warm solid presence of a person anywhere along the stairs or in the narrow opening at the top, I would have screamed and fainted from sheer terror. Yet I fully expected someone to be waiting there, somewhere, knowing I could leave the cellars only through that arch. Like a cat outside a mousehole, he could let me come to him.

Turning in the direction of the hall, I found my way by touch. But I had scarcely taken a dozen steps before light flared at the far end of the passage and then Matthew walked around the bend that opened into the hall. Face to face, with only some thirty feet separating us, we stared at each other in stark silence.

I don't know what thoughts ran through my mind or his during that long moment, or what he would have done if Freya's voice hadn't snapped the invisible thread of tension stretching tautly between us. She had spoken from the hall, and he answered almost at once.

"Here she is! She just came back through the gardens." And he came flying down the passage toward me, his heels ringing on the stone flagging.

Startled and still in a panic from my earlier fright, I didn't wait for him to reach me but turned and ran back the way I had come. He caught me easily, his hand gripping my wrist and whirling me about just as Freya came rushing down the corridor, her dark skirts billowing behind her.

"Vixen!" she cried so furiously that I involuntarily swung away from her. "Did you think to return to your bed, all innocence and surprise?" she went on, catching my other arm and dragging me forward. "This time you have been too clever for your own good!"

My godmother, followed by Hal Langdale, came hurrying toward us. "Oh, Elizabeth, I don't understand!" she said bitterly. "How could you bring that man into this house!"

"What man?" I asked stupidly, and then knew. George Askham.

"We'll wake the servants," Matthew interrupted curtly. "Here, into the cellars." He lifted his candle and stepped into the archway, taking me with him. I had no choice but to follow, for Freya was right behind me, her feelings toward me easily read in her face. Loathing and contempt were exposed in the flickering light, and a hatred that frightened me. We hurried down into the cavernous chamber, our shadows hastening before us, and stopped near the crocks filled with dried fruits, spices, and mother of vinegar. Matthew released me, and Hal took the nightstick from my fingers, lighting it from his brother-in-law's candle.

They were ranged before me, all four of them, blocking any hope of escape, even if I had had somewhere to go. Their distaste was almost tangible, and I braced myself for the confrontation with a reminder to myself that I had done nothing wrong and therefore had nothing to fear. But I had to clasp my hands before me to still their trembling.

"He has taken my son," Freya was saying. "Philip is gone. Tell me where he is!"

I couldn't believe Askham would do such a thing, but Freya's face told me that it must be true. She was ablaze with anger, her eyes dark and full of fire, her burnished red hair falling over the shoulders of the black velvet gown she had hastily donned. No avenging goddess could have looked more magnificent—or more deadly.

"If he has taken Philip, it is for the child's sake," I said. "He wouldn't harm him, you know that as well as I do!"

"You don't know what you are talking about!" she said, nearly beside herself. "He'll use Philip against me. He must have guessed what Hal did to him over those regimental funds. He suspected it even before he left here. That's why he wouldn't marry me, even though I told him—" She broke off, her lips suddenly forming a thin grim line.

But it was too late. In her anger she had said too much.

"So that *was* the reason for the quarrel between you and Charles," Matthew said slowly, his face twisting with pain. "Why you agreed after all to go through that mockery of a wedding. *Philip was Askham's child!*"

"No, no! It was all a lie! I tried to hold George with a *lie!* But he laughed in my face and said that I was no better than my brother." Her voice broke, the hurt still vivid in her memory. "I hated Charles Carrock, but he had money and you didn't. I desperately wanted to marry well and as quickly as possible, to show George that I wasn't heartbroken over him. Only after Philip was born too soon and proved to be as fair as George did my husband begin to grow suspicious. Of course he knew how mad I had been for a year and a half,

256

throwing myself at George every time he came to Ravensholme. Yet when Charles asked me point-blank that night, I was wildly angry and foolishly told him he'd always have to wonder. I only wanted to wound his pride, his precious pride. But I had gone too far. He said he was finished with both of us, that Philip would never inherit Abbot's Thorston. I was frightened at that. When he started to the door, I tried to stop him."

"I thought there was too much blood to have come from the cuts on your hand," Aunt Charlotte said faintly. "*You* tried to kill *Charles,* not the other way around!"

"Yes, I stabbed him in the back with all my strength, but he pulled the knife free and took it from me. That's how Matthew found us, and I cried out that Charles was attacking *me.*" She took a deep breath. "*But my husband walked out of Ravensholme!* Whatever I tried to do in our bedchamber, *I* didn't kill him!" Her eyes turned slowly to Matthew's. "And I don't care who did!"

"I heard you screaming and found him with a bloody knife in his hand. We fought over possession of it, and in the passage just outside your door I wrenched it free. He was like a madman. I couldn't hold him, even though I was in a blind rage myself. I was afraid if he got free he'd turn on you again and I wouldn't be able to stop him. So I stabbed him, but only in the shoulder. I never told anyone about that. And then we fell together, the side of my head struck the door, and for a moment I was half stunned. By the time I could stagger to my feet he was gone." Matthew faced his wife squarely. "Yes, I followed him. But I never caught up with him. If I had, I'd have brought him back. I wanted to step into his shoes, but I wouldn't have cold-bloodedly killed him!" He looked down at his broad, capable hands. "Whatever else I may be, I'm not a murderer."

Hal Langdale leaned his shoulder against a row of

shelves. "It is time we sorted this matter out. I was on the fells trying out a new pack of hounds." His golden eyes turned to me. "We hunt fox up here, but it is a little different from the Quorn. We have to make allowances for the terrain. When Torver reached me with the news of what had happened, two hours had elapsed, and we still had to come down for horses. Since I didn't know the reason behind the quarrel, I expected Carrock to be headed for Abbot's Thorston and went there to talk to him. Freya can tell you I met her on her way back from there with Philip." He swung around. "Only one person could have set out after him and killed him on the sands. Weak as he was from lost blood, he'd have been no match by that time even for a woman. You weren't blind then, my dear Charlotte. But you have *always* been in love with Matthew, and would do anything for his happiness!"

"No!" she cried in dismay, her hands out before her as if to ward off a physical attack. "No, it isn't true! I couldn't have!"

"Ask Torver where she was that night or the morning after it," her husband said inexorably. "She is unbalanced and always has been. She has blamed me for her own barrenness, tried again and again to harm herself and to pretend afterward that *I* wanted her dead. I've even questioned her blindness itself. It can cover many . . . peculiarities . . . because of our pity."

My godmother's eyes searched blindly for our faces as we stared speechlessly at her. Her fingers pressed into her lips as if to stifle any attempt at protest or defense. And then, before anyone could move, she whirled and raced for the stairs, her feet tripping over themselves and the obstructions that littered the main aisle.

We watched her go in stunned silence. Then Freya said uneasily, "It *is* possible . . ."

I thought of the accidents I had had and the strange

comment at the ball that my godmother had always been deeply jealous of my mother.

And Matthew's voice almost answered for me. "No," he said firmly. "I won't believe it. Anyone but Charlotte."

Freya's face flamed. "Because she seems so helpless? Don't be a fool! But it doesn't matter about Carrock. I'm concerned about Askham. And my son."

"You said he didn't believe you when you told him you were with child," Matthew replied. "How could he use Philip against you now?"

"He had eight years of exile to think about it! To brood on his wrecked career, to wonder if I really spoke the truth, even to twist what I said to his own advantage! I've lived in a nightmare since he returned to England, waiting for him to come north! Instead he has sent *her* to spy, to sow dissension and fear until I'd give anything at all to be rid of him. Can't you see? He even used her to get into this house!" Her hand lashed out, catching me across the face, her rings cutting into my cheek. "You miserable little wretch! *Where did you take my son?*"

My fingers, cold and shaking, pressed against the hot welt on my face. "I haven't seen George Askham or anyone else tonight!"

"You left Ravensholme to meet him somewhere, just as you tried to do at Abbot's Thorston. Matthew saw you coming back through the garden door!"

"But I wasn't! I—" Breaking off in the midst of that heated denial, I realized what I had almost betrayed. My eyes flickered across Hal Langdale's impassive face, then to Matthew's tense one.

Freya, watching me closely, laughed coldly. "Where are the protests of innocence this time, the tears and outrage at our mistreatment of you?"

"To use Martin's death in this way, knowing we were grief-stricken and vulnerable, that is unforgivable,"

259

Matthew added contemptuously. "You and Askham deserve to be horsewhipped. If you care for the boy, don't leave him in that man's hands."

"I don't know where Philip is!" I said wretchedly, regretting that I had told George Askham the truth and been indirectly responsible for what was happening, even if I had had no other part in it. "I'll help you search."

"How kind!" Freya replied curtly. "No, my dear, you'll stay here, in the cellars, until I have found Askham and my son. Let the rats keep you company in the darkness and whatever else creeps on the floor or walls."

We had been too absorbed to hear the footsteps approaching until Aunt Charlotte arrived precipitately in the doorway, her face parchment white, her hands trembling as she held them before her to find her way.

Matthew was the first to turn. "Charlotte!" he exclaimed, and Freya wheeled. Hal straighted up, a frown on his face as he stared at his wife.

"He has come for her! He is already in the house! I heard him calling her name. In the darkness he must have mistaken me for Elizabeth—"

There was the clink of spurs on the stone steps leading down to where we stood frozen in surprise.

Aunt Charlotte gasped. "He has followed me!"

Matthew threw Hal a swift glance and they ran to place themselves at the foot of the stairs. The candles, left on the floor near me, sputtered and streamed golden fire in the sudden breath of air. Freya was beside me, one hand gripping my arm, the other clapped hard over my mouth before I could cry out a warning. I tried to struggle, but she jerked my head back against her shoulder, wrenching my neck.

And then he was coming through the opening, a tall man in riding boots and a cloak, exactly as I remembered him from the sands of Morecambe Bay. He saw me standing in the aisle, held fast by Freya Ryland, and my godmother poised in fright beyond us. The shadows played across his face just as Matthew and Hal sprang from their place of concealment and brought him down.

Freya was screaming now, her voice rising in terror and rage. I was forgotten. Her hand fell away from my mouth, her grip on my arm loosened. I pulled free and put a row of flour sacks between us. Hal and Matthew were shouting as they scuffled with their prisoner, but he was giving a good account of himself. My godmother shrank from their thrashing feet and clung to a partition between bins, her knuckles as white as her face.

Before I could think what to do to help him, Askham fought free of his captors. His cloak swirled away from his right arm as he moved swiftly to stand with his back to the stairwell, facing us. And he held a pistol in his hand, leveled at the five of us, keeping us at bay in the looming shadows of the cellars. What I could see of his face sent a shiver down my spine. The resemblance to Philip was gone, lost in an implacable determination that bordered on icy rage.

"Now," he said in a cold, even voice, "I shall at last have the answers I have come here for. You will tell me precisely what I want to know and then we shall consider what must be done to set matters right."

Impotent tears were streaming down Freya's cheeks. "You monster!" she cried through clenched teeth, "Oh, God, *how I hate you!*"

He smiled grimly. "How well I know, my dear Freya. You have given me ample evidence of it."

Matthew, breathing hard like a man who had just lost a race, was gray-faced and beyond anger. "Why did you come back?"

"I'll tell you why," Hal said, his fists clenched and his

261

strange eyes ablaze with frustrated fury. "For revenge. But we outnumber him. If we stop him now, before anyone comes, we can go on as we were, in peace. After all, it is no crime, none at all, to kill a man who is already dead."

13

Stunned and disbelieving, I stared from Hal's harsh face to the stern, shadowed features of the man holding the pistol.

"No . . . it can't be!" I stammered disjointedly.

"It shouldn't be. After all, *I* identified the body," Hal replied.

"But—but this man is George Askham! Isn't he?"

"*Askham?*" Freya repeated, her derisive laughter too brittle. "Don't be a fool!"

"I saw him on the sands. He was in the hall of Abbot's Thorston and up on Gable! And at the ball—"

"You called me George Askham, and I neither confirmed nor denied it," the stranger said quietly. "You seemed to be expecting George and I wondered why. The last news I had of him, he was still in London."

"Then who has taken Philip?" Freya demanded sharply.

"I have. He is quite safe, believe me. I thought it wise to remove him until we have settled our differences."

"How dare you use my own son against me!" she raged, but his face never changed.

"Your son—and mine. Or am I wrong in assuming that?"

Her eyes were black with revulsion. "I won't give you that satisfaction. I'll see you in hell first!"

"Freya, tell him the truth," Matthew replied, his voice tired. "You owe him that much."

"I owe him *nothing*," she snapped.

"That's true," the stranger said. "You did your best to kill me in this house. And then you followed me to the bay to finish your work. Only I proved stubborn. I refused to die."

She lifted her chin and made no answer.

"You were very nearly a murderer that night," he went on softly. "Hichen was not so fortunate."

Matthew took a step forward. "You are wrong. I caught up with you in the bay, not Freya. And I killed Hichen to silence him."

I heard a gasp of pain from my godmother.

"The poor drunken fool," Charles Carrock was saying. "He came back at the wrong time." His glance held Matthew's.

"And I stopped him from talking," Matthew said steadily, his eyes never wavering.

"And your own brother as well?" Carrock asked. "Oh, yes," he went on in the face of his shock and disbelief. "Martin was very likely murdered too. If Philip *is* my son, what was the need, Freya?"

"I hated the sight of you. I still do. But I never reached the bay. Hal always said he believed Matthew could have. Tonight he told us Charlotte had followed you." She shrugged. "Take your choice."

"It isn't a matter of choice. You see, I have proof. I was very weak from loss of blood, but I thought I could make it across the bay. You caught up with me and my horse bolted. As we struggled in the water, I saw you. So did Hichen. That's why he fled Cartmel. The moon came out and your hair was clearly visible. I couldn't be mistaken, my dear Freya, not in that."

"Believe what you please!" she returned scornfully.

"Hichen is dead. It is your word against mine. Will you drag your son's mother through a trial for attempted murder?"

"No. But I shall take Philip from you. If he is wise, Matthew will do the same with his daughters."

Before Matthew or I knew what she was about, she threw herself down the room, heedless of the pistol in her husband's hand. Matthew caught her arm as Carrock raised his hand to shield his eyes from her clawing nails. In the commotion, my godmother, bewildered and disoriented, stumbled away from the confusion just beyond her. I cried out in warning, too late to stop her from brushing against the candles on the floor. The hem of her wrapper flared and a pillar of flame ran up the silk folds. Matthew dropped Freya's arm and dashed toward my godmother. We reached her at the same moment, flinging her to the cold cellar floor in an effort to smother the flames. Matthew snatched at my shawl, beating out the fire as I tilted the nearest crock of liquid and poured it over her shaking body. The pungent odor of smoke and vinegar sickened me. With only the thin silk to feed upon, the blaze died as rapidly as it began, leaving Aunt Charlotte sobbing hysterically in Matthew's arms.

Charles Carrock was still struggling to control Freya's reckless attack, one hand holding the pistol out of her reach. A shot rang out in the cavernous chamber, bringing me to my feet in alarm, but it was Torver, standing on the last step, who had fired at point-blank range. As I watched Charles Carrock falter, blood streaking the light brown hair at his temple, Hal was beside me, gripping my arm. He pulled me away, toward the stairs, shutting out my last glimpse of his brother-in-law. Torver moved aside to allow us passage through, then blocked the opening again.

Hal sent me ahead of him, racing headlong up the

steps and down the passage to the garden door. I heard a crash, then the shattering of glass, muffled but echoing, and tried to twist free.

"Let me go! They have killed him!" I cried.

"He tricked you too. Why should you care?" he demanded, turning in the direction of the stables. And then he must have seen Carrock's horse, reins down, by the tall hedge that bordered the gardens.

"Much better," he growled. "We won't have to wake the grooms."

Though I struggled frantically, he led me inexorably toward the great black animal silhouetted against the brilliant night sky. Pleading, wild with despair, I fought him every step of the way. He was swearing viciously, now, dragging me the last few feet. And then the wary horse reared suddenly, looming above me like the towering mass of Gable.

Hal shouted a warning, but my mind had ceased to function. I was back in childhood, crouched in terror against the wall of the loose box, watching the hideous form above me pawing the air and neighing shrilly like some spirit in torment. My father had taken me in the afternoon to see a new foal, and I had been enchanted with the long-legged, shy creature. Venturing back to the stables after my dinner, I had inadvertently entered the wrong box, startling the high-strung hunter into taking instant exception to a white-clad four-year-old entering his private domain. By some miracle he hadn't struck me, but the incident had left worse scars.

There was no stout oak wall behind me now, pinning me here. Pulling away, I threw dignity and common sense and every other consideration to the four winds. I only knew that somehow I must escape those iron-shod hoofs, the great black body that threatened to fall and crush me at any moment, the bared teeth and flaring nostrils. Not even Hal could hold me here. I wrenched free and ran as if my soul depended on my fleetness. The only direction open to me was back the way I had come—back to Ravensholme.

He caught me before I had gone too far, slapping me twice across the face with the flat of his hand. Gasping and momentarily confused, I tried to shield my face with my arms. He stooped, tossed me over his shoulder, and walked back. Jerking at the reins, he quickly brought the frightened horse under control. I was set in the saddle in spite of all I could do, and then he was mounted behind me, an arm tight about my waist. My reeling senses shut out the sight of the horse's mane flying like a banner in my face. I leaned weakly against my captor, unaware of where we were going or why.

"You'll stay the night in the schoolmaster's cottage," he said in my ear almost as if he had read my mind. "Tomorrow I must decide what is to be done about you."

There was the sound of hoofbeats behind us. Hal growled and glanced over his shoulder. Although he changed direction at once, he made no other effort to elude pursuit. But I could feel his body, tense and ready, in the saddle behind me.

We rode up the fellside behind the schoolmaster's empty cottage, and then along a steep flank of loose scree high above the head of Wastwater. The horse skittered and slipped, but Hal drove him relentlessly toward a plateau where sheep grazed over the sparse grasses of the fell. The hunched white shapes scattered before us, and I saw the rectangular mound, partly rock and partly turf, just beyond. The old Viking grave mound where I was afraid the schoolmaster had been buried.

Hal reined to a halt and slid from the saddle, holding me before him. As the horse ambled away, I saw the other rider approaching and realized with deep relief that it was Charles Carrock. My knees felt like water as I waited for him to come up with us.

He drew rein some ten paces away and said quietly, "It is over, Langdale. Let her go."

Hal laughed, the same terrifying sound deep in his throat that had followed me into Kurt Raeder's cottage.

"Oh, no. It is far from over. You are already dead, Carrock. You only lack a formal burial place. With a stake in your heart to *keep* you in your grave in future. I'd have sworn that wreck of a man they pulled out of the water was you. You gave me a nasty turn when you walked into the cellar tonight."

"I imagine I did." He swung from the saddle. "It was what I intended, after all." For an instant his hand rested on the saddlebow, and I recalled the blood I had seen on his temple. Then he straightened, dropping the reins.

"No one knows you are here except the family. If you vanish as quickly as you came, who will wonder at it? And I am afraid that you have sealed Elizabeth's fate by not dying more tidily at Torver's hands."

Charles Carrock took a step forward. "My solicitor knows I am here. Or will, when he receives the letter I sent this morning. And if you are waiting for Torver now, I ought to tell you that he is dead. So is Freya. The shot that was meant for me grazed my head, but it struck her down. As he realized what he had done, he lowered his guard long enough for me to disarm him. Matthew knocked him into a rack of empty wine bottles. It fell, pinning him to the floor. He didn't live long, but he told us everything we wanted to hear. Matthew will kill you if I don't. He loved Freya, and in his own way, he loved his brother."

I stood very still, watching Charles Carrock move another step in my direction.

Hal's hands tightened on my shoulders. "Martin was

too curious for comfort. He tried one scheme after another—cheating at cards, blackmail, extortion—anything for money. We were all at one time or another his intended victims. Who can say why or how he died?"

"Torver said Martin discovered what is in the mound. You followed him from Abbot's Thorston that night, didn't you? And caught him here. So you drowned him in Wastwater, poor devil. But he had the last laugh. Somehow he came free of his chains and floated to the surface. Neither you nor Torver was prepared for that unexpected problem. Your note led everyone to believe he had returned to London. No one would ever have thought to search for him in Wasdale."

"A clever supposition. There is no proof, of course."

Charles ignored him. "I always believed your sister attacked me on the bay. I was nearly senseless from loss of blood, but I *did* see the top of her head—or so I thought. After all, she had already tried once to kill me. She also knew I was angry enough to disinherit Philip if I survived. You forced her to marry me, Langdale. You persuaded Askham to gamble beyond his means and then to use those regimental funds to pay his debts. *You* sent that letter to his commanding officer, informing on him. He sailed for India, and Freya went through with our marriage. You led Matthew to believe that *she* had killed me, to keep him from guessing the truth about you. And you told Freya that *Matthew* had followed me that night. Torver was the only one who knew where you were. Not tramping the fells as you claimed. You were halfway up the drive when you saw me ride out. And Torver met you with the whole story, didn't he? He always knew what was said and done in Ravensholme. It was you who caught me on the sands. It was your hair I saw. In the moonlight I mistook it for hers. And you did your best to kill Elizabeth, certain that she had some connection with Hichen or Askham. But for some unknown reason you suddenly changed your mind and tried to kill Charlotte instead."

I gasped. "*Hal* planned those accidents? But . . . he said he wanted to marry me!"

"Because you showed courage in spite of your danger, the sort of courage I'd like to see in my sons. Tonight I hoped Charlotte might take the blame for Carrock's death. Freya believed it readily enough. Even Matthew would have come around if she wrote a 'confession' before she—ah—took her own life. But Charles spoiled it all by reappearing damned inconveniently. Yes, I killed Martin and Hichen, and did my best to kill you on the bay to clear the way for Philip— through his mother—to sell me this land with the Viking burial mound on it—land my grandfather foolishly sold to pay his debts!"

"It was empty. Why was it worth so many lives?"

"Torver didn't tell you that?" He lifted his hand toward the mound. "If you can walk that far, see for yourself."

"No, don't," I cried. "I can tell you what is there! The body of another victim, a—a German schoolmaster. I don't know who the other grave belongs to. I thought it was yours. It may be the real George Askham's."

Hal Langdale ignored my interruption. "The mound has been empty of treasure all through the centuries, though it contains the bones of a Viking chieftain and his wife. My father discovered the story in the old records. When Harald Bluespear and his family were expelled from Iceland, they found a new home here and prospered. But Bjorn, the eldest son, became a Christian. Harald was furious when he discovered that the priest who had healed his son's broken leg had also secretly converted him. Harald was Thor's man. But in the end he let Bjorn believe as he pleased. And Bjorn betrayed him. When Harald died, a staunch follower of the old religion, he expected to be sent to his gods in a flaming long ship, his woman and his treasure about him. Bjorn didn't honor his father. He buried him in the earth with Christian rites and gave the treasure to the priest to build a church and say perpetual mass for his father's pagan soul. Only the goblet was kept as a token, because it had brought the family good fortune."

"What has this to do with Martin's death? Or mine?" Charles asked.

"I wanted this land, and you wouldn't sell, not even after you married Freya. But I got it anyway and did what I could to restore the honor of a Viking whose spirit was exiled from Valhalla. See for yourself. What does a 'dead' man have to fear from ghosts?"

Charles Carrock walked slowly toward the mound and pushed the flat stone from the entrance. Behind it was a narrow passage covered with a hide curtain. I heard a match scrape and an indrawn breath. In the sudden flare of light his face turned back toward us. "Are you *mad*?"

"No," Hal answered calmly. "Merely righting an ancient wrong. I can't build the long ship or send him to sea with a handmaiden and his treasure, but I *can* give him back the pomp and glory of a Viking warrior. The Christian shroud was poor apparel for a man who terrorized Europe in the name of Thor. I've put every farthing I could scrape together into setting his soul at rest. And my own. His betrayal has haunted me since my father told me about it as a child." He led me to the door. "Everyone believes the mound is empty. The treasure will be safe enough. And I always worked at night. You nearly caught me once, covered in filthy rags, just returning from an expedition here."

"There was no *prisoner* in the cellars?" I asked in surprise. "It was *you* with Torver?"

"Of course it was. For years I collected my . . . ah . . .

supplies in the old stone house beneath Ravensholme. This winter I began to move them up here." He shoved me forward and I stopped on the threshold, awed.

The low-ceilinged chamber was larger than I expected—some six feet by twenty. And I could see no sign of fresh graves. But in the light Charles Carrock held high lay an incredible display. Around the walls were piled golden jewelry, bright with gems, amulets and cups, church plate and reliquary chests, ancient armor and a long blue-black spear. A great two-handed sword next to a shorter wider-bladed one, an axe and wrought-gold daggers, finely made clasps and rings and sword belts thick with Celtic carving and studded with cabochon rubies or emeralds. A king's ransom—or the booty of a great warrior.

Charles took my hand, leading me down the cluttered chamber to show me an ornate crown delicately wrought in gold filigree, then gave me the stub of candle as he bent to touch the blood-red stone set in the pommel of a sword.

"It isn't Harald Bluespear's lost treasure, perhaps, but I had my agents scour Europe for the finest specimens of the period. He would not be ashamed to claim it. Good-bye. After you are dead, I'll bury you here. Future generations may believe you are a Viking and his woman. I grieve to lose you, Elizabeth, but you know too much now for my safety or yours."

Moving with the swift grace of the warrior he had so long admired, Hal Langdale scooped up the great battle-axe and hurled it toward Carrock. But Philip's father was ready for him. Shoving me aside, he was already deflecting the blade with the short sword he had been—seemingly—admiring. It snapped in two under the force of the axe, and as Hal took a step forward to finish his victim, Charles hurled the heavy hilt into his face. Staggering back, brushing aside the blood that welled from his cheek, Hal retrieved his axe and blocked the narrow entrance. There was a strange fire in his golden eyes, an excitement and blood-lust that had wiped out his first intention of disposing of us quickly and efficiently.

Charles had taken up the two-handed broadsword, heavy and unwieldy in this confined space. I cowered against the cold stone wall, clutching the candle stub for dear life, terrified of darkness descending and putting us at the mercy of that flashing, unpredictable axe.

Metal clashed on metal in the long chamber of the mound. As I watched in surprised fascination, Charles Carrock parried the huge blade of the axe with the great sword, a ballet in terrible parodied grace as they moved in response to the danger threatening both of them. Either weapon could split a skull or sever a limb, though the axe offered more flexibility in close combat. Slowly, inexorably, Hal was driving Charles backward. And then he stumbled on the clutter of golden objects, his foot slipping on an amulet and bringing him to one knee.

As I cried out in alarm and warning, Hal brought the axe blade down with all the force of two hands. Charles Carrock rolled away, almost to my feet, and the shimmering blade split a golden plate. Hal was breathing hard as he retrieved his weapon and leapt back. Charles had risen with the agility of a cat, light flickering along the sword in his hands. I backed away to the far corner to give him room, for he was already at the disadvantage of having to stay between me and danger. Almost numb with fright, I watched the red-gold head and the brown one dodge and strike, advance and retreat. And then the sword sliced through the handle of the axe in one great sweep. Hal swore viciously, his breath coming in gasps, and then he wheeled to disappear outside the hide curtain. We could hear the stone being shoved forward and Charles Carrock jammed the sword's length through the curtain and into the opening to wedge it there.

"Stay here!" he panted, and flung himself against the stone, forcing Hal to give way. And then they were both outside and a cold draft of air sent my candle leaping and sputtering into darkness.

On my feet and running, I paid no heed to the heaped treasures but thought only of escaping this hateful smoke-filled tomb.

The two men were grappling with each other, the great sword between them. Starlight twinkled on its blade as they circled the shelf of meadow. Below lay the long dark face of Wastwater.

"Take the horse and get away from here!" Carrock ordered, flinging the words over his shoulder to me. But I couldn't. My fear of approaching either of the nervous high-strung animals outweighed my fear of what might happen to me if Hal succeeded in killing his brother-in-law.

Both men were suddenly sliding on the loose scree, their boots scrambling for a foothold. The edge of the shelf was too near, sloping at a gentle angle toward the rocks below. Charles Carrock released the sword and threw himself flat as a last resort. Hal, overbalanced by the weight of the weapon, cried out as he realized his danger and then went cartwheeling into the night. As he struck the first bank of rocks, the blade pierced his body. I turned away, sickened, and raced to help Carrock, who had caught himself on the rim of the plateau, drawing in his breath as he laboriously pulled himself to safety. I reached out a hand and he grasped it gratefully, lying at full length on the cold, hard ground for a moment and staring up at me.

Matthew and Philip came running over the grass toward us, scattering the huddled, frightened sheep. As

Matthew stood staring down at the body scarcely visible below, Philip bent to look at the man on the ground, puzzled and uncertain. Father and son stared silently at each other for a long moment. Then Philip whooped in glee, casting himself on Carrock's chest.

"I knew you would come back! *I knew it!* But what happened to your whiskers? And why is your hair different? Can you see without your spectacles?"

I sank to the trampled grass, my knees suddenly too weak to bear my weight. Could it be? Dear God!

Charles Carrock turned his head and met my eyes. "I'm sorry. I meant to tell you in a gentler way."

Looking away, I felt confused and somehow betrayed. Charles went on gently to Philip: "It is a long story. And well past your bedtime. You shall hear the whole of it tomorrow, I promise."

A terrible story of death and imposture and suspicion. I trembled. How would Philip comprehend it?

Matthew came forward to take the child as Charles got wearily to his feet. "I'm sorry," he said briefly. "You had married Freya before I could return. I didn't let it happen out of maliciousness or spite."

Matthew nodded. "We'll find a way to deal with the scandal. Somehow. Charlotte will keep the girls for the present, if you'll allow her to remain at Ravensholme. It belongs to Philip, now."

Charles touched his son's shoulder and said carefully, "I had rather see it go to Freya's daughters. They don't deserve to suffer. And my memories of that house are not pleasant. Charlotte will need your help in managing the property."

Matthew turned away. "It is generous of you." He held his hand out to Philip, who took it with surprising readiness.

"Ride the horses back, will you?" Charles asked. "We shall walk."

I thought Matthew hadn't heard, but he glanced over his shoulder and said with difficulty, "I did love her. It wasn't the money. The difference between you and me is that I would have taken her, whatever she had done." And he lifted the tired boy to the horse's back and swung into the other saddle. As they trotted away, Philip waving over his shoulder, Charles Carrock reached out and took my hand.

"I deceived you twice, but only for Philip's sake. Can you understand and forgive me?"

"I don't know," I replied quietly, watching the sheep drift like fuzzy ghosts higher up the fellside. "I thought you were Askham. You let me believe you were. And I never guessed that you—" I could not say the name. My throat was suddenly constricted. "I was so afraid Hal had killed you. When I saw Martin's body—" I broke off, unable to continue. I walked away and after a moment he followed.

"It was damnable to love you and yet to be forbidden to speak. You came into my life like a whirlwind, changing it irreversibly. I wasn't prepared for you. And . . . I had a wife."

"You asked me to marry you at Abbot's Thorston," I said accusingly. "Freya was there, nothing had changed."

We stopped by a rock and watched the light spilling from the windows of Ravensholme. I had never seen it so brightly lit. A party of servants with torches were making their slow way down toward Hal's body. I drew the shawl about me against the wind and the uncertainty that chilled me.

"I had come there to make it change," he said gently. "At the ball I planned to confront Freya publicly. It seemed the only solution. Whatever she might claim privately, she wouldn't dare brand Philip a bastard before the assembled guests. And as I was ready to seek a divorce, she might have used him as a weapon against me. I couldn't take that risk. You see, I no longer cared whether Philip was my child or Askham's. I loved him for what he was and wanted to keep him. When I arrived, I found you in the gardens. I expected you to recognize me as quickly as Philip did just now. But you called me Askham, leaving the impression that he was invited, that there might be trouble later. I thought you would be safer if you weren't involved. And then you told me that Philip was very likely my son. It came as a shock. It also meant that there was no *need* for an open scandal. Freya and Matthew and I could arrange matters privately. So I left, saying nothing to you and avoiding her. Tonight I slipped into Ravensholme, got Philip out and to the cottage without waking him, and then returned for you. Only you took fright and fled from the cellars before I could stop you."

I looked at him in surprise. "It was *you* in the cellars?"

"You were just starting down the stairs when I opened the garden door. So I followed you. I was certain you had returned to your bedchamber and went there to see. I was frantic with worry then, but fortunately Charlotte led me to you. You know the rest."

"But why were you pretending to be a schoolmaster?"

"It is a long story. Freya's father and mine arranged our marriage several years before they died. When she met George Askham, one of Hal's disreputable friends, and lost her head, I offered to release her from the agreement. But Hal wouldn't hear of it. He said her feelings were no more than a girl's infatuation with a dashing uniform. I realize now that he wanted both the marriage settlement and this grazing land. God knows, he tried repeatedly to interest me in taking part in his drunken gaming parties. When that failed, he must have decided Freya could eventually persuade me to sell. The wedding date was set, Askham was suddenly posted to India under a cloud, and scarcely a month later Freya became my wife.

"It went wrong from the beginning. But we were young—Freya was nineteen and I was scarcely twenty-two—and might still have made it work if she had cared. Philip was her only interest. He *could* have been Ashkam's child, and he was so fair into the bargain. I began to wonder but said nothing until he was nearly two. That night at Ravensholme, Freya had flirted outrageously with Matthew to annoy me, and we quarreled violently after we went upstairs. She told me then that Askham had been her lover, that Philip's parentage was open to doubt. I was in a cold fury by that time and made it plain that I was going to disinherit the boy. She did her best to kill me. Matthew came bursting in, saw blood everywhere, thought it was hers, and went after me. I managed to stop him, took the first horse I came to in the stables, and got out of there. But someone followed me. I realized then that the odds were against my reaching Abbot's Thorston alive. Trying to lose my pursuer, I turned toward the bay. But she—he—caught up with me in the water. I was badly hurt, but I did what I could to protect myself. The last thing I remember was seeing that distinctive red-gold hair and cursing Freya. Naturally I believed it was she.

"When I came to my senses, I was floating with the tide. I couldn't swim far in my condition and the current was too strong anyway. By the time the ship picked me up, I was all but dead from loss of blood and swallowing half the bay. The captain nursed me himself. He said the cold had saved me, that he'd seen a man pulled from a Swiss lake and revived after half an hour under water. I was very ill, but they were outward bound with the tide. When we reached Rio I was still delirious. Before the captain could make sense of what I was saying we were in the South China Sea. I was bent on revenge, asked him repeatedly to put me ashore as soon as possible. He always answered that revenge was for the dead, not the living, that I had to work my passage first. I hated him, then, but understood later what he was trying to make me see. Kurt Raeder—"

He broke off at my start of surprise. "Oh, yes, Kurt Raeder did exist. He was an intelligent, compassionate, very stubborn man. I wish you could have met him. I'd never known a world like the one he showed me on that voyage. I began to realize that revenge was petty, that there was more to life than burning myself out with hatred. When we docked in Hamburg nearly a year later, I was a different man from the one who had been fished out of the bay. I was ready to come back here and set my affairs in order, not to demand blood for blood. Only, Fate took a hand. Raeder was killed in a stupid, senseless brawl trying to help one of his men. He died in my arms, asking me to look after his children, afraid his brother might try to cheat them of their rightful inheritance. The man had already been caught once embezzling from the firm. For the next four years I worked to build the family business into a prosperous, going concern with investments in shipbuilding and the China trade as well as merchant vessels. It was a challenge as well as a debt. Neither wealth nor family name was there to smooth the way for me as the new manager. Only my own ability. When Hans reached seventeen, I turned the firm over to him. Ilse was betrothed to a fine man who could finish what I had begun. The time had come to make a decision about my own life."

He paused, staring up at Gable's black profile blotting out the stars. "I wanted to learn the truth about Philip before I accused Freya openly. And I wanted to know him better before I made any decision about his future. It seemed best to return secretly. Can you imagine the shock of finding myself declared 'dead' and suspected of attempted murder, with my wife remarried? So I took the name of Kurt Raeder and came here in the guise of a schoolmaster. It seemed to be the perfect answer. Who would look for a dead man behind the dyed hair and heavy beard, the glasses that obscured my eyes? Because I was a 'foreigner,' the villagers had little enough to do with me anyway. And I could go away again if I wished to do that. I'd already proved my ability to make a new start. But you came the night I crossed the bay in search of Hichen, unaware that he was your driver. I found myself wanting roots again, a home—a wife." He turned, his hands gripping my shoulders. "Have I ruined every chance I might have had? Neither the schoolmaster nor the man you thought was George Askham exists any longer, except in your memory. Is there a place in your heart for Charles Carrock?"

I met his eyes and said, wavering, "I fell in love with Kurt Raeder, and then discovered he loved someone else. Hans's sister. I can't tell you what attracted me to the man—you—on the bay. But in the garden at Abbot's Thorston I listened because you seemed familiar, someone I had met. I thought it was the likeness to Philip that made me trust you. Perhaps I saw Askham because I expected him, but in my heart I may have recognized the schoolmaster. I don't know the answer. You were three men, and I don't know any of them very well. But I can tell you this—when I saw Martin's body and thought it was Kurt Raeder's, the world seemed a bleak and empty place."

His hands slipped down to my arms. "It is a beginning. I can be happy with that for the moment. When you are comfortable with Charles Carrock, I shall ask you again to marry me."

"And I will give you my answer," I said unsteadily. He

drew me closer, and I let my head rest on his chest, weary and in need of comfort.

"I love you, Elizabeth," he said softly, his lips against my hair, and there was the resonance of the schoolmaster's voice in the words. "I tried to send you away until I could come to you honestly. There was no one else and never has been. Ilse is a charming child, as lovely as she is good, but she has only a small corner of my heart as her father's daughter. You will see for yourself one day when you meet her."

I listened to the beat of his heart beneath my cheek and knew he told me the truth. I had misunderstood Philip because I had been so vulnerable to hurt.

We stood there, his arms holding me close, for a while, until I felt calm and reassured. And then, as if he sensed the change in me, he bent to touch my lips lightly with his, then released me. "There is a hint of dawn in the east. We must go back to Ravensholme. I'll take you to Abbot's Thorston today, and Philip with you. He'll need you, my love, until he can come to terms with the changes in his world. I have an estate in Gloucestershire. Neither of you has seen it. Will you both go there and start a new life until I can find a place for myself in it?"

"Yes," I said simply, and could almost feel the tension draining out of him.

We started side by side down the fell toward Ravensholme, now a gray smudge against the darker shape of Gable in the gathering light. I stopped to look back at the mound, almost invisible from this distance. "What will you do about Hal's pagan treasure?"

"Leave it where it is. It has caused enough unhappiness and death. I'll come back later today and seal the entrance. Only you and I know what is in the burial vault. Let the spirit of Harald Bluespear rest in peace now, and his namesake as well."

He smiled down at me, his hazel eyes alight with love and something else that burned in the depths, waiting patiently. With a lifting heart, I took the hand he held out to me and turned my back on the past.